MACKENZIE HEAT

by

S. T. Mugglebee

ISBN-10: 0615473385
ISBN-13: 978-0615473383

Author's Note: Readers will find there is no Chapter 13 in the story. The author could claim it was intended to be another mystery in the story, but it was only a mistake that occurred during reformatting when the novel was first published as an ebook on Amazon/Kindle. No part of the original manuscript has been omitted, however, to avoid any confusion from renumbering chapters for those who have already read the story as an ebook, the error remains in place. Please forgive any inconvenience this may have caused you.

DEDICATION

This book is dedicated to all the members of the greatest class ever, the class of 1959 at Beverly High School, Beverly, MA. I am proud to be one of them.

ACKNOWLEDGMENTS

This book could not have been written without the encouragement, support and love of my wife, Sharon. She was my guiding light, my taskmaster, and my helper, and I miss her every day. I also acknowledge the countless hours spent by Roland Enz, a good friend and former banker, who helped me put together such a diabolical plot. And to my son, Christopher, who came up with, and designed the fabulous cover, goes my enduring love.

Chapter 1

Wednesday: June 10th (morning)

THE PACKAGE arrived in one of those expandable, manila, intra-office envelopes; the kind with a red string wrapped around two little buttons. The mailroom kid dropped it in the middle of my desk and took off before I could stop him. I could tell it was a bunch of crap; most of what I get every day is crap. My name is scrawled across the flap, and below it is the stupidest message I'd ever read: "YOUR EYES ONLY."

"I know where you live," I yelled after the kid. I could smell his after shave lingering in the air.

For the past half hour I've been shoving an unlit Camel cigarette in and out of my mouth, holding it there long enough to drag in some of the fresh tobacco smell and taste a little of it on the tip of my tongue.

It's been three weeks since my last smoke, and my lungs are begging to be filled with tar and nicotine again. I'm like a 12-year-old kid trying to give up masturbation, "Please, one last time, then I promise I'll give it up forever."

The weather forecast came over the radio and grabbed my attention. "Hey, all you horse lovers out there, it's going to get toasty at Suffolk Downs today. When that lame nag you bet the rent money on stumbles in at last place, the temperature is going to be in the nineties, and the humidity will be out in front by a nose. So, forget that crying towel you usually drag along with you, you're going to need a really big sombrero and plenty of cold beer to wash down all those hot tips you got from the corner bookie."

"Goddamn it, I hate the weather in this town." I'm alone in my office, so no one tells me to, piss-off.

The DJ is talking about me. An hour from now I plan to be on my way to the track to enjoy an afternoon of beer and betting, my two favorite pastimes. Sid Moore, head of operations at the bank, the guy who sent the package sitting on my desk, was supposed to be joining me, but he chickened out. Come to think of it, he probably sent over that new pile of crap, and wrote that stupid message on it, just to get even with me for calling him a "pussy."

My gut was trying real hard to convince my brain to ignore the Trojan horse, or, better yet, dump it in the trash. Hit the road you numb-nuts; get your ugly butt over to the track like you planned, and screw the office. Whatever's in there can wait. Only a "whuss" would check it out.

Besides, I already know what's inside; a pile of lousy numbers just like all the other piles of lousy numbers that get dumped on my desk every day. "Yah, right, so how come Sid put that dumb message on this one?"

"I hate Boston in the summertime." Yah, I guess I said that already, but it deserves repeating. Think of heat and humidity, the two things that can really aggravate the hell out of a guy. *Beantown* comes loaded with both in the summertime. Your shirt collar gets all wet and slimy, and by the end of the day you feel like you've taken a shower with your clothes on.

The only thing worse is coming to work on an ordinary Wednesday morning, during a summer heat wave, and finding some new mess has been dropped in your lap. Today is sure beginning to look like one of those times.

Stop procrastinating you old fart. Make up your goddamn mind. You gonna open it, or not?

I shoved the unlit cigarette into the corner of my mouth, stood up, untied the envelope, and slid out a thick wad of paper. On top of the pile was a one-sentence, hand-written memo from Sid: "Mac, I think someone stole $5 mil!"

"Sid, you're an asshole," I yelled out.

How in the hell does the Director of Operations get away with only *thinking* he lost five million bucks? I mean, shouldn't he at least *know* if someone stopped by and swiped a bundle of cash the size of a small truck?

Harry Houdini couldn't grab that much dough without all hell breaking loose. Cops and feds should have been swarming all over the place by now, along with an army of TV reporters trying to get interviews for the 'six o'clock' news.

What in the hell is going on here? Has anyone told "The Lord?" I smell something, and it sure ain't that mail kid's after shave.

I stared at the stack of papers sticking out of the envelope for another minute, thumbed through part of it just to satisfy my curiosity, and confirmed it was exactly what I'd predicted; a ream of computer printouts full of lousy numbers. The paper zombies were back in full force, oozing out across my desk like some green slime in an old, horror flick.

Underneath Sid's one-page memo was a hand-written report, several pages long, dated yesterday, and signed by one of the computer analyst at the bank, a gal named, Audrey Simone. The whole thing sounded phony to me, like a joke with a screwed-up punch line. If Sid is pulling my leg, I'll make him pay. He knows I hate practical jokes.

I need a drink. All this talk of heat, humidity and numbers is making me crave one of the tall tin soldiers packed in the refrigerator at my empty house. I'll have to settle for a little diversion. I turned around and walked over to the glass windows behind my desk and stared out at the clear skies spread over downtown Boston.

The 27th floor of Sterling Tower, in the middle of Boston's financial district, facing north, gives a body one hell-of-a view across the harbor and beyond. The title on my door, "Director of Security, Sterling Bank & Trust of Boston," comes with a few perks, but for my money this was the only one that really counted.

I stood there for a moment, fascinated as usual, watching the tiny, toy ships moving around the bay below me. Street guys like me don't usually get a chance to see the big picture, and this was definitely a prime time show. The never-ending cycle of planes taking off and landing at Logan on the other side of the bay blows me away every time I stop to watch.

My telescope is aimed at the City of Revere, just north of the airport and I move behind it and focus in on Suffolk Downs. I watched the horses being trotted out for their early warm-up, and heard them calling to me, "You're such a whuss."

Maybe so, but only my bookie really gives a damn. My gut had already given up on the argument with my brain the minute I opened that package. My plans for an afternoon at the track had evaporated in the heat wave going on right outside the window. Only my creditors are happy.

At 55-years-old, losing out on an afternoon at the track isn't my only frustration in life. You want the truth, my best parts crapped out a long time ago. What's left? Just another old fart, standing around chewing on his tie and going bald.

Ten years ago it was considered dangerous to be on my bad side. Word on the street was I didn't handle confrontations very diplomatically. But, I could back it up, and on the street that was all that really counted.

Now, though, every morning when I step out of the shower I see a 6'3", 230 lb. pile of sagging flesh, who couldn't swat a fly. I stand there trying to remember what it was like to be a cop. Sure, I still see the mutton-sized hands and thick forearms, but they're only a small reminder of the real power I once held in this town.

The life-sized, cardboard, cutout cop standing in the corner of my office is another reminder I keep around. When I quit the Boston P. D. eight years ago, my daughter, Cathy, dug out a picture taken at my graduation from the police academy a million years ago, and had it blown up and turned into that poster for my retirement party. The singer, Billy Joel, sure got it right when he sang, "I'll never wear a younger man's clothes." Maybe that's why I keep the damn thing around, to remind me that I'm not a cop anymore. I'm standing in line like every other poor schmuck, waiting my turn.

Get on with it, slugger. No one's listening to you.

I turned around and picked up the analyst's report and tried to read the first page. Bad idea. It was full of technical garbage; "batch controls" here, and "identifier codes" there; about as clear as my morning coffee. Worse yet, my head started to itch. That definitely wasn't a good sign. Anytime things don't sit well with me, my head starts to itch.

One thing was real clear. Someone had done a hell-of-a job clamping a lid on things, and I didn't have to think twice about who that someone might be: Philip Cabot Lord III, Sterling's lord and master. If "the Lord" was already on the scene it meant I had to figure out the score and what inning we were in, and fast. I dialed Sid Moore's extension.

Sid stands a few inches taller than me, is several years younger, and has a lot more hair. We grew up in similar neighborhoods, but on opposite sides of Boston. That meant neither of us gets away with bullshitting the other. For a partner in this boring world of 'suits' I could do a whole lot worse than Sid.

"For Christ's sake, dummy, if you needed to borrow a few mil why didn't you just come and ask me?"

"Screw you, you bald-headed flatfoot. I'm the poor bastard who had to tell the Lord the good news."

"Wait while I get out my violin. This pile of crap on my desk is a day old. What in the hell is going on? If we got hit, how come I haven't heard any noise?"

"Because that ain't what happened. Didn't you read what I sent you? Oh, yah, I forgot you were absent the day they taught reading at Rindge Tech. Pay attention, you mushmouth Scot, because I'm about to clue you in on something that's going to bite both of us on the ass, big time." He sounded agitated, but then Sid always sounds agitated.

"Near as I can figure, exactly five grand was electronically transferred out of a thousand individual accounts and sent, via *Fedwire*, to that many banks all over the frigging country. No one dropped by and handed a note to the teller saying give me all your dough; it was all done through the computer. It happened right under our noses and we didn't smell a thing.

"After the customers' statements went out last month, we started getting calls bitching about money that had been transferred out of their accounts without permission. Naturally, I figure this has got to be some kind of computer screw-up. So I have one of my analysts look into it. She comes back with that report I sent you."

"Audrey Simone, right?"

"Yah. She's a little on the weird side, but a hell-of-a numbers cruncher. You want to talk to her?"

"Maybe later. Let her know I'll be in touch."

Sid continued on with his story. "Audrey can't find any connection between the accounts the money came out of and the accounts it went into; they don't belong to the same people. There's also no pattern to suggest we had some computer screw-up, so I'm starting to get a little nervous. I'm thinking maybe someone is deliberately messing with our customer files.

"I tell Audrey to go dig around in a couple of the receiving accounts and see what she can find there. I nearly have a heart attack when she comes back and says, in every goddamn account she checked out, as soon as the dough gets there, the account holder on that end withdraws it, in cash."

"You saying you wouldn't do the same thing if you found an extra five grand in your account?"

"What I'm saying, shit, I can feel my nuts getting squeezed on this one pal, is, once you pull cash out of the system there's no way in hell of tracing it. It's gone, man. Unless you can somehow grab the assholes who did this, we got zip."

"When did all this go down?"

"Audrey says the transfers started at the end of April, right at the beginning of the next billing cycle. Once she figured out the bogus transfers were all for the same amount, five large, she used the *Fedwire* transfer numbers and figured out when they were online. The assholes did this a couple of hours each day, five days in a row, then, just stopped. I told her to make up a list of every stinking, five grand, *Fedwire* transfer that went out of here during that period of time. That's how we came up with the $5 Million dollar figure."

"Maybe I'll run a check on little Audrey, after all."

"It won't do you any good, Bozo. I'm telling you, she's *Forrest Gump* with a Brooklyn accent. Oh, I almost forgot, a memo's coming at you from The Lord. He wants a meeting tomorrow afternoon at 4 o'clock. In the meantime, no one says squat about what happened."

I jotted the time down on my calendar. "I thought I detected his holiness' presence. You know, if I was in your shoes, buddy-boy, I'd wear a sports cup to that meeting tomorrow." Sid grunted and slammed down his phone.

The person who reports a crime always gets checked out; that's an old rule of thumb from my past life. As Lt. Duncan MacKenzie, I was the guy in charge of the elite undercover squad working out of the North End, and knew the drill. Back then there was even talk of captain's bars coming my way, but, of course, that was before 'bloody' Saturday.

I stared at the pile of paper stacked up on my desk again, and an odd thought crossed my mind. My mother would say this was a "cornucopia of glad tidings." It meant all kinds of wonderful little surprises were coming your way. So far, though, the little surprises coming my way this morning weren't making a whole lot of sense, and I certainly didn't feel glad about any of it.

Computers aren't my bag. Being dropped in the middle of a high-tech heist on a Wednesday morning wasn't something I looked forward to. Why can't perps stick to the old-fashioned way of robbing a bank? You know, pull out a gun, hand the teller a note, and grab the dough. Why does it have to be goddamn computers?

I poked the intercom button on my phone for Sheila Woburn, my chief deputy, and shouted, "Hey, I'm gonna make your day."

The day I gave up my badge and walked into Sterling as the new chief of security, Sheila was part of the welcoming committee. The fact that she was taller than everyone else, with a full figure stuffed into a dress that was tight enough to show exactly what was there, wasn't the only thing that made her stand out. Underneath all that sex appeal was the toughest, hardest working, most loyal, broad I'd ever known. She turned out to be the perfect 'yin' for my 'yang.'

Sheila dropped herself into one of the worn leather chairs in front of the old library table I use for a desk and, as usual, mocked my appearance. "Looks like someone didn't manage to get by the laundry on his way home last night like he was supposed to."

"Did I ever tell you, you sit like a goddamn truck driver?"

"You don't like the show, don't watch."

"Sid sent us a little present." I nodded at the stack of papers and added, "He claims some computer geek snuck inside our cool new system and e-mailed five grand presents to a thousand of his closest buddies."

Sheila sat up at attention. "You're kidding. That's five million bucks. Where are all the feds and reporters?"

"Tell me about it. The Lord has once again miraculously parted the waters."

"Come on, we still should have heard some noise by now."

"Not according to Sid. He says the perps wired the dough all over the country so no one knew what was happening. If Sid's right, one fine day, a thousand guys walked into a thousand different banks and left with five mil of Sterling's money. The guards probably held the doors open for them, and said, 'have a nice day.' Now we're left sucking our thumbs."

Sheila cocked one eyebrow. "That doesn't make any sense at all. What are we talking about here, some paramilitary group out to give their local cells a few bucks each so they can go out and buy a couple of Uzis? There are way too many people involved to make it worthwhile. What's the payoff?"

"It gets weirder. A gal over in operations, Audrey Simone, figured out what happened and made up this nice little list for us." I held the ream of paper in the air and let it drop onto the desk with a thud. "I can't even read this crap.

"Oh, and I saved the best for last. The Lord wants a prayer meeting tomorrow at 4 o'clock."

"I guess that means you don't get to kiss the ponies this afternoon," she said with a shameless grin on her face. She knew what I had planned for the day, but before I could get out a comeback, she added, "You start from the front, and I'll work it from the back."

That was exactly what I was about to say. By some odd coincidence, Sheila has this uncanny ability to anticipate whatever I'm about to say; like "Radar" O'Reilly in M*A*S*H. At first, I chalked it up to female intuition and bitched at her whenever she sprang it on me. But after so many years of working together I admit, in private, it comes in real handy every once in a while.

"I told you to knock off that shit."

She ignored me, as usual, and divided the stack in half. "I'll make up a form so we can look at the results and see if there's any kind of pattern that shows up."

Sheila was out the door before I could think of anything cool to toss back at her. Having her around was like having a second conscience. I wished I could smack that well-rounded butt of hers. Christ! she probably knows that, too.

The cigarette was back in my mouth and lit before I realized what I'd done. Just as I inhaled that first deep, satisfying drag, Sheila stuck her head back in the doorway and said, with a big grin, "Little boys just don't have any will power."

"Screw you!"

Embarrassed over getting caught, and angry at my lack of willpower, I fell back into the soft leather and thought about the mess sitting on my desk. In spite of being disappointed over a lost afternoon at the track, I had to admit there was a little excitement hanging in the air. My stagnant brain had received a minor jolt. This new caper had some "shine" to it. It certainly wasn't another one of those goddamn credit card schemes that bored the hell out of me on a daily basis. This one had "special" written all over it.

And nothing I'd heard so far made any sense. That always got my attention.

I dug up the phone number for BancAll, the first bank on the Simone list, and placed a call to their headquarters in Minneapolis. When the receptionist answered, I asked to be connected with their chief of operations.

"That's Mrs. Howell," she answered, and put the call through.

"This is Ellie Howell. How may I help you?"

"Ellie, my name's Duncan MacKenzie. I'm head of security at Sterling Bank & Trust of Boston. I'm trying to run down some wayward *Fedwire* transfers and one of them ended up in an account at your bank. I was hoping you'd provide me with a little customer info so we can clear things up."

"Well, now, sounds like ya got yourself a little pound of trouble back there in Boston," she answered, with a little giggle. "Got any ideas how it happened? I always like to take a stab at figuring things out before I get going. Yaah, you know, just to see how close I can come. Adds a little spice to my day, don't ya know. Well, sure, I'll be glad to help if I can. So, Duncan, you want to share your ID number with me?"

I've always thought the movie *Fargo* was a documentary. Every mid-westerner I ever talked to made me feel like they were scraping their fingernails across a chalkboard. I figure they were left out there in all that cold, empty country, in the middle of nowhere, far too long. It was enough to turn anyone into Mr. Rogers, or Jeffrey Daumer. I'll take pissed-off, city freaks that bitch all the time and don't want to be my buddy and swap recipes, anytime.

The ID number Ellie was after was a special code assigned by the American Bankers Association to each member bank, and a sub-number identifying individual executives. I gave her my code number and waited for her to check it against an index. I knew she'd honor my request because it was part of an ongoing theft investigation: something akin to law enforcement agencies sharing arrest records. Only in this case, the BancAll customer I was checking out probably had every right to expect the information Ellie was about to give up, would be kept private.

Ellie came back on the line, and asked for the number of the account I was investigating. I read it to her off the list, and she promised to check it out. She took down my special e-mail address to send me everything she had in the file. The whole conversation took less than three minutes and I moved on to the next bank on the list. This was going to be a long day.

The fat, old, gray mouse climbed back on his little treadmill and started running as fast as his tiny feet could carry him. The big question, as always, would he get anywhere?

Chapter 2

Wednesday: June 10th (afternoon)

I never fit in with the executive washroom crowd at Sterling. Give me cement sidewalks under my feet, not wool carpeting, and I'm a happy camper. The 27th floor is about as high up in Sterling Towers as I can breathe. I need to suck in the smell and dirt of Boston at street level in order to feel right, not all that purified, canned air they pipe into Sterling's "mountaintop."

By mid-afternoon, the thought of my upcoming meeting with The Lord was making me antsy. I felt confined. Running down all those account numbers was shitty business and being stuck in an office and not out on the streets cramped my thought process. It was like putting your shoes on the wrong feet, you feel stupid, but you can't keep from looking down. I started marching in and out of my office, again and again, without saying a word to anyone.

I feel like I'm being programmed and I hate it. Someone, somewhere, somehow is pushing little buttons on a crazy remote control device, forcing me to carry out this dumb assignment, like one of them mechanical bears in a carnival shooting gallery. Back and forth, back and forth, just waiting to be zapped.

Sheila and I spent all day chasing down dozens of accounts and by the time 5 o'clock rolled around we hadn't made a dent in the list. It still looked as long as when we started.

This heist showed all the signs of being a top-rated scheme. The kind where the bad guys do everything right, and the good guys end up looking like shit. If I couldn't come up with some answers damn quick, I'd be the one wearing a "kick me" sign at the meeting tomorrow.

Mad as I was over being manipulated by some anonymous perp, and anxious to put off assessing my inadequacies, I decided to take a break. Earlier, I'd called down for Audrey Simone's personnel file and it was now sitting on my desk. I settled back in my chair to catch a look at this would-be heroine.

It didn't take me long to realize what Sid had in mind when he described her as *Forrest Gump*. According to her file, little Miss Simone is a 33-year-old, single gal, who, since her mother passed away last year, lives alone in a rented apartment in the North End, not far from my own house. She left Brooklyn, NY five years ago to accept the job at Sterling as a computer analyst. Her only relative, a married sister, lives in Cleveland, Ohio. On the employment application, in the section for hobbies and special interests, she wrote in, "not applicable."

Not much of a party girl.

Employment-wise, the information was even more boring. The only company she had ever worked for, before coming to Sterling, was Quality Life Insurance. She started there as a data processor, right out of high school. Along the way, she attended evening classes at NYU, eventually earning a degree in computer science. That degree qualified her for her current post.

A blind man could see Audrey Simone wasn't going to turn out to be Madonna in disguise, but then I wasn't looking for a sexy, femme fatale at this point in my life. I needed a better handle on how the dough got transferred. I dialed her extension hoping to get a quick lesson in computers and maybe a line on which direction I should be headed.

An image formed in my head as I dialed her number. I saw this shy bookworm, with big glasses, intravenously connected to her computer and constantly looking over her shoulder for would-be attackers. Like too many of my bets at the track, I wasn't even close on this one. Audrey Simone turned out to be a lot more like a mafia hit man, in drag.

"Yeah, who's calling?" she challenged after the first ring.

"Audrey, it's Mac MacKenzie. I'm head of security for the bank."

"Yeah, Sid said you was gonna call." She sounded tense, but then Brooklynese always sounds tense to me.

"I've read your report, you know, the one about you finding them bogus transfers. If it turns out your numbers are right, I think we've got ourselves a local hero." I figured it couldn't hurt to do a little stroking, maybe build up some rapport with her before we got down to business.

"Can the hero bullshit, and as far as my numbers go, they're straight. Figures don't lie, and neither do I."

I walked right into that one, and my attempt at a recovery fared even worse. "Hey, did I say anything about anyone lying? I only meant your memo is based on some stuff that got stuck in the computer by someone else. That's all. I figure the other guy could have made a mistake when it got entered. That happens, right?"

She wasn't buying.

"Maybe you don't read so good. Whenever there's a screw-up, I trace it back to the source. I showed how each one of the legit transfers got entered and ID'd every document backing them up. Everything's accounted for except the bogeys. Like I said in my report, there ain't no entry codes or documents backing up any of them suckers."

This broad was definitely from Brooklyn, and a tad too tightly wound. She obviously took her job a whole lot more seriously than I did.

To be fair, it takes a special kind of nut to deal with all them numbers day after day. This broad sounded like she ate numbers for breakfast. She certainly wasn't coming across as your average, thirty-something, MTV freak. More important from my standpoint was the message she was sending out loud and clear; anyone who messed with her records is in for a world of hurt.

An odd duck can sometimes turn out to be a real asset in an investigation. Then again, she could just as easily turn into one big pain-in-the-ass. So before I went any further down the road with her, I figured I better find out which side of that coin my little charmer belonged on.

"Look, I follow what you did after you got around to checking out this little mess. What I don't get is how come you headed in the right direction in the first place. Sid says there's no pattern. So how come you spotted one?"

"Oh, yeah—well—uh—see, that's kinda personal. You'd probably laugh and think I'm just screwin' which you."

Suddenly, she is going soft on me, like some switch got flipped inside her head. As if I'd just asked her if she was a virgin, or something, and embarrassed her.

"I never laugh when it comes to bank jobs, especially when five million bucks goes walking out the door." My pulse rate said I wasn't lying.

"Awright, pal, but I hear so much as a cough outta you and your next paycheck gets screwed up. You got that?"

There was a pause, like she was trying to dig up some courage, and then she blurted it out. "It's in the rhythm. See, I get a rhythm goin' when I'm running my numbers. So, every time one of them five grand transfers shows up it's like a beat, like I'm hearing a bad note or something. You get me?"

Sid was right on the money about this chick.

"Not exactly. Are you telling me this whole thing is on the weird side? I already know that. What I want to know is how they did it?"

"Now you're into the juicy part." Her voice shifted back to its original, you're-a-real-dumb-ass tone. "See, the system automatically assigns a batch control number every time a teller handles a transaction. That's how I match things up so nothing gets lost or entered twice, you know, shit like that. If a transaction gets entered and there ain't no documentation backing it up, the document totals for that batch won't match-up with the transaction totals. Makes sense, huh?"

I was still stuck in the starting gate and kept my thoughts to myself.

"But let's say some slick-dick tries to stack the deck with funny money so's the document totals match up with the transaction totals. The automatic match-ups in the computer can't always pick that up. My job is to spot the phony stuff; you know, like a bogus check or some other puppy. Only trouble is, I don't find nothing like that. The batch totals for each day match up with all the receipts, and everything is legit, except for them dumb-ass, five grand, Fedwire transfers.

"The system never assigned any identifiers to them. That means the assholes somehow walked into the main customer files, sat down, and started mailing out the dough. You gettin' any of what I'm tellin' you yet?"

She might be weird, but I knew she belonged on my team. "Every bit of it," I lied. "Sounds like you're telling me someone hacked into the bank's computer system?"

"That's pretty lame Mac, even for a cop."

"Ex-cop. What you're saying sounds too easy. Don't we have programs in the computers that keep out the riffraff?"

"Beats the hell outta me. You're gonna have to talk to one of them computer wonks to get that kinda info. All I know is what they done, not how they done it."

Well, can you beat that, I've got my first lead. Granted, it's small, but it's a lead nonetheless. The perps somehow managed to get inside Sterling's super duty, whiz-bang computer system that was installed last year. Now I can walk into my meeting with The Lord tomorrow afternoon wearing my usual "what-me-worry" expression, and throw down that tiny morsel of information, letting the world know the cop is on duty.

"Audrey, I want you to drop everything you're doing and dig me up some samples of them things you just said. Maybe crank up a few charts or something to make it easier for dumb-asses like me to follow along. Have everything ready by 4 o'clock tomorrow. And don't worry, I'll make it straight with Sid."

"What happens tomorrow?"

"Just sit tight and I'll get back to you."

"You know you're kinda weird, Mac."

I smiled. "Yeah, well coming from you I take that as a compliment."

Audrey's explanation raised more questions than it did answers, but I now knew which ballpark the game was being played in. Audrey had provided me with some direction, and that was a whole lot more than I thought I'd have when The Lord started asking his own questions.

Two hours later, I glanced at my watch and decided this day was over. I hollered out to Sheila, "It's after seven.

Get your butt out of here and go on home to your horny husband."

I figured we'd made contact with less than a hundred banks. All that effort and so little gain made me think about some of the questions Sheila brought up during lunch. How in the hell did the crooks manage to pull cash out of so many different accounts in only a few days? Did they have some big, well-organized army on standby, ready to move whenever the boss said jump? If so, where's the profit for the big guy? And why did they stop when they did?

We still didn't have any answers and on my way out of the office I stopped by Sheila's desk to look over the information she was charting. Full customer info had come in on every receiving account; the account holders' names, addresses, phone numbers, even their social security numbers. It was all there, nice and neat, like a present that's almost too pretty to open. The perps were thoughtful enough to make sure whoever came along got every bit of information they needed so they wouldn't get lost in the wilderness. I scratched my head and shut off the lights.

The bank records showed all of the receiving accounts had been set up within the last few months. There were two names on each account and 50 bucks, in cash, was put on deposit to open each account. The activity sheets showed some small amounts of cash moved in and out of the accounts, once or twice, before the five grand arrived. Then, with military-like precision, the five grand arrived and was withdrawn on the day after the transfer. Most of the original 50 bucks was still sitting in each account like so much loose change that had fallen out of someone's pocket. By anyone's calculations those little savings accounts had thrown off a pretty hefty rate of interest.

I wasn't ready to cry myself to sleep, yet. Years of playing cops and robbers taught me at least one universal truth; crooks and politicians can't stand to walk away and leave money behind. Every one of them is born with some internal greed buried deep inside their warped little minds. The kind of greed that eats away at your insides until you can't stand it anymore. Even if every bit of information, on every one of those lousy accounts turned out to be bogus and there wasn't a snowball's chance in hell of ever tracking them down, I'd wager a long-shot that someone in the organization will slip back to all those banks someday to scoop up the last few bucks.

From a practical standpoint there were way too many banks involved to even think of staking out all of them. My plan was to apply some pressure on The Lord, at just the right moment, and sweet talk him into authorizing a stakeout on a few of the receiving accounts. All I need is for one member of the gang to show his ugly face and the whole caper will go down like dominoes.

Sure, the odds are long, but that's what I usually bet on. Long odds gets you the big payoffs. Anyway, it was the only thing I could think up for my offering at tomorrow's prayer meeting.

Chapter 3

Thursday: June 11th (afternoon)

At 3:56 p.m. the elevator I was standing in shot past the 50th floor on its way to the 56th floor of Sterling Tower. If things were working right, the TV camera in the ceiling was now switched on and I was being watched on a security monitor. It was part of an anti-terrorist program I had installed on the executive floors shortly after I took over. At the first sign of trouble my men would flood the compartment with a knockout gas. So far, we hadn't had to test it under fire, and I hoped things stayed that way.

I was standing beside Sid, and Audrey Simone was standing in front of us, fidgeting in obvious discomfort. My guess was her discomfort came from the black pumps she had squeezed on her chubby feet. When she stepped into the elevator I watched as she teetered a bit and figured she'd left her Nikes back in her office and gone all out to dress up for this special occasion.

Plain-looking, in a dark sort of way, she struck me as the sort of gal who never took the time to brighten her face with anything more than an occasional touch of lipstick. The mousey-brown hair was cut short and left naturally curly, probably for convenience sake. Given what she had on, the limits of her fashion outlook amounted to throwing on whatever she could find that was clean and loose fitting enough to hide her stubby body.

I decided to make some light conversation with her. "Ever been to the mountaintop before?"

"Oh, yeah, I used to come up here all the time to do lunch with The Lord until they changed chefs."

"When we stop you'll have to hold up your bag for the camera before they'll open the doors. They want to know if you're just an ordinary pain-in-the-ass jerk coming to complain about the company picnic, or one of them really disturbed persons who wants to make a big statement about bankers." My attempt at humor brought no reaction.

"Just make sure you genuflect when The Lord comes into the room. He expects that."

Sid got on me. "Knock it off, asshole, she's nervous enough." He jabbed me in the side with an elbow and nodded at the dark spots spreading out from under Audrey's arms.

"Oh, yah, kid," I added, anyway, "don't forget our agreement. As soon as The Lord comes in the room, we both point at Sid and say, 'He did it.'"

Sid grunted, and Audrey started to giggle as the elevator came to a stop and a voice from above called out, "Please open your cases."

Paula Harding, The Lord's spectacular, executive assistant, led us into his private conference room. A large, round conference table made of highly polished wood and metal dominated the room. It matched the rest of the decor; sleek, high-tech, and very expensive. First class was the way our CEO liked things, and he always got his way.

Audrey dumped her papers on the table and started to check out the place. "Geez, this is great. Like being on the Enterprise."

"That would make me Captain Kirk." The voice came from the open doorway at the far end of the room. Philip Cabot Lord III, tall, lean, and Republican-looking, was standing there in his elegant, dark blue, tailor-made suit.

He walked up to Audrey and took her hand. "You must be Audrey Simone." He sounded like a Kennedy, and looked directly into Audrey's eyes. She stared back at him, her mouth hanging open, as if she'd gone into a trance.

I often wondered if it was that specially blended cologne he wore that was responsible for the incredible effect he had on people, especially women? No, it's probably just all that money.

Phil didn't wait for a reply. "I'm very proud of the way you spotted this problem for us. I respect ingenuity and loyalty. Please, have a seat, young lady. I'm quite anxious to hear everything you can tell me about this unfortunate affair." He pulled out a chair for her, then moved over and shook hands with Sid, then me, addressing us both by name.

Paula jotted down our drink orders and told us dinner would be served at 7 o'clock in the executive dining room. When she left to see to the details, Phil drew Sid off to one side to question him quietly on another matter. I hung out with Audrey until a steward delivered our drinks. Phil made a quick toast and added, "I invited Sunny Childe to sit in on our meeting. She should be arriving at any moment."

"Not that I ever mind Sunny hanging around, but why bring in an outsider?" I thought it needed to be asked.

Phil gave me his patented "isn't-that-an-amusing-question" smile, and answered, "I've read Audrey's excellent report and it sounds like we have a clever hacker at work. Who better than Sunny to track down someone running amuck inside our new computer system? After all, it's her creation."

So much for my breaking news, but when Phil mentioned Sunny's name I noticed a wide grin broke out on Audrey's face. I knew why I was always happy to see Sunny Childe, but I couldn't help wondering what was going on inside the Brooklyn Bomber's head.

* * *

Sunny Childe's lush, red lips were curled upward in an unmistakable smile, as she stood alone in the elevator on her way to the 56th floor. The smile would be gone by the time she walked into Phil Lord's private conference room, but in the privacy of the elevator she could enjoy her thoughts. She closed her cat-like, green eyes and let those thoughts expand, savoring the moment.

The great, all-powerful Philip Cabot Lord was about to stand before her and praise her work. He would say the bank needed her to pull it through this latest crisis, and then would bow low in recognition of her talents. The thought of that taking place was almost as thrilling to her as all the money Sterling would end up paying her for this job. Almost.

Security alerted Paula Harding of Sunny's arrival, and Paula was there to greet Sunny when she stepped off the elevator. The two women were equal in every important attribute: physical attractiveness, remarkable intellects, and an over-abundance of feminine charm. Rumor had it they displayed an instant dislike for each other the first time they met. If true, it would have been a classic example of the proverbial irresistible force meeting an immovable object.

The two women embraced with a perfunctory hug, smiled at one another, and walked off arm in arm. Paula held open the door to the conference room with a slight look of polite disdain on her pretty face. It was a familiar circumstance for both of them. Not long after the new computer system had gone online, Paula held open that same door for Sunny as Sunny stormed out of the conference room following a very unpleasant confrontation with Phil.

* * *

When Sunny walked into the conference room, a thought crossed my mind. How is it this broad always manages to pull off just the right mix of business and glamour? The expensive, tight-fitting, linen suit she was wearing with a bright scarf hanging off one shoulder, showed off the color of her auburn hair and made her the perfect blend of sex and professionalism. I caught a whiff of her expensive perfume and noticed Sid, like me, couldn't stop grinning.

"Please don't get up gentlemen, you all know I'm just one of the boys."

Yah, and I'm a Rockette.

I watched her greet Audrey, giving her a hug, and addressing her by name. Then she moved on to Sid, me, and finally Phil, giving each of us a little air kiss and a personalized greeting that included her recollection of a past encounter. When she finally sat down next to Phil and mentioned, rather cryptically, the last time she had been in that room, she had the spotlight, and I for one am a very happy guy.

Phil reached over and patted her hand. "Sunny, the job you performed designing and installing our new central computer system was nothing short of a miracle. I'm very proud of you. Believe me when I say this, yours was the only name I even considered when it came to getting some outside help on this latest misfortune. We need the best and that is why you are here. So, let's get down to business and see if we can't bring you up to speed on what has taken place."

Sid led off and gave an overview of the theft. The meeting pressed on for several hours, due in part to the interruptions every time Phil had to take some urgent phone call, or put his John Hancock on some document brought to him by Paula. To no one's surprise it didn't wrap-up until after we had finished a great meal of baked halibut with roasted almonds and wild rice, served in the executive dining room. I would have preferred a steak, but then Phil isn't really a red meat kind of guy.

Around 8:30 p.m., Phil summarized the results over brandy. "Sunny will set up shop in the operations department and report directly to me. Mac, you've got authorization to stake out several banks during the next three months and will be in charge of coordinating all the field activities. Audrey will be temporarily assigned to Mac so she can translate anything Sid and Sunny dig up. Their jobs will be to figure out how these criminals managed to get inside our system and stop them from doing it again."

He stood up as a signal to the rest of us that the meeting had come to an end. "I want all of you to treat this as top secret. Until we know exactly what we are up against, I don't want a word of this to escape. I'm not even going to let internal audit know anything, yet. At this moment the only people who know what happened are the five of us, and the crooks. I want it to stay that way.

"Your number one priority is to figure out the identity of the thief, or thieves, and how he, or she, or they, did it. Then we'll dig them out of the hole they are hiding in and put them behind bars. No one steals $5 million from this bank and gets away with it. I simply will not allow that to happen. Please don't disappoint me."

One interesting tidbit floated to the surface during dinner: a past relationship between Sunny and Audrey. A year ago, while Sunny was installing the new computer system, Audrey got assigned to help enter a lot of the data needed to make the thing run. No biggy. But that, it turned out, wasn't their first duet.

While she was a student at NYU, Audrey attended several lectures given by Sunny, and during one of those lectures, according to Audrey, she decided Sunny

Childe was, "without a doubt, the most intelligent and the most beautiful lady, she'd ever met."

I couldn't disagree with her on that score, and in the elevator on the way down to the lobby, I proposed stopping off for a nightcap. Sunny, to my great surprise, readily accepted. Sid and Audrey begged off. With that kind of luck going for me, I should have headed for the track.

Sid and Audrey took off for the "T" station, while Sunny and I left through the main entrance of the building onto Pearl Street. Outside, we headed north toward Franklin. The tide was out and the smell of saltwater was heavy in the muggy, nighttime air. The sidewalks around Sterling Plaza were nearly empty except for the last of the commuters hurrying to get home.

It was tough trying to keep from glancing over at the knockout walking beside me. I thought of the few times we'd had contact last year while she was hanging around the bank working on the new system. Mostly, those memories were of the smoothest curves and the sharpest brain I'd ever seen, getting together in one really great package.

Anyone would be impressed with Sunny Childe's professional background. She had a brilliant academic record from a couple of the best, MIT and Stanford, followed-up with advanced research in artificial intelligence at Carnegie-Mellon. Being magna-cum-everything gained her a quick reputation in the cyber world. Authorship of a half dozen books on computer programming, along with a visiting professorship at NYU, helped polish her star. Lucrative private consulting contracts followed on a regular basis and all that dough made for a super lifestyle to go along with that super body. As the saying goes, "Them that has, gets," and, boy, she had it all.

A resumé like that usually went hand-in-hand with one of them weirdo computer geeks and, in a way you could say that was partially true in Sunny's case. No one, male or female, had a better handle on computer software, and how to use it, than Sunny Childe. But the lovely lady also possessed an even more valuable gift.

Beneath all that fantastic packaging was a woman who could anticipate a user's needs and figure out how to meet those needs in ways that no one else could match. It wasn't just that she understood "computerese" better than everyone else, her systems worked better. All the other geeks out there came in a distant second. Phil never wasted the bank's money on second best.

We reached Jake's Tavern, a nearby watering hole that I liked to call home. I held open the door for her and as she slipped by me close enough so that her perfume had the intended effect, I closed my eyes. Christ, how can anyone be so sexy and still so goddamn smart?

The Thursday night crowd had thinned down and I motioned to the bartender, Dugie Russell, as I led Sunny to a booth in the back. The dark woodwork and red naugahyde in the joint gave it a real masculine feel that I found comfortable. Besides, Dugie and I go way back. The place reminds me of every neighborhood bar I've ever stuck a foot in.

Sunny ordered a Black Russian and I nodded for my usual, a boilermaker. Out of respect for Sunny's obvious class, and probably to gawk at her cleavage for a few extra seconds, Dugie wiped off the table and put down a paper coaster in front of the lady.

Dugie and I go back to when we were picking our noses together on the playground. I've lost track of the score on who carried who home drunk, the most. In a tough spot, he is a good guy to have covering your back.

I was feeling a little unexpected nervousness and decided to break the ice. "So, are you fair and wise and gay?"

"Pardon me?"

"You know, `Sunday's child is fair and wise and gay.'" Her full name was Sunday's Childe, a bit of anti-establishment humor on the part of her parents, who were hippies back in the 60s. "My daughter used to have that poem with all the days of the week hanging in her room when she was little."

"Oh, that," she laughed. "Well, maybe two out of three, given today's politically correct interpretations."

I laughed, too, and tried to keep the conversation moving. "I got the impression you weren't too keen about my plan to stake out those bank accounts. If you know something that makes it a waste of time, I'd like to hear it."

"If I thought that way I would have said so in front of everyone. I'm not anxious to see the bank waste it's time, or money, on a fool's errand. What you probably sensed was my suspicious nature."

She leaned toward me. "Do you really think this whole thing is going to go down so easy? I mean, come on. Just grab the crook when he comes to get that last $50 and make him rat on the whole bunch. You must have doubts along those lines yourself."

My palms were getting a little clammy. "Between you, me, and the fencepost, sure I got doubts, but it's still a lead. And right now it's the only one I can handle."

"That's why I didn't burst your balloon. If I'm going to crack this case, and I will, I'll need every suggestion you, or anyone else on the team, can dream up. I see that honest, handsome face of yours as an asset, not a liability." Her beautiful green eyes were staring directly into mine.

"Lady, you're one hell-of-a salesman. I'll buy a subscription to whatever you're selling."

"That's saleswoman, in case you haven't noticed."

"Believe me, I noticed. So now that you've shot me down, care to share where you're headed?"

"That's why we're here, isn't it?"

* * *

While Sunny and Mac were enjoying their drinks at Jake's, trying to win each other's confidence, Phil Lord sat in his office staring intently at a bank of TV monitors. He was watching a video replay, on multiple screens, of the meeting that had just taken place in his conference room.

Hidden cameras, strategically positioned around the conference room recorded every facial expression, under the table "footsie," and even private notes that were being written down during the meeting. The remote control console he held in his hand allowed him to select any one of several different camera angles and zoom in on a portion of a selected frame. No one at the bank, except he and Paula, knew the system existed.

"That minx figured out she was being recorded," Phil said out loud, as he studied Sunny's reaction to his opening remarks.

Paula walked toward him, slowly undoing each button on her white, silk blouse. He looked up at her and watched the perfectly manicured red nails as they moved so slowly, and with such seductive purpose.

"What's that darling?" she asked.

"It's Sunny, she's too damn smart. But I have to admire her style."

"What are you talking about?"

"See for yourself," he said, pointing at the monitors.

Paula turned and looked at the screens. A close-up shot taken from behind Sunny appeared in stop-action. Phil zoomed in on the pad in front of Sunny where she had just written down, in block letters, the word, "GOTCHA."

Chapter 4

Monday: June 15th (morning)

The smell of Sunny's perfume was a lingering memory when I got a call from her early this morning asking me to put in an appearance at her new office. She had appropriated an office in the operations department for her new command center, and when Audrey and I walked in we caught Sid studying the fabric of Sunny's tight skirt instead of what she was writing down on a large whiteboard.

"Looks like we're late for our class in Bank Robbery 101, Audrey," I offered, parking myself in a chair next to Sid. "You're wasting your time Sunny. Sid's too dumb to make it as a crook."

Audrey put a box of donuts and four coffee cups she was carrying on the desk. "I remembered you drink tea, Sunny." She handed coffee to Sid and me, and left the tea on the desk for Sunny.

Sunny continued making her point to Sid. "Let's see if we can agree on some kind of a base line. I see the figure, $5 million, as symbolic, something meant to get our attention." She wrote the figure on the board. "Do you agree?"

"That depends," Sid stammered, trying to catch up with her thinking, "on whether you think they could be taking more if they wanted to. I still don't see how in the hell anyone can make that many transfers in such a short time span."

"Well, the bank isn't doing anything different from what it was doing before this happened, is it?"

"No. How can we?   We don't know what to change."

"Then what's going to stop the bad guys from coming back and doing the same thing all over again?"

"What makes you think it wasn't a one-time thing?"

"Then why stop at five mil? Why not go for 10, or 12, or even 50? The statement cycle had just begun and they still had another several weeks before the next statements got mailed. Why stop after only five days? Why five days? Think about it, Sid. It all boils down to one thing. They wanted to reach the figure of five mil and stopped when they got there." She kept writing numbers on the board as she talked.

"Okay, so they picked five mil as a figure. What's that supposed to be symbolic of," Sid asked?

"It's a number that's big enough to get our attention, but not so big that the bank can't keep it under wraps. Don't you see, the crooks are letting us know they understand how things work at Sterling. They're sending us a message."

"So what's the rest of the message?" Sid was having a hard time following her logic.

"I'm not sure."

"Then what's your point?"

"Only that I don't think we should be wasting our time on the amount of money they stole. It's not an indicator of how they did it. We have to assume they have the ability to take as much as they want, whenever they want."

Sid thought about that one for a moment. "If you're right, we should be getting some kind of a ransom note telling us what to do next."

"Now you've got it," she laughed. "So, our initial premise is that the crooks have access to our main data files and can take all the money they want. And, they aren't using our network terminals, so they have to log in. That's why I need that list of everyone who has your current login codes."

"Whoa. Take me through that part again. You're telling me someone hacked into our system from an off-site computer? I thought that's impossible?"

"All I'm telling you is they had to log onto one of our servers using a computer that's not part of our system. I don't know of any other way they could have done it. I agree with you, logging on wirelessly from a remote location is impossible. So they must have made a physical connection right here in the building, probably through one of the department servers.

"Regardless of how they managed to make that connection, in order to get online they had to login. So who's got the login codes?"

"Are you kidding?" Sid offered meekly sipping his coffee and staring down at the floor. "How in the hell should I know?"

"What," Sunny shouted.

It looked like she was going to send him to detention.

"Don't tell me you never changed those damn codes after I turned over the system?"

"Hey look, everything was up and running. No bugs were showing up, so why would I take a chance on screwing everything up just to change a few lousy codes?"

"Because lots of people had access to those codes when we were running the trials. The whole idea was to make sure only authorized people could log on after the system went online. That's why we have a firewall. I told you that before I signed off. I even put it in the "hand-off" checklist."

Sid was between a rock and hard place: too many balls in the air, and too much pressure to get results. He did his job well enough, but like most suckers around here, was overworked. Out of necessity he did what he had to do to get the problem solved and move on to the next one.

He saw not changing the codes as one less headache. He didn't want to run a risk of ending up in front of The Lord trying to explain why things that had been playing so well suddenly decided to jump in the crapper. I didn't blame him one bit.

"Even I had those login codes," Audrey offered, trying to take some of the heat off her boss. "In fact everyone I know, except for maybe Mac here, had access to them at one time or another."

"Well, that sure makes life easy," Sunny commented sarcastically, and turned her attention to me. "Mac, I asked you to come by this morning so we could go over a list of everyone who could have gained access to the files and start running down those names. Now it looks like that list includes me, all of my staff, and damn near every employee at the bank."

"What do you want from me?" Sid apologized.

Sunny showed us how to really win friends and influence people. She stepped behind Sid and began gently stroking the top of his head in a calming gesture. "For starters, get me a list of the names of everyone you can think of who absolutely must have access to the codes; and the operative word is, absolutely. I don't know how the crooks got hold of the codes the first time around, but if I change them now they'll at least have to dig them up again. That might buy us some time."

"What if they're already in the system?" It was my turn for some attention. "Based on what I heard the other night, having those codes is only part of what's needed. What about the rest?"

"What in the hell are you mumbling about?" Sid asked with a puzzled look on his face.

"Those codes you guys keep talking about might have got them online, but they still had to be hooked up somehow. You know, "jacked in" or "patched up," whatever it is you computer freaks call it."

I didn't understand a lot of what was being tossed around that night, but one thing definitely made me sit up and take notice. In order to gain access to the files and make the transfers, the perps had to have access to the customer files through one of the department servers. In my book, that meant we were looking at an inside job.

"Mac's right," Sunny joined in, excitedly. "You just mentioned that a minute ago, Sid. We need to check out every server in the system and see if they've been tampered with. That sounds like a hardware question and you know there's only one person I recommend calling in to handle hardware."

"You and Dennis still an item?" Sid asked, with a cheepish grin on his face.

"We are. You have a problem with that?"

"Only from the standpoint of my long-enduring jealousy," he answered with a shrug. "How about you Mac? You got anything against bringing Dennis back in to help out?"

"Me, hell no. After all, we're just one big happy family. Ain't that so, Audrey?"

Audrey just nodded and continued smiling at Sunny.

Chapter 5

Wednesday: June 17th

The investigation wasn't going anywhere when a letter suddenly landed on my desk. The envelope was addressed to me, with a Minneapolis postmark. It contained a two-sentence warning. `You know too much. Get out of our lives!'

Out of habit, I held the plain piece of white paper up to the light to see if there were any unusual watermarks, or smudges that might show up as fingerprints. Nada. It looked like a laser printer was used so there was little chance of ever tracing down its origin.

"Sheila, get in here," I shouted over the intercom. "We've just been contacted."

I also put in a call to Sunny. "Sunny, it's Mac. I just got a calling card in the mail. You want me to read it to you?"

"I'll be right there."

Sheila came running in, grabbed the note and quickly read it. "How the hell should I know?" she said in anticipation of my question.

"You agree it's from who I think it's from?"

"There's nothing else going on that's even close."

"Why send it to me?"

"That's easy. Everyone knows you're the head of security here. The perps probably figured the bank knows about the theft by now, so security's bound to be involved. Makes sense to me."

"Go grab that chart of yours, the one with all the information about the bank accounts. I want to check something."

While Sheila was gone, Sunny walked in and picked up the note. I studied her gorgeous face, hoping for a reaction. She didn't like to share her thoughts, but this time the corners of her bright red lips turned upward in a definite smile.

"I was right, it's not about the money."

"How in the hell do you know that?"

"Simple, they didn't mention money. They didn't even make it a point of negotiation."

"What the hell's that supposed to mean?"

"The figure, five mil, was only meant to get our attention. They can take as much as they want. Otherwise they would have threatened to take more."

"So, are they gonna do it again, or not?"

"I'd say, yes, unless they get some reaction from us."

"What reaction? What are we supposed to do? Do you have any idea at all what they're talking about?"

Sheila returned, handed the folder to me, and took a seat beside Sunny and explained the document to her. "It's a chart I made up to show various categories of information we got from all the banks that received the stolen funds. So far, it looks like the banks were chosen at random, but the procedures the perps followed were the same for every account."

Sunny shifted her attention back to me. "In answer to your question, Mac, I'm not sure. I need more time to think about it."

She reached over and rested a hand gently on Sheila's arm. "Is there anything at all about the location of the banks that were used that might point us in a particular direction?"

"At first we figured they stuck to metropolitan areas. You know, high volume, low customer recognition, that sort of thing, as a cover. But that theory got shot down when we found a number of accounts set up in small-town, out-of-the-way banks. If there's a clue in there we sure haven't been able to dig it out."

Time for my two cents worth. "This envelope is postmarked from Minneapolis and if I'm not mistaken, several banks from that area made the list."

I ran a finger down the first few pages of Sheila's chart and nodded affirmatively. "There are at least a dozen banks located in and around the twin cities that were used to flush the dough. I've been trying to decide where to put my stake-outs and that looks like as good a spot as any."

Sunny was skeptical. "I hope you remember what we talked about the other night. The chances of them actually showing up while your people are there is somewhere between slim and none."

"I know that. But when you add up all the money left in the banks in that one area, it's close to a grand. One person could easily spend an hour running around town, scooping up the last of the dough, and head off into the sunset."

"Rick's in Atlantic City chasing down a paper hanger," Sheila offered, anticipating what I was going to ask.

"Who is available?" I asked.

Sunny suggested, "Why don't you get one of the local banks to recommend someone from their area. It would be a lot cheaper and you could keep them on the job longer."

"Maybe so, but you heard The Lord. He wants things kept quiet. That's why Sheila and I have been busting our humps instead of calling in some help."

The phone rang and I hit the speaker button, "Mac MacKenzie."

"Mac, it's Dennis. Have you seen Sunny?"

"What is it, Dennis?" she shouted.

"I'm on the 12th floor, in payroll. You guys ought to get down here. I think we found where they cut into the system."

The three of us ran out of my office, picked up Audrey on the way, and headed for payroll. By the time we got there, Sid was standing in front of Dennis, nodding his head up and down like a bobble-head doll, while Dennis ragged on him.

"I'm sorry. I forgot," Sid kept repeating.

"It's a damn false alarm," Dennis called out, throwing up his hands when he saw us coming. "I found a splitter on a cable behind this server and followed it to that room over there." He pointed at a small storage room at one end of the accounting department.

"I thought the bad guys made the connection, brought in the necessary boxes and did their thing in there when no one was around. But it turned out Sid authorized the installation of that cable two weeks ago, to handle a new payroll monitoring program. He just forgot to mention it to me."

"Hey Dennis, I already said I was sorry. It's not like it's the only thing on my mind these days."

Dennis grabbed Sid by the shoulder. "I don't mean to bust your balls, Sid. I'm just so damn frustrated. This was the first thing in two days that looked even remotely promising."

I wedged myself between them and slid an arm around each guy's shoulder. "Denny, my boy, I read somewhere that some company, maybe it was Apple, came out with this gizmo that allows computers to talk to each other without wires. Is that really possible?"

Dennis and I had become drinking buddies two years ago when he was installing all the new hardware necessary to run Sunny's computer programs. He's the same age as my son, Brian, and maybe that's why we got along so well.

One night at Jake's, over boilermakers, I found out we shared two very important things in common: we're only comfortable in crowded cities, and a fantasy involving Sunny. Of course, there was one big difference. Dennis got to live out the fantasy bit, while I had to settle for a goddamn wet dream.

"Sure it's possible. I've seen it work, but so far it's limited to a special environment. Transmitters and receivers have to be built in on both ends and the signal's got to be shielded somehow from any interference."

"Like when they beam people up on the Enterprise," Audrey tossed in. She gave Dennis a little shot in the arm.

"Cute, Audrey," Dennis replied and turned to Sunny. "If that's what I'm supposed to be looking for you're talking a search that could take months. I'd have to open up every single box in the entire building, maybe all the branches, too. I don't think The Lord's going to be real happy to hear that."

"I'm not ready to hear it either," Sunny answered with a dismissive wave of her hand. "For the time being let's just continue on with what we're doing. If we reach a dead end, then I'll start thinking about sci-fi possibilities."

Chapter 6

Sunday: June 21st (morning)

The black Mercedes sedan raced across the picturesque Belgian countryside until it reached a grove of tall poplar trees on the outskirts of Antwerp and began to slow down. A quarter of a mile further down the road it turned off the main road onto a long, perfectly groomed, gravel driveway and came to a halt in front of a large, well-maintained, chateau. Philip Lord stepped out of the back seat and glanced up at the thick stone turrets silhouetted against the gray afternoon sky and thought, this picture hasn't changed in over three hundred years.

The pleasant ride in from Paris allowed him an opportunity to appreciate the tranquil beauty of the Belgian countryside. As the car sped past farmers working their ancient fields, Phil often thought about the many benefits one could derive from such a simple way of life: a life so different from his own. Such thoughts were generally shaded with a touch of envy.

A short, rather slight, gray-haired man, impeccably dressed in a gray, cashmere suit, stared down at Phil from a second floor window. Henri Bettancourt, the owner of this magnificent chateau, was a true aristocrat who always wore the enigmatic expression of royalty so no one could ever be totally certain of what was going on behind those steely eyes.

Phil's heels clicked on the polished marble flooring as he entered the second floor library. There was a satisfied smile on his face. The room was adorned with intricate, hand-carved woodwork and magnificent old-world tapestries. A large conference table occupied the center of the room and the group of people seated around the table became still the moment he arrived.

"Ladies and gentlemen, I hope I haven't kept you waiting," Phil apologized, and took his customary seat to the right of Henrí.

"Not at all, Philip. You are prompt, as always." Henrí, as chairman of the cartel, played the role of gracious host, and always welcomed each of his honored guests with genuine sincerity. On this particular occasion, though, it was clear to everyone in the room, including Phil, that Phil's late arrival had been planned. "I trust your flight was comfortable?" Henrí inquired, avoiding any awkwardness.

"I've always said the Concorde's cabin is too small," Phil answered. "Hopefully, we Americans will get it right with the new Boeing SST."

A servant inconspicuously placed a crystal flute of Dom Pérignon next to Phil, and Henrí rose to give the opening toast. Phil stood along with the rest of the delegates and lifted his glass.

"As chairman of this conference," Henrí intoned, "I salute all of you and wish you inspiration and good fortune as you carry out your responsibilities." Henrí raised his glass and added, "To God, and to our mutual good fortune."

"To God, and to our mutual good fortune," came the retort.

A gesture from Henrí and the servants quickly vanished. At the press of a button, the room was secured against any un-welcomed intrusions. Automatic door locks snapped into place and special covers dropped down over the tall windows, preventing any outside electronic eavesdropping.

To further insure against anyone making a record of what was discussed at this conference, all note-taking or recording devices of any kind, were strictly forbidden. The only recording device a delegate was allowed to bring with them into the room was their mind. Any plans, or resolutions adopted during the meeting, would have to be delivered to the delegate's regional group, by the delegate, strictly from memory.

The very existence of this organization remained one of the most closely guarded secrets in the world. Countless stories have been passed down through generations, speculating on the possibility that such a cartel existed, or what the nature of its activities might be if it did exist. Some claimed it was a mother group operating behind the scenes of the high profile, international banking organizations, such as, the World Bank, or the IMF. Others were certain that such a group, if it existed at all, was a clandestine arm of one of those organizations, used to carry out more surreptitious and nefarious activities.

No one with any first-hand knowledge had ever violated the strict code of secrecy demanded of each participant. Except for members of the cartel, past and present, it remained a figment of peoples' imagination.

The selection process by which each delegate was chosen to serve was another carefully guarded secret, unknown even to the delegates themselves. In fact, the twelve regional delegates who attended this conference had no idea of the identity of any of the member institutions, even those within their own region. That rule was intended to create a fail-safe security measure, a plan that had achieved great success, in one form or another, over the past four hundred years.

Regional meetings, similar to the global conference, were conducted under the strictest security measures. A private meeting room was chosen at random, and a screen erected to separate the region's global delegate from the representatives of each member bank in that region. The global delegate always arrived last and left first. That unusual precaution was taken to prevent the delegate from ever knowing, for sure, whom he or she was actually representing. For that simple reason, no person who had ever served as a member bank's representative was ever allowed to serve as a global delegate, and vice versa.

At the global conference, such as the one now in progress, the delegates were known to each other by name and the geographic regions they represented. The particular financial institution they happened to be personally employed by was also available, but considered of no consequence. It didn't matter because a delegate's selection in no way insured that the financial institution that person worked for was even a member of the cartel. Each delegate, at the time they accepted their post, pledged to share any information they received only with their regional group and never the particular institution they worked for.

In Philip Lord's case, a notice of appointment as the global delegate representing the North American Group came to him eight years ago. It was delivered shortly after he took control from his father at Sterling Bank & Trust of Boston. A bonded messenger arrived at his home and handed him a small sealed envelope, then waited patiently while Phil read the short, unsigned letter.

Dear Mr. Philip Cabot Lord III:

You have been appointed to serve an indefinite term as a delegate to a special global conference on finance. You will receive notification in advance of the next meeting of the regional group that selected you, as well as, the next global conference, which you will be expected to attend. The code name for all future communications regarding these matters is, "God."

You must burn this letter in the presence of the messenger and no copy is to be made. Do not keep any record of this or any other communication or documentation you may receive from God.

To God, and to our mutual good fortune.'

Like most people who gain access to the highest levels of the financial world, Phil was well aware of the rumors and tales of secret cartels. The idea of a cartel capable of influencing economies and the flow of money around the globe, conceptually at least, made sense to him. It offered reason and logic in a world that often provided little of either in his estimation. Thus, in spite of receiving such an arcane message, he decided to take it seriously, and undertook to follow the instructions.

Within a month he received his first call from "God," telling him to be at a certain restaurant, on the top floor of a Manhattan skyscraper, at 11:00 o'clock sharp that same evening. During that meeting, and at every one thereafter, names were never used, and Phil never recognized any of the voices coming from the other side of the screen.

Even if the opportunity had presented itself for him to identify who was on the other side of that simple barrier, he would have avoided doing so. The anonymity of his constituency allowed him to maintain a clearer sense of the power being wielded by the cartel, and helped generate a secure confidence that the cartel's desires would be carried out. He saw in that body, along with the other regional groups around the world, the true brokerage of worldwide economic power, greater than any single nation or potentate. The unnamed cartel was greater, through its unobserved existence, than even the World Bank or G7. He believed only fate and the unpredictable foibles of man could ever deter them from achieving whatever they set out to accomplish.

"Philip, perhaps you will be kind enough to fill us in on the recent problems that have come to light at your bank." Henrí's patrician voice sounded flinty, matching his gray eyes. As usual he took a direct approach and went right to the heart of the matter. The cartel never tolerated anyone wasting its time on subtleties.

"An unusual theft took place," Phil began, without hesitation. "Unusual from a standpoint that $5 million was stolen electronically and we have not been able to determined how it was done." He anticipated this subject would come up during this hastily called conference, and was fully prepared to respond. "Our computer files were compromised and the precise amount of $5,000 was transferred out of 1,000 customer accounts and sent to the same number of accounts at banks all across the U.S."

Lee Yamagato, the representative from the Pacific Rim Group, interrupted. "If they were electronic transfers there should be a clear trail to follow. I don't understand the problem."

"As soon as the funds were posted in the receiving accounts, the money was withdrawn ... in cash."

The last two words, "in cash," were meant to send furtive glances and startled expressions flashing amongst the men and women seated at the table, and so they did. Phil paused for a moment to let the full impact of his statement settle in before concluding his brief remarks.

"The $5,000 was withdrawn, in cash, from every one of the transferee accounts and I suspect the entire $5 million has since found its way to an off-shore account to avoid detection."

Sir Edward Saulte quickly challenged Phil. "My good man, you will recall that I warned of this sort of vulnerability when *Operation Sine Dinar* was first introduced." Sir Edward represented the Western European Group, and liked to think of himself as the unofficial inquisitor of the cartel. "A rather naïve presumption on our part, I dare say, going around hoping no one would discover such a weakness before we managed to eliminate the bloody stuff completely. Foolhardy, I warned."

"I must respectfully disagree, Sir Edward," countered Mai Wu Chung from China. "The very act of this theft, assuming it has a connection to our plans, no longer becomes a risk once *Operation Sine Dinar* is fully implemented. It demonstrates to me, most emphatically, why we must move ahead and eliminate cash, as quickly as possible."

Henrí returned everyone's attention to the central question. "May we assume at this point that the thief was only after the money?"

"It is too soon to make any assumptions," Phil answered, displaying a deliberate calm. "I suspect they will be back for more unless we can figure out how they gained access. So far, they've made only one other contact, a note sent to my director of security."

"And will you share with us the contents of that note?"

"It consisted of two sentences: `You know too much. Get out of our lives.'"

Murmurs spread around the table again, as delegates nodded to one another in recognition of the dire portent of that short statement.

"Sounds a bit odd to me," Sir Edward replied. "Could have been meant for Philip's security chap and nothing at all to do with our plans. What do you say to that, Philip?"

No one expected a direct answer. The question was meant to put Philip on notice that the people sitting in that room wanted assurances. They wanted to be assured that a cryptic note and an unusual theft of cash would not develop into the unthinkable, a breach of the cartel's security.

Phil was not in a position to give them any such assurances, at least not yet. "Until my people have developed some kind of profile on who is behind the theft, it is quite impossible to determine, with any degree of certainty, who the note was meant for, or what it refers to. I have my staff working on it, and I am confident they will succeed."

His attempt to convince them the mystery would get solved in short order was only partially successful. A success that cost him a good deal of the cover he was hoping to maintain until the real confrontation, the one he knew was shaping up on the horizon, finally took place.

The cartel would never allow the integrity of Operation Sine Dinar to be compromised, under any circumstances. More significantly, it possessed the resources and dispassionate will to see that nothing interfered with that plan, including Sterling Bank & Trust, or its esteemed Chairman.

"Timing is most important, as we all know," Henrí offered closing out the subject with an icy stare at Phil. "For now, I'm sure everyone here is satisfied the matter is in capable hands, and that Philip will keep us well-informed of his progress."

The words Henrí chose were benign, but the tone he used had all the charm of a ninja assassin on a deadly mission. The look in Henrí's eyes left no doubt in Phil's mind as to the real message that was being delivered. Results were the only things that counted with the cartel. Excuses were never tolerated. Control of the economic lives of everyone on the planet was at stake, and there wasn't a soul in that room who thought Philip Lord and his insignificant bank mattered one wit against *Operation Sine Dinar*.

For the time being, the matter would be left in Phil's hands, but there was no telling how long he had to get it resolved. If he failed to achieve success quickly enough, it would be snatched away from him, and that was something Phil could never afford to let happen.

* * *

Phil sipped his brandy during the late-night chartered flight back to Boston, while he peered through the thick glass into the dark abyss streaming by outside. For the moment, he let his thoughts wander into the past, an unusual act for someone who took so much pride in being forward thinking. Phil was a planner, always focused on the horizon. Patience and fortitude were his medals of honor. He was able to realize all of the pleasures his privileged life could provide by sticking with those two simple virtues.

There had been so many triumphs, and so few disappointments. Now, though, as he replayed the events of the last few weeks in his head and watched the dark clouds collecting in the distance, he could see he was on the brink of his first serious fall from grace. The favored existence he had enjoyed could easily turn ugly, even dangerous, if things got out of hand.

Chapter 7

Monday: June 22nd (morning)

Audrey came storming into my office, threw herself down in a chair, and shoved a Nike clad foot up against the top of my desk. "I figured somethin' out." A broad smile was plastered on her round face.

"Don't wait for a drum roll." The kid's bulldog attitude and droll sense of humor was beginning to get to me.

"Instead of trying to think about them accounts that got hit, I decided to take a look at how they fit in with all the other accounts in our files. So guess what?"

"You heard some new notes?"

"Don't strain your brain. I found a pattern. I ain't sure how they did everything, yet, but I know part of what went down."

"I'm all ears."

"Every one of them accounts that got hit ends up in numeric sequence once you know they all had five-figure balances. Sid didn't see any pattern because the account numbers don't have any relationship to each other. The perps didn't take every tenth account, or some other horse pucky, so they looked like they were just random selections. But, if you ask the computer to go through and sort all our customer accounts and report on only the ones that got a balance of ten grand or more, you get the same list I came up with.

"The way I'm seeing it, that must'a been a qualifier the bad guys set up in their program. Probably, to make sure the withdrawal of five grand didn't set-off any bells and whistles."

She was hyped on this shit, and it gave some attractiveness to her pudgy face that normally was lost in all the dark shadows. You've got to appreciate a kid who's found the true meaning of life.

"They must have used some slick program that reads through all our accounts and sorts them based on the current balance. Every time it finds one with five-figures, bam! it gets targeted for a transfer. Once they got all the target accounts identified all they needed was a list of receiving account numbers set-up and ready to go. Their computer matches up the two accounts and sends the dough on its way. A walk in the park."

"Could they do all that within the time-frame we're looking at?" I asked, having no idea how tough it might be to pull off what she had just described.

"No sweat. I checked out the dates and timing of each transfer so I could figure out just how long it took. Them fuckers were doing their search and completing a transfer within seconds. I mean, we're talking class "A" work here, using heavy duty hardware."

"What about all the legit transfers Sterling was making at the same time? Wouldn't they mess those up?"

"Nah, you're talkin' big numbers when you take on our whole system. Their stuff got lost in the mud. That's how come no one knew what was going on until after the show was over."

I grabbed the phone and dialed Sunny. "Sunny, it's Mac. Our "numbers-eating" plant from Brooklyn just came up with something outstanding. We're on our way up to your place. See if you can dig up Sid and Denny. They ought to hear this, too."

After everyone listened to Audrey run through her thing, Sunny walked over to her, took Audrey's face in her hands and planted a kiss on her cheek. "Sid, this lady deserves a bonus."

"Don't go getting carried away, Sunny. Even if I had a budget on this project, which I don't, I'd be way over it by now."

My own reaction to Sunny's generosity traveled along more personal lines. I was thinking I should have pulled rank and presented the information myself, and it wouldn't have been to get a two-bit bonus.

"But, does it get us anywhere?" I asked, shrugging off my lost opportunity to put a lip-lock on Sunny.

Before anyone could give me an answer the phone rang. It was Sheila calling from Minneapolis. Sunny put her on the box so everyone could listen in.

"Mac, I think I'm onto something. I'm in Redwing, just outside St. Paul, checking out one of the local banks. I was having a talk with the tellers to see if they remembered anything, when one of them says to me her boyfriend came in one day to make a deposit. He tells her he's been hired over the phone to look after some lady's sick mother. The lady who hired him, had him open a bank account at this bank so he could run errands for the sick mom. Now here's the kicker, the account I'm checking out at that bank has this guy's name on it."

"Way to go, Wo-be-gone," I shouted, sending my fist in the air and beaming like a proud papa. "I'll grab the first flight I can get and leave word at your hotel on my arrival time. Any action on the accounts?"

"No, nothing yet. Anything new on your end?"

"Audrey came up with how them scumbags lined up the accounts. We were going over the details when you called. I'd say the varsity's running up the score today. I'll fill you in when I get there."

"Love and kisses, folks," Sheila shouted, before hanging up.

"You aren't fooling me, asshole," Sid snarled. "You and her have that game down to a science. You get a few days in the sack at a nice hotel, on the bank's money. How come I never get to pull any of that duty?"

I laughed at him. "When Maryanne sews your balls back on, come talk to me."

"Aren't the Scotch supposed to be frugal," Sunny added, good-naturedly. "Seriously, do you really feel this lead is worth spending money on?"

"Oh-oh, she used the 'S-word,'" Sid warned.

"First off," I answered, sucking in my gut, "scotch is a drink. And second, this is the only lead anyone's come up with so far that doesn't require a goddamn degree in computereeze. You're damn right it's worth following up. I'm going to make a collar."

Everyone laughed, but I wasn't joking. The team had been in the dumps, lately. Twelve days, and while the weather stayed hot, the trail was rapidly growing cold.

Dennis came to my defense. "I'm with Mac. We should grab anything that moves. All I want is one tiny clue, one piece of loose cable, that's all I ask. I'm sick of dead-ends."

Sunny was standing behind Dennis and put her arms around him. The rest of us watched as she started to rub his chest in an unconscious effort to mollify him. The look on her face showed her brain was busy processing all of the bits and pieces, dropping them into neat little storage compartments for future retrieval. Her bright red fingernails were spread across Dennis' chest, moving in an undeniably sexual way. It was one hot show.

"Don't worry, honey," she whispered, "we'll find something for you to play with real soon. Things are finally starting to fall into place, I'm sure of it."

"I changed the login codes today, so if the crooks do strike again, we'll know they're hiding somewhere online. Sid, in light of Audrey's discovery I think you should assign some people to monitor the activity on all accounts with five figure balances. Audrey is absolutely right, that's where they'll come at us."

Chapter 8

Monday: June 22nd (midnight)

In the elegant Marlborough Street apartment, the high-ceiling bedroom was pitch black, and the man and woman lying naked on the bed were not discernible to each other. The woman raised herself on one elbow and casually stroked the thigh of the man lying beside her.

"Everything's in place," she whispered. "All I have to do is alter one little priority." Her touch set off a tingling sensation in the man, as her fingers slowly glided up his thigh, over the hipbone, and then lightly across his stomach.

"I know we're set up for it, I'm not questioning that," he continued to argue. "I'm also quite aware of the impact that another attack would have on the investigation. What I'm questioning is the timing. Is this the right time to make another hit, or should we just send out the next message?"

"They need to feel more helpless," she responded. "The mindset we want just isn't there yet. We need to bring home the hard reality that anything they try to do to stop us is meaningless."

"I admit that would help."

"So will this," she moaned, and wrapped her fingers around his erection, then squeezed hard. Her body arched against him in the dark.

"You're fighting dirty, again," he complained. "Why do you always bring sex into it? Afraid your logic won't get you what your body can?"

She climbed on top of his naked form and pushed an aroused nipple into his mouth while he grabbed her by the hips and pushed downward, impaling her wet warmth. "This isn't about sex," he gasped, as his pelvis thrust upward in an irresistible need to join with her.

"You're wrong," she cried out, as the enjoyment of him filling her spread through her body. "It's all about power, and power is sex."

Her hips began moving rhythmically, up and down, as she leaned down close to his ear and sighed. Her words were forming in short, seductive gasps, conveying a wanton release of inhibition mixed with absolute self-control. "Right now ...you wants me so bad ...you'll do anything to fuck me."

She moved faster and faster, pushing him closer and closer to the edge of control. "Do it!" she panted. "I want you. Fuck me! I own you. Do it! Now!"

Their naked bodies undulated wildly, like two giant snakes entwined in an erotic dance. An agonized cry announced the explosion of his climax as the man surrendered to her overwhelming passion. Exhausted, and drained of every drop of energy, his hands dropped to his side as he struggled to regain control of his heart rate.

"Are you trying to kill me?"

"I have that power ... through sex."

"Maybe so, but how do you plan on getting a bank sucked into that deadly paradise between your legs, so you can kill it?"

"Maybe, I already have."

She rolled off him onto her back and stared up at the darkness. He took hold of her hand and said, "You're right, of course, about hitting them again. But I'm still concerned about number one. How much time will you need to get ready for the pick-up?"

"Two days max. All of the adjustments to the program can be made in the meantime." She was hardly out of breath and raised his hand up to her lips, and began kissing his finger tips. "Will you be recovered enough by then? I want you to fuck my brains out, like last time, right before it happens."

"You're such a romantic," he laughed.

Chapter 9

Wednesday: June 24th (afternoon)

It was 1:30 in the afternoon, and Sunny and Dennis made an exceptionally attractive couple tucked away in one of the small booths at the *Bistro* restaurant, in Boston's financial district. They stared into each other's eyes, oblivious to everyone around them.

Dennis kept glancing down at the opening of Sunny's red silk blouse to study the exposed curves of her perfect breasts. Sunny reached out with one hand and let it rest on top of his. She began lightly tracing one of his veins with a perfectly manicured, red fingernail.

"Are you nervous?" She posed the question without warning.

"No, excited," he responded.

"I feel the same way." Her voice had a low, seductive-sounding mystery to it that aroused him. Throughout lunch, she had been toying with his emotions, using her words and the tone of her voice to increase his level of excitement. "I really can't wait any longer," she added with a smile. "My panties are soaked. God knows I've been horny all morning."

Dennis dropped two $100 bills on the table and they quickly exited the restaurant. They walked across Franklin Street, turned down Congress, and headed north toward the Singleton Office Building. A gentle summer breeze came blowing in across the Commons and played at their backs, carrying with it the sultry heat of summertime in New England.

They arrived at the 12th floor of the building and walked down the corridor to Room 1212. Dennis reached out to unlock the door, but Sunny pulled his arm back and embraced him. The passion in her kiss demonstrated how much she wanted to savor the moment and revel in the thrill of what they were about to do.

The sign on the door read, "Jane's Secretarial Services." The couple stepped inside and locked the door behind them. Alone, anonymous, and unnoticed, they were now hidden away in the drab corridors of a nondescript office building; the perfect setting for what they had in mind.

Chapter 10

Thursday: June 25th (morning)

It was the middle of summer, but the Agricultural College at the University of Minnesota in St.Paul was a busy campus. Young people, dressed in cool casuals, were passing by me in every direction as Sheila and I crossed the quad trying to follow the directions we'd been given. When we found the right building and knocked on the door at Room 327, a young preppie answered and invited us in.

The room was stuffy, typical of a guy's space, with sports photos sharing wall space with pin-ups. Clothes were scattered about and all the furniture looked like it came as a matched set. Brad Holtzman told us his roommate had gone home for a visit so he had the place to himself.

"So tell me, am I in some kind of trouble or something?" he asked.

I settled my sweaty bulk into one of the two straight chairs. "What makes you ask?"

"Come on guys, I'm not stupid. You ain't checking me out for the honor society. You're doing some kind of investigation, so you must be cops."

That was a good answer. I have the kid pegged as a straight shooter. Sheila already checked him out through the school and found nothing in his background to suggest any involvement in criminal activity.

Brad was the middle child of five kids from a Norwegian farming family in the southwest corner of the state. The young bank teller who brought up his name was a high school classmate, and currently his girlfriend.

"We aren't cops, and you aren't in any trouble, yet. We are investigating something, though, and you can help us out. What we're looking for are some straight answers."

Sheila added, "Andrea wouldn't have given me your name and telephone number if she thought you were in some kind of trouble, right? So what do you say Brad, will you help us out?"

Brad was having a hard time trying to avoid looking at the amount of flesh Sheila had on display. She knew exactly how to play a young, red-blooded, all-American, college boy. She settled herself on his bed with her legs curled up under her, pushing the skirt mid-way up her thigh.

"So what's this all about?" he asked again, turning back to me.

"Andrea says you've got this job helping out a Mrs. Sinclair in Redwing." I pulled out my little notebook, and Sheila reached over and placed a small tape recorder on the desk beside Brad. "I'd like to know how you got hired for that job and exactly what it is you do for her."

"There was a card stuck on the job board at the student union. They wanted someone to run errands on a part-time basis for some, bed-ridden old lady. It gave a phone number to call. I figured it wouldn't take much time and I needed some extra cash, so I called."

"Do you remember the number you called?"

"No way, but I do remember it was an 800 number. I thought that was kinda cool."

"Was it a male or female who answered, and did they give any company name?" Sheila asked.

"A female, but I don't remember the rest." He looked at Sheila and let his eyes drop downward again. "She might have given a company name. The whole conversation was real short."

"Let's get back to what this lady wanted you to do." So far, none of what the kid was giving us sounded suspicious, and I wasn't scratching my head.

"She says she lives out of town and can't handle things on a daily basis for her sick mother. I'm supposed to open a bank account in her mother's and my names. That way, she can put money in the account and I can get it out if I need to pay for something, without having to disturb her mother. I didn't see a problem with that, especially when she says she's willing to pay me $25 a month cash to be on-call, and every time I run an errand I can take another $25 out of the account for myself."

"What happened next?"

"She sends me a letter with $50 in it. The letter has the name of the bank where I'm supposed to set up the account, and her mother's name, social security number, address, all that stuff. Like I said, I'm supposed to sign for the account so I can withdraw money."

"So what did you do?"

"Hey, I only did what she told me. I put the $50 in the account and sent her the account number. I always put everything she sent me into that account. I never took anything for myself that I wasn't supposed to. If she's saying anything different, it's a lie."

"Calm down, Brad. Nobody's accusing you of doing anything wrong. We're just trying to find out what took place, that's all. Did you ever meet the old lady, or go by her place?"

"No way. My instructions were clear, don't go near it unless I'm told to."

"Then what kind of errands did you run?" Sheila asked, shifting her position on the bed.

"No big thing. One time I took some cash to a church and left it as an anonymous donation. I got a message saying how much to take out and where to take it. It was never a big deal kinda thing."

"But, one time it was?"

"Yeah. How did you know that?"

"That's not important, just tell us what happened."

"I got another message telling me to go to the bank and withdraw five grand, in hundred dollar bills. She wanted them in one "bundle." Says the bank will know what that means. I figure she's kidding because I'm thinking there's like maybe 25 bucks in there. But somehow the money's there, just like she says."

"What did you do with the cash?"

"I mailed it to the same P.O. Box in Chicago that I sent the account number to, just like she told me. That was about a month ago and I haven't heard from her since. You think it would be okay if I take out the $25 she owes me for this month?"

"Maybe you should wait a little longer and see if she contacts you again. If she does, we'd like you to let us know so we can follow-up. In the meantime, you think you can remember the P.O. Box in Chicago you sent that money to?"

"I got a receipt here somewhere." He started shuffling through some papers on his desk. "I didn't want to take any chance on someone saying I never sent that money, so I did it registered mail. Here it is."

Chapter 11

Thursday: June 26th (morning)

"Them slimy suckers did it again," Audrey shouted, as she charged into Sunny's office, looking as hot as the weather outside. She was waving a sheath of computer printouts in her hand and added, "Mac's in Minneapolis with Sheila, so I figured I ought to bring this to you guys."

"Who did what, my clever little detective?" Sunny asked. She and Sid were in the middle of sketching out the latest plan to guard against another attack.

"Them fuckers, they hit us again, this time for a quick mil."

"Give me some details," Sunny demanded. "How close on their trail are we?"

"That depends on if you think they're going after the same payday as last time. They went on-line for two hours yesterday afternoon and hit 500 accounts for two grand a pop."

"She's right. We don't know how much they want this time," Sid moaned.

"My guess is they'll come back online again this afternoon," Sunny added. She was out of her chair and on her feet pacing back and forth, excited over this latest turn of events. "We have to be ready for them." Then she stopped and stared at Audrey. "Didn't we have all of the five figure accounts under surveillance?"

"That's the bad news, Sunny. They didn't go after accounts with five figure balances. It looks like they changed programs. So far, it looks like they only hit on six-figure accounts."

"Damn it," Sunny swore. "Are you absolutely sure of that?" She asked the question slowly and clearly, as if trying to force Audrey to concentrate on every word.

"Yeah, I know. It sucks," Audrey replied. "I guess the fact that they changed the amount of each transfer from five grand to two grand don't mean much by itself. Hell, anyone could figure the bank would be watching for five grand transfers. But going to the trouble of changing their program so it looks for accounts with six-figure balances instead of five-figure ones means only one thing; we got us a snake-in-the-grass. Right?"

"We'll have to worry about that later," Sunny offered, putting aside any signs of disappointment. "Right now I want to be ready for them if they come back online this afternoon. Sid, our latest plan to trace their route through the system better work."

Sunny put in a call to Phil. "Paula, it's Sunny. Is Phil available?"

"I'm sorry Sunny, he's on the phone and it may be awhile. Is there something I can help you with?"

"Just tell him I'll be in my office and the electronic pick-pockets have been at it again."

"Oh, no. Stay put and I'll slide a note in front of him. I'm sure he'll want to get right back to you."

Phil returned Sunny's call within minutes. "How close are we, Sunny?" he asked, without any introduction.

"They hit us yesterday. I'm not sure if they're coming back today for more, but we're ready."

"Mac is in Minneapolis. Did any of the money get transferred to the accounts he was looking into there?"

"I can't say yet. Audrey just brought me the printouts. From a quick glance, I'd say it's a whole new list."

"Have that checked out right away. If Mac can get there quickly enough, his plan to catch someone might work."

"I'm scanning the list into my computer as we speak. As soon as it's done I'll run a cross-check to see if any accounts match-up with the old list."

"Do you have any clue yet as to how they're getting into the system?" His question came almost as an after-thought.

"No, but you do realize the implication of what has happened. The list of people who have access to the new login codes is pretty short." Her message came through loud and clear.

"So it is," he responded, without recrimination, "and no one on that list is above suspicion."

"You and I are on that list."

"No one is above suspicion," he repeated with finality.

Chapter 12

Friday: June 27th (morning)

News of the latest attack caught up with me when I landed at O'Hare in Chicago. It fit in nicely with my itinerary, but wasn't the kind of thing I was hoping to hear.

I was hoping another hit might tell us where their overall game plan was headed. If they followed the same strategy as last time, cash from the new theft ought to come sliding into that post office box right around the same time I got there. I might even get lucky and nab one of assholes at the scene. Nah, my luck has never been that good. Besides, the crooks came up with a whole new list of banks for receiving the dough. It wasn't likely they would stick with their same old collection points.

When we left Brad's dorm, Sheila and I took another stab at the list of banks to see if we could figure out some kind of pattern. Sheila finally spotted the common element. All of the receiving banks were located close to colleges or universities. The campuses provided a convenient and unlimited supply of young people ready to act as a silent, unsuspecting army.

College kids made perfect foils. Young and anxious to make a few bucks, they wouldn't ask too many questions. And, like Brad Holtzman, they wouldn't have many answers when, and if, someone like me came along with questions. They would also be gone from school as soon as the semester ended in May, so the perps would have more time to cover their tracks. The whole thing was well thought out.

The genius in that plan was that it could be carried out anywhere and everywhere. Using electronic transfers made even the smallest bank, in the remotest corner of the country, an unsuspecting participant. All the boss man had to do was notify his army of students, at the right time, to go collect the cash and mail it off to the collection box. And it only cost a couple of bucks to rent the kids for a few days. Fuck, it was much too good a plan to have any convenient flaws.

By the time I climbed into the rental car and left O'Hare, headed toward downtown Chicago, my enthusiasm for this trip was long gone and my head was itching like crazy.

I drove south on the Kennedy Expressway into the downtown area and at the Loop, crossed over onto the Eisenhower. When I stepped out of the car at the main Post Office, straddling the Eisenhower Expressway, I could smell the stink of exhaust fumes from the passing traffic and the humidity turned my whole body into a wet sponge. It felt like a substantial part of Lake Michigan had somehow been absorbed into the air.

"Christ, Chicago's worse than Boston."

The temperature was almost 90 and it was only 10:00 a.m. By noon, the entire city would be one big steam bath.

"My name's Duncan MacKenzie. I'm Director of Security at Sterling Bank & Trust of Boston," I announced, as I was lead into the Postmaster's office. A tall, African-American man stood up and shook my hand. "A theft took place at my bank recently and I'm on a mission to track down the money."

"Your office called and gave me a heads up, Duncan. I'm Bob Ridley. Have a seat." Bob had the broad, smiling face of a politician.

"As long as you know why I'm here, I hope you won't get offended if I wait until after I've checked out what I came for, before doing any socializing. I'd hate to miss my bus."

"Like I said, have a seat, Duncan. I promise you won't miss any bus." He sounded like he had something to say and it wasn't anything I wanted to hear. "Your folks told me why you were coming and I told them, I'm not sure I can help out."

"Maybe my folks didn't make things all that clear." I sat down and tried hard not to sound too obnoxious. "See, we figure a very large amount of stolen cash is coming into one of your boxes either today or tomorrow. If I'm not there to grab whoever comes to pick it up because I'm in here, chatting it up with you, my boss is likely to cancel my Christmas bonus."

"Don't worry, I'll send you a turkey. Relax, Duncan. No one's going to haul away any sacks of money today. The problem is we can't go handing out confidential information, or turn over mail to you, just because you're trying to catch a crook. Normally, the feds come calling on a bank job, especially if it involves the US mail. They handle all the paper work, give us some official looking documents to cover our butts, and everybody's happy. So how come they aren't in on this case?"

"Feds have a habit of ending up on the evening news and my boss wants this kept quiet. We haven't quite figured out how this little caper went down and that wouldn't look too good in the papers."

"What do you mean you don't know how it went down? That doesn't square with you following the cash here."

"We know they transferred the cash out of our bank, electronically. And we know the wise guys pulled it out in cash from the receiving accounts."

"Clever. How much?"

"I'd rather not say."

"I understand. So, then they mailed the cash to a collection point, namely, here at this post office. Sounds pretty slick to me. The only way I can imagine stopping a heist like that would be to eliminate cash entirely. We both know that'll never happen."

"I've got a little different plan in mind. I plan on having a nice long talk with them scum-bags about their career choices whenever they get here to pick up the dough."

"I'm afraid you're not going to get much action at this bus stop, Duncan. The box you're interested in is just a pass-through, everything that comes in, gets passed through to another location."

"Why did I know you were going to tell me something like that? Ain't that kind of arrangement a little odd?"

"Not in the least." A phone call interrupted the discussion for a moment before Bob continued on with his explanation. "Lot's of businesses prefer to advertise a location in some big city when, in fact, their operations are really located elsewhere. It's pretty common."

"So you're telling me the owner of this box is Acme Incorporated, in Kalamazoo, right?"

"I'm only saying that's a likely scenario, not that it's true in this particular situation. Until I get some paper work in my hand that protects my butt, I'm not saying anything specific about the owner of that box." Bob was turning out to be precisely the politician I thought he was when we first shook hands.

"How about cluing me in on how this pass-through stuff works. I mean you guys don't forward the junk for free, right?"

"Right. The customer maintains an account with us, authorizing us to draw on it to cover any expenses. As long as there's money in the account to cover the postage and handling, we'll forward the mail."

A light went on in my head. "So you must have records showing where the money came from to fund the account?"

"That I don't know. I'll have to check our files. They could have paid in cash, you know."

The light switched off. "Yah, that's true. It's funny how everyone else in the world is into using plastic these days, but these creeps always show-up with cash in their pockets."

"Sounds like drug business to me," Bob added.

I put in a call to Phil Lord, who in turn called someone in Washington, D.C., and eventually word came down to Bob Ridley to release the information. Along the way Bob dug out the records for that mailbox.

The records showed Box 1105 was rented to Chicago Special Enterprises, a company listed at what turned out to be a phony address in nearby Oakbrook, Ill. No record of any such business was registered in either the local or statewide business records. As Bob suspected, the rental and forwarding deposits were made in cash.

The forwarding address on record was another P.O. Box, located in the middle of downtown Manhattan. The records also showed that a large number of envelopes were forwarded there within a few days of the original theft, but not nearly enough to cover the entire $5 million. That meant the crooks were using more than one collection point.

Several sites had probably been set up on some kind of a regional basis. Again, a very smart move, intended to keep the cash in amounts that never matched-up with the amount stolen.

"I'm beginning to really hate those guys," I said to Bob on my way out the door and back into the summertime heat.

Chapter 14

Friday: July 3rd (morning)

Chasing my own butt around the country wasn't a very satisfying experience. I was turning into a stupid cartoon character again. My stop in New York turned out to be a dead-end, just like Chicago. A bogus company rented the box and the cash had already been picked up and disappeared. My gut was usually right and it had been telling me all along that I was stuck in the sights of whoever was holding that damn remote control.

"I'm pissed," I growled at Sheila. "I want dinner and drinks before I get screwed."

"I didn't know you were such a romantic."

"I'm being played for a goddamn stooge."

"I think you've got more pressing problems."

"What's that?"

"Stop and think about it. The perps made some really smart moves during the latest hit. Doesn't it strike you as a little too coincidental that they just happened to switch over to six-digit accounts when we were set up to monitor five-digit ones? And how convenient for them that none of the cash went through Chicago while you were sitting there."

"You saying a member of the varsity squad is in on this? Hell, if that's true we're in deeper shit than I thought."

"All I'm saying is, before we go planning our next move we ought to make sure everyone's wearing the right team colors."

"You pointing the finger at anyone in particular?"

"No. But everyone on the squad, including The Lord and Lady Paula, has enough smarts and access to the files to be able to carry this thing off. Except, of course, for you and me."

"I'll tell you right now if it turns out to be Audrey, she deserves every penny. She'd have to be the best goddamn actress I've ever seen to pull off that routine of hers. Any day now I expect to see her come walking in here wearing military camouflage and carrying an AK-47."

"If she does, my guess is she'll dig her foxhole right in front of Sunny's office."

"No, kidding. I wondered about that." The thought amused me. "In that case I'll let you check her out, along with Sunny and Dennis. I'll take Sid, Paula, and The Lord."

"You're all heart."

"It's just that you can relate better to that kind of broad."

"That ain't funny. The only closet I'm coming out of is the one you keep trying to grab me in. And, yes, me and your ex-partner will be at Brian's tomorrow."

Every year on the Fourth, my son throws a big shindig at his home in Beverly, a small city along the coast, just north of Boston. Brian is a teacher and the head football coach at the local high school. He broke with MacKenzie tradition a year before his mother died, and decided to become a schoolteacher instead of a cop.

When the time came to turn in my badge I knew it meant there wasn't going to be a MacKenzie walking a beat in Boston anymore, and it made me think long and hard about what I was doing. That's bullshit. I didn't really have any option.

Who would have figured it would be my little girl who would be the next member of the clan MacKenzie to wear a Sam Browne belt and pin a Boston PD badge on her chest. But that's exactly what happened. My daughter entered the academy right after she graduated from law school.

"I hear Cathy's bringing someone," I mention to Sheila, nonchalantly. "You know anything about that?"

She gave me a big grin. "His name is Michael Jordan."

"The basketball player?"

"First, the guy is doing his residency at Mass General. Second, he's white, not black. And, third, I can't believe what a racist pig you are."

"Why, because I get a little surprised when my daughter brings home a married, millionaire, black, basketball player?"

"I don't know why she even bothers with you. Try to be on time for once."

"Yah, yah. I only show up late so I don't have to keep company with the latest housefrau Sally's dug up for me."

"Don't worry, by now you've scared off every gal over the age of 40 on the North Shore."

Sheila headed for her office with Audrey's personnel file in hand, but turned around and added, soberly, "I agree, checking out The Lord is definitely going to be tricky."

If Phil Lord had anything to do with these thefts it certainly wouldn't be for the money. His family was old money, as they say, which meant they've had dough for at least several generations.

The various characters that make up Sterling's special investigation team, divide neatly into two categories, those with lots of bucks, and those who could use a loan. On my way to the Human Resources office to collect the personnel files on Sid, Paula, and Phil, I decided to start my investigation with the one guy on that short list who I knew fell into the latter category.

* * *

Sid Moore is 51-years-old and 27 of those years have been spent working for Sterling. Actually, he started at the bank a few years earlier than that, while interning through the work-study program at Northeastern University.

He grew up in Milton, Massachusetts, a suburb south of Boston, and was now raising his own family in Quincy, a few miles from his hometown. Maryanne, his wife of 20 years, was also a Massachusetts native, and their lives centered around a close-knit circle of family and long-time friends.

The birth of three daughters presented Sid, a former high school and college basketball standout, with some initial misgivings. He was hoping to re-live some of his past glory through the efforts of a son, but none popped out. Fortunately for him, the recent rise in popularity of female sports gave him a chance to fulfill all of his macho yearnings, as each one of his daughters became a star athlete. All of which ends up on the positive side of the ledger.

On the negative side, Sid, like so many fools who dedicate their business careers to the low-paying banking industry, has a sizable mortgage, car payments, orthodontic bills and an unending supply of clothing to purchase; not to mention three weddings in the not too distant future. In short, Sid has money problems. $5 million would go a long way toward making those problems disappear.

Armed with Sid's personnel file and a credit report I pulled off my computer, I sat down with enough information to check out nearly every corner of his life, right down to his last visit to the dentist. Like most people, Sid tried to simplify his life by using plastic whenever possible.

His paychecks were deposited automatically. He paid his regular bills by computer and used plastic for the family groceries. Even on the rare nights out when he and I sat in the Fleet Center watching our beloved Celtics, he hardly ever had more than $50 in cash on him.

Peeking into someone's life and poking around, makes me depressed. The fact that a person's spending habits are constantly being captured and stored away in computer files, at some anonymous organization, isn't something I feel good about.

My basic aversion to paying bills drove me to use cash for most things. I don't like to leave a record behind every time I make a stop at the liquor store, or lay down a $100 bet at the track.

When I studied the details of Sid's life, I felt a certain sense of relief knowing that my own spending habits would never be subjected to that kind of intrusive scrutiny. In Sid's case, fortunately, I didn't find anything I didn't already know.

I moved on to Paula's file and the first thing that jumped out at me was her home address. Her apartment was located on Marlborough Street only a block or so from where Sunny and Dennis were shacked up. I remembered Sunny mentioning that she lived on that street the night we stopped for drinks at Jake's. It made me wonder if the two women were aware of the fact they were neighbors.

I called Sheila on the intercom. "You have Sunny Childe's address handy?"

"Yah, what's up? It's 525 Marlborough Street, Apartment 5C."

"That's what I thought. I just noticed that Lady Paula lives at 635 Marlborough. Coincidences always get my attention."

"It doesn't mean they're buds, you know. My guess is they don't even realize they're neighbors. Trust me when I tell you those two don't get along."

"What's their problem?"

"My take is that it has something to do with The Lord."

"I always figured Sunny and Dennis were real tight. What makes you think Phil made a move on Sunny? Or was it the other way around?"

"I didn't say that. It could be that Paula just doesn't like taking chances where Phil's concerned. Maybe, she figures he's one of them horny toads, who needs to be kept out of the way of temptation. I'll bet you've had a dream or two about Sunny, yourself."

"Stay the hell out of my dreams. It's bad enough having you know what I'm going to say."

"For what it's worth, I hear The Lord wasn't seeing eye-to-eye with Sunny by the time she finished getting the new system online."

"That's interesting. I didn't know that. Sunny made some crack when she showed up at that meeting a few weeks back, but I didn't think anything about it at the time. I wonder how many other little secrets are out there that nobody's bothering to share."

Paula Harding's credentials were nearly as outstanding as Sunny's. Born in Seattle, she grew up in London, England, where her father managed an operation for Boeing. She came back to the U.S. to attend college, graduated from Smith, and went on to Georgetown University where she picked-up a Master's degree in economics. After that, she landed a staff position in the office of Senator Warren Mills of Massachusetts. During her

5-year stint with the Senator, looks and brains made her an easy standout, and she quickly rose to become Chief-of-Staff.

It was at one of Senator Mills' campaign rallies that she ran into Philip Cabot Lord III. Rumor has it, the heated looks she and Phil exchanged during their brief introduction left no doubt as to the timing or purpose of their next encounter. They were in bed at the Parker House before noon the following day.

Six months later, Paula resigned from Senator Mills' office, hired on as Phil's executive assistant, and settled herself into an expensive apartment on Marlborough Street, not far from the Commons. It was the beginning of an interesting, yet common, relationship.

Not too surprising, she was able to save most of her paycheck in spite of having rather expensive tastes in apartments and clothing. At four grand a month, her rent seemed a little high for someone earning only $60,000 a year. When you threw in a first class wardrobe, money should have been real tight. Her current bank balance suggested The Lord might be supplementing that picture, and well he should. Considering how much time he spent at that apartment and inside those special silk panties she regularly ordered from a company in London called, *Janet Reger*, he was probably getting off cheap.

Paula clearly had a taste for money and could use a lot more of it if she ever wanted to get set-up on her own, and away from Phil's wallet. She also had an almost perfect cover. Her position as Phil's Executive Assistant put her close enough to the action to know what was going on, without actually participating in anything. For a lot of different reasons, I put a big checkmark beside her name, as a prime suspect.

It came as no big surprise to me when the manager of Human Resources told me he didn't have a personnel file available for the bank's esteemed, commander-in-chief. A file did exist, somewhere, but I knew it would take special permission to get access to it; permission that could only come from Phil, himself, or from a special resolution by the bank's Board of Directors. In light of everything that was going on, I didn't feel real comfortable with the prospect of approaching either one of those sources on such a mission. There had to be another way to skin the cat.

Chapter 15

Friday: July 3rd (afternoon)

The second ransom note arrived on my desk without fanfare. I slid the single sheet of paper out of the envelope and read the brief statement. "Cancel *Operation Sine Dinar*, or face the consequences."

I didn't bother with the intercom. "Sheila!"

"What's it say?" she asked, as she rushed into my office.

"Cancel Operation Sine Dinar. What in the hell is Operation Sine Dinar?"

"You're asking me? Sounds like something from the Pentagon. Hell, maybe the bank is funding another Iran-Contra on the sly."

"Get serious. The last time Sterling was involved in a military operation a bunch of tea got dumped in the harbor. Something's going on here and we're probably the only ones who don't know what it is. Somebody better have some answers for me, and I mean now."

I grabbed the phone and started making calls.

"Sid, what the hell is Operation Sine Dinar?"

"Say what?"

"You heard me. Just tell me what you know about it."

"I don't know what the fuck you're talking about."

I knew Sid well enough to recognize when he was lying and this time he was definitely on the level. "Skip it. I'll get back to you." I punched the cancel button.

My next call was to Sunny. "Sunny, tell me about Operation Sine Dinar."

"What's that?"

"You saying you've never heard of it?"

"Are we playing 20 questions? What's going on?"

"I'm asking a simple question and I'd like a simple answer. Have you ever heard of Operation Sine Dinar?"

"No. Now, will you tell me what's going on?"

"I got another note from my pen pals. It says, `Cancel Operation Sine Dinar, or face the consequences.'"

"That's the second time they failed to mention money. This whole thing must be related somehow to that Operation, and not the money."

"Does it mean they're going to hit us again, or not?"

"I'd say, yes."

"Well we can't just sit back and let them get away with it. Can't you do something?"

"What do you have in mind?"

"Christ! I don't know. Shut down the goddamn computers or something."

"Mac, get a grip. You better give Phil the bad news. Maybe he has some ideas on what that operation is all about. In the meantime, I'll try to think of something that might make it more difficult for them if they do try to hit us again."

When I rang Phil's private number, Paula came on the line. "I'm sorry, Mac, he's already left for the day. He's spending the holiday at his place in Wenham."

"Another note arrived this afternoon and I need to discuss it with him, privately."

"Sounds important. Don't you always spend the Fourth at your son's place in Beverly?"

"You'd make a good cop."

"I can give you Phil's home number and you can call him from Brian's, then make some arrangements to get together. His place is practically next door. I know he's anxious to be kept up on anything going on in that matter."

What she was really telling me was, Phil's spending the holiday with his family instead of me, so I don't give a shit if you interrupt him. Well, it would be convenient for me, and slipping away from Brian's place for a few hours might be a welcomed excuse. It would get me out of the clutches of the latest date Sally had waiting for me.

Chapter 16

Saturday: July 4th (noon)

My retirement from the Boston PD came one year after Karen's death. A few months later, Brian held the first of his all-day block parties on the Fourth. The kid was never big on putting reasons behind his actions. I didn't press him on why he started doing it. If a party somehow fit in with how he wanted to handle his mother's death, so be it.

The thing grew bigger and more complicated every year, taking on a life of its own. Now, the Beverly Times sends out a reporter and photographer to cover things, and people come in from all over Essex County.

The weather on the Fourth always stinks in Massachusetts. It hardly ever rains, but you usually end up feeling like you've been caught in a shower. You know, hot and sticky, with the collar thing.

I turned off Rt.128 and drove through the quiet neighborhoods feeling my usual discomfort. Tree-lined streets divided into squares of green carpets don't reach out to me the way they do for others. I'm a confirmed city guy, comfortable only when I've got cement beneath my feet, and a tall building to lean against.

When my kids were growing up I never considered moving out of the city. Suburbia is okay for a visit, but like some Transylvanian vampire I have to be back on my native soil before dawn. It was a constant source of irritation for Karen.

I slowed down at the little pond next to the Cummings Center. The little stink hole always reminded me of someplace Thoreau probably would have hung out at. I turned onto Matthies Street and saw the crowds already milling around up ahead of me. When I came to a stop at the barricades set up to block off traffic, I spotted Brian's latest star fullback, Tony Riccio, hanging lights from a telephone pole for the evening dance party.

Every year, I stand around and stomp my icy feet on the sidelines at the traditional Beverly-Salem, Thanksgiving Day football battle; the price I have to pay for one of my daughter-in-law's great turkey dinners. As the coach's old man, I generally got to know some of the players who came and went and this Riccio kid was a sure winner.

"Hey, Riccio, give us a hand over here," I yelled at him.

The kid ran over and leaned in the window. "Yah, Mr. Mac. What's up?"

"Grab these cases of beer and take them in the house for me, while I park the car. And you better only take one for yourself, or I'll have to break both your legs and you won't run so good."

"You got it."

Everybody parked their cars in a small, neighborhood playground a block away. It was already filling up when I pulled in, and seeing as how I was planning to head out to see Phil Lord later that afternoon, I found a convenient get-away spot along the edge of the field.

As I walked back along the black asphalt road I began to realize how much I had in common with that old fart staring back at me in the mirror every morning. Not being able to get a handle on the investigation so far made me feel stupid. Feeling stupid is the same thing as feeling old.

What is it with this crazy sounding, "operation" crap? And how am I going to check out The Lord? What if he's involved in this whole mess? It all sounds like one giant swamp, just waiting to suck me under.

Eric Mahan, a local cop, was standing on a ladder painting his house when I walked by. I waved to him, and shouted out, "Hey, Eric," but didn't stop.

Every year Eric pulls me aside at the shindig, hands me a beer, then asks if the Boston PD is doing any hiring. The guy is never going to make any big changes in his life, but I guess asking the question gives him something to look forward to. New Englanders are like that. Eric has lived in this town all his life, and the house he is repainting for the 10th time, is the same one he grew up in. He'll never leave it.

The front door of Brian's house was wide open. Just as I stepped inside, I saw my three-year-old granddaughter, Maeve, carefully making her way down the stairs. It looked like she'd gone up to her room, unnoticed, and put on a bathing suit. I was pretty sure she had the top on backwards.

"Grampy!" she squealed, leaping fearlessly into the air.

"How's my sweet pea?" I said, reaching out quickly to catch her in mid-air, and enjoying the feeling of those tiny hands pulling on my ears.

"I got a new bathing suit, and Colly had a firecracker in his room and broke a window. Did you bring me something?" She talks nonstop, just like her mother.

"Sure I did, but I want my smooch first."

"No, I'm gonna lick you like Roscoe does," she giggled and proceeded to lick my cheek like the family's great dane.

I reached into my pocket and pulled out a little stuffed whale.

"It's a Beanie Baby," Maeve squealed, as I carried her into the kitchen. "Mama, Mama, Grampy got me a Beanie Baby."

"Hi, dad." Sally smiled up at me with those warm brown eyes. She was in the middle of cutting up a bucket of potatoes and stopped long enough to give me a kiss on the cheek and twist Maeve's top around. "You're early, your date won't be here for another hour. Just kidding. Maeve, honey, go play with Gillian and Pam, and show them your new Beanie Baby. Sheila and Les are here. They brought someone with them, Audrey something. She works with you. Kinda odd, but in a funny sort of way. Definitely from Brooklyn. Cathy hasn't shown up yet, but she promised. And she's a little nervous about you meeting this new guy, so go easy. We haven't met him either, but he sounds great. Just think, a doctor in the family."

If there was a breath in there somewhere, I never noticed. It was her Irish blood. My daughter-in-law talks so fast, and says so much, that she often carries on both sides of a conversation. I can live with that. At least she doesn't close me out like Cathy.

"I've got to go make a call, and I'll probably have to run over to Wenham for a little while this afternoon." I glanced out the kitchen window at the crowd spreading across the rest of the neighboring yards on the block.

"Sure. Anything wrong?"

"No, just business. I missed The Lord yesterday and need to go over something with him."

"Invite him over. He'll get his picture in the paper, and Tony Riccio would love to give him his autograph. We just found out he's made the Parade Magazine High School All-America Team. You sure everything's okay, Dad?"

"No big thing. I'm gonna go say hi to the Brooklyn Bomber."

Instead of walking out to the backyard, though, I detoured into the den and dialed Phil Lord's number. Phil actually sounded pleased that I called, and asked me to come by for a drink around 3:00 p.m.

It comes so easy for guys like him to schedule other peoples' lives. As a cop, I learned early on there are certain people you can tell what to do, and others who tell you how and when to do your job. That was just the way things work.

I made my way through the people moving in and out of the house and walked out to the backyard. Standing there for a minute, taking in the crowd. I spotted Brian.

He saw me and dropped what he was doing to come over and give me a hug, and kissed me on the cheek. That was another one of those odd little habits he picked up right after his mother died.

"Hi, Dad. You're early for a change."

"I thought I'd get in and out before my date arrives."

"No such luck, I think Sally talked Anita into taking another swing at you. She's over there getting it on with someone Sheila and Les brought along. "

Anita Boisvert is Brian's cute neighbor, three houses down. She is about my age, divorced with two grown kids, and some grandkids. Sally says we make a cute couple, because we both swear a lot. I have news for her, compared to Anita, I'm a sweet-talker. Actually, it might have worked out between us except for that time I stayed over and she woke up in the middle of the night with all them ghosts and goblins flying around. It scared the shit out of her.

"I've got to take care of something in Wenham," I said to Brian.

"Yah, Sheila mentioned that to me. Well, I'm in the middle of getting this game set up, so grab a beer and make yourself comfortable. You know everyone. I'll catch up with you later. Cathy's not here, yet."

Brian is 32-years-old and stands a little taller than his old man, with a leaner build, but the same thick forearms and large hands. A natural athlete, he was a standout in three sports. His talent got him a spot on the All-Ivy League football team during his last two years at Dartmouth College.

Like most things in Brian's life, his decision to teach and coach instead of following in his dad's footsteps, turned out to be fortuitous. Three years after he signed on as an assistant coach at Beverly High School, the local legend, Bill Hamor, decided to retire and handpicked Brian as his successor. Two state championships and three undefeated seasons later, he was already receiving offers from a number of local colleges. There is no doubt in my mind that the kid will always make the right decision, at the right time. He also would have made a great cop.

I grabbed a beer from behind the portable bar set-up in the yard, stopped to shake hands with Brian's next door neighbors, Al and Anne DePiero, and headed toward Sheila, waving to me from Al's yard. She and her husband, Les, were seated at a table with Audrey and Anita, in one of the eating sections set-up on the DePiero's patio.

Les Woburn was my partner for more years than either one of us care to mention. As we shook hands, I grinned and said, "Hey, Buddy, your old lady looks like she's working vice in the combat zone." Sheila had on a pair of shorts and a tank top. The local teenage boys, and their dads, were going to have wet dreams for a month.

"Yah, she's undercover. We hear there's a big hooker-housewife sex ring going on around here, and Sally's the madam."

Les and Sheila got married two years ago. They figured they might as well make it legal, seeing as how they were spending so many nights together pulling me through endless bouts of depression. Their shared loyalty saved my ass on more than one occasion.

"Hey, Nita, you look good enough to eat," I offered as I bent down and gave her a peck on the cheek.

"You always said the way to a man's heart is not through his stomach, it's through his dick."

"I was just trying to get in your pants."

"So, Audrey," I asked, sitting down beside her, "anyone ask to see your green card, yet? You know, New Englanders consider Brooklyneese a foreign language."

"Yeah, well anyone who says, `pahk the caah,' ought to learn to talk right before they go throwin' stones." She had grown pretty comfortable around Sheila and me by now, and the friendly atmosphere of this gathering gave her another reason to relax.

People were roaming everywhere in the neighborhood. There were a dozen activities going on at once. At Anita's house a horseshoe-pitching contest was taking place, and under one large weeping willow tree, several chess and checkers games were being played out. Brian was supervising an egg-rolling contest for two dozen little tots and nearby a bunch of youngsters, including my 10-year-old grandson, Colin, were trying to pass a water balloon from one to another without using their hands. It was all pretty corny, but it worked.

I see a lot of Brian in Colin. If there is a risk to be taken, Colin will be first in line, and if trouble is nearby, he knows how to find it. Fortunately, he also has his father's charm and his mother's gift of gab to help get him out of most scrapes. Above all else, though, what I really like about that runt is the way he adores his baby sister.

It was exactly the same way between Brian and Cathy. Brian is only three years older than Cathy, but you would have thought he was her father the way he looked after her when they were little; and still does.

In a roundabout way, I guess their close relationship came about because I was always trying to keep my family separated from my job. I wanted Karen and the kids protected from all the filth and violence I had to wallow in every day. The only way I knew how to do that was to be distant and unapproachable, just like my old man. Only Karen knew how to get inside. Brian just naturally filled in for the missing dad in Cathy's life.

Everything changed on that rainy Saturday afternoon, nine years ago. It was my day off. Karen dragged me along when she went to do her shopping at a neighborhood grocery store. Two whacked-out punks showed up to rob the place, and in a matter of seconds, gunfire broke out. The punks were dead, and I was lying on the floor with my left knee torn open, clutching Karen's lifeless body tightly in my arms. I tried, God knows I tried, to hold back the blood, but Karen bled to death in the middle of all that sawdust and overturned shelves. There wasn't a thing I could do except scream at God.

A year later, I had a plastic knee that worked pretty good, and my life was supposed to move on. But no amount of stitches could ever sew up the real hole. A part of me was left behind on that blood-soaked, wooden floor; the part that tried so hard to hold onto Karen's life. I never found it, and my life never really got back to the way it had been.

One thing I eventually was forced to face had to do with my service revolver. I couldn't manage to draw it, let alone use it in the line of duty. On "bloody Saturday" I drew down on those punks out of force of habit. Since then, every time I tried to pull my gun from its holster, I saw the image of Karen in my arms, bleeding to death, her eyes pleading for me to save her. I couldn't manage to separate one thing from the other.

On the day of what would have been our 25th wedding anniversary, I turned in my badge and accepted the job as head of security at Sterling Bank & Trust of Boston. Even now, eight years later, I'm not sure I did the right thing.

I spotted Cathy coming around the corner of the house and the minute that halo of shiny, black hair surrounding her beautiful face was in view, a big knot formed in my stomach. The blue eyes are so much like her mother's. I watched her search the crowd looking for me as the dull constant ache in my heart spread like a cancer eating away at my insides.

"Hi, Daddy," she said, wrapping her arms around my neck and kissing me.

Whenever I got to hold her in my arms it was like getting shock therapy. If I closed my eyes I couldn't tell if I was holding Cathy, or Karen. My mind played tricks on me, and Cathy became a child again, long enough for Karen to be alive. There was no defense. It hurt like hell.

"I want you to meet Dr. Michael Jordan. Michael this is my father, Duncan MacKenzie."

"You look a little different on the court," I joked, shaking the man's hand. "I always figured you to be taller."

"It's all the make-up I have to wear so everyone thinks I'm black. Actually, there aren't any black guys in the NBA." He obviously was used to getting ribbed.

Cathy introduced Michael to Anita and Sheila, and Sheila introduced Audrey. While Sheila gave Michael some good-natured grilling, I pulled over a seat for Cathy and she sat down next to me.

"So, how come you didn't call me back the other day?" I asked.

"I thought you weren't going to do that anymore."

"Do what. I can't call my own daughter anymore?"

"Daddy, I know Les told you about the big bust going down. That's what you were calling about."

"Look, I only wanted to go over a few things your Sergeant probably didn't have time to mention. Those kind of deals can get tricky, there's a lot that can go wrong."

"You promised you wouldn't interfere anymore."

"What, interfere? I was only trying to give you the benefit of a little experience. A lot of rookies would cream in their jeans to hear what I have to say, but my own daughter thinks it's all a load of crap."

"I'm not a rookie anymore, and I don't think it's crap. I just want you to let me do my job and stop trying to protect me. I can handle things on my own."

It began the day she signed up to be a cop. Cathy wanted me to respect her as an individual, and not treat her like a daughter. But I had a hard time getting beyond the image of her in a shoot-out. Ever since she joined the force, it was her face that began appearing in my recurring nightmares.

Maeve interrupted us as she climbed up on Cathy's lap. Brian and Sally were close behind and a new round of introductions got under way. I used the opportunity to pull Sheila aside and see if she'd come up with anything new on the investigation.

"How's it going?"

"Nothing out of the ordinary, so far. I think we can safely eliminate Audrey, but Sunny and Dennis are still a real mystery. As rich as he is, I can't imagine why Dennis even gets up in the morning. And Sunny's got so much going, I can't see her jeopardizing everything to get involved in some stupid bank job. By the way, Audrey's come up with a new slant on things. I'll let her explain."

She called Audrey over.

"Tell Mac what you mentioned to me yesterday."

Audrey followed me over to the grill area to pick up a few burgers and fresh beers.

"The way I see it, Mac, we've been trying to figure out where the scumbags jacked in and it's getting us nowhere. So I'm thinking, what if that ain't their style. What if they can get on the right road without being hard-wired."

"You mean using wireless communication? You heard me ask Dennis about that and he said they'd have to install transmitters and receivers on both ends."

"I know, but what if he's wrong. What if the transmitter and receiver only has to be on one end. The remote computer would act just like it was in the system except there'd be no record of it being there."

"What's that bit you said about getting on the right road?"

"The crooks need to get to the main data base, right, where all the customer account records are kept. That stuff is at a particular address on the main server. To get there you gotta know the right codes."

I must have had a blank look on my face because she immediately tried a different approach.

"Look, getting into a computer is like landing at Logan: you're in the right town, but you still gotta get to the right address. To land at Logan you need some codes, but once you start running around town you keep bumping into these one-way streets. You have to figure out which ones to take before you can get where you're going.

"Say you've got a map of city streets and you're a cabby trying to figure out which ones to take to get to a particular address. You know the general layout and the direction you need to go, so you start trying some standard codes to get there. That's the hacking part, figuring out which streets or codes will take you where you want to go. Once a hacker gets online, as long as he knows the address, sooner or later he's gonna find a way to get there."

"You're giving me Star Trek crap, again. Can someone do what you're saying or can't they?"

"You mean connect remotely with another computer? How the hell should I know? But if you give me the okay, I thought I'd try it out on one of my old profs at NYU. If there's anyone in the country working on that shit he'll know about it."

"Okay, do it, just don't use any names and don't mention why you're asking. The Lord ain't too happy over our progress so far, and he's going to be even less pleased once I give him the latest news. So keep in mind what he said about no leaks."

"Yeah, I hear you. I don't blame you for being nervous. That guy has a way of looking at you and all of a sudden you're as dumb as dirt."

"Who said anything about being nervous. I said he wasn't going to be happy about what I'm going to tell him."

"Which is?"

"The latest note from our pen-pals."

"No shit. Another note. This is really getting juicy."

Chapter 17

Saturday: July 4th (afternoon)

If Phil Lord wasn't camped out at his Louisburg Square townhouse a few blocks from the Capital building on Beacon Hill, or visiting Paula Harding's swanky digs, he usually checked in at his quaint little cottage; a 30-room, stone castle located in the tiny hamlet of Wenham, next door to Beverly. The Lord estate sits on a gentle rise, that, get this, is called 'Lord's Hill.' It has a great view of the surrounding properties and the obligatory church steeple pokes through the ancient elm trees beside the village green, in the center of town.

As the current lord of the manor, and also head of the Lord Foundation, Phil presided over the locals with a certain restrained sincerity. He kept a yacht, the *Lordship*, moored close by in Manchester-by-the-Sea, and on Sundays, during the fall season, he often brought out his horses to participate in the polo matches at the Myopia Hunt Club. In short, the guy lead a life that was about as close to aristocracy, as Americans would tolerate.

Whenever I drive through Wenham I get the feeling I've fallen into a Norman Rockwell painting. People coo over the place calling it, "a lovely New England village." Well, I ain't one of them. I like to imagine there are ritual sacrifices going on behind those shuttered windows.

This was my first visit to the Lord mansion, but it didn't come as a big surprise when a butler answered the front door. "Sir, the guests are gathered on the west terrace. Please follow me."

I was lead down a wide corridor through a large, well-stocked library and out onto a stone terrace. As I stepped through the tall, French doors onto the terrace, I found myself standing beside Charlotte Lord, Phil's wife.

"It's Mick, or Mac, or something like that, isn't it?" she asked, pointing her drink at me. "I remember talking to you at the Sterling Christmas party last year."

"It's Mac, Mrs. Lord, Mac MacKensie."

"Call me Char, everyone does. Now I remember," she added, resting a warm silky hand lightly on my bare forearm, "you're a cop, or you were a cop, and now you're the head of security at the bank."

"You'd make a good cop, yourself. I'm sure you met a lot of people at that party."

"Oh, I remember you. You weren't at all like the rest of those plastic drones." Her open smile filled an attractive face, but the bloodshot eyes gave away her secret. She started drinking long before the party was underway. Her figure was attractively slim, but I guessed she had to work hard to keep it that way.

Phil quickly joined us, and Charlotte just as quickly lost interest in me. "I hate boy talk, so I'll leave you to it," she said, and let her hand slide off my arm   As she sauntered away, displaying a shapely backside that moved suggestively beneath her thin dress, she glanced over her shoulder and added, "Don't be a stranger, Mac."

"I'm so grateful you could manage to come by," Phil added, as he motioned to a waiter carrying a tray of drinks. "Holidays are supposed to be a chance to relax, but somehow they always end up being so hectic."

He handed me a fancy glass of champagne, lifted his own and offered a quiet toast. "To our success in catching those wretched crooks."

I took a long swallow as Phil turned me around and led me back inside the library. "We'll be more comfortable in my study."

We headed from the west wing over to the east side of the mansion. Along the way, I was surprised to see rooms and furniture that were the complete opposite of the style Phil liked to maintain at work. At Sterling, he insisted everything be super modern and high-tech, creating the impression that Sterling, although steeped in tradition, was right up there with the best in the new technological age.

This place, on the other hand, looked like the Vanderbilts had a hand in the decorating. Old-looking paintings in large, ornate frames cluttered the walls, and heavily carved, dark furniture, built to fit the large, high-ceiling rooms, looked ancient and immovable. I looked around for a sign that said, "no metal or plastic allowed."

"This is quite a place. How old is it?"

"Actually, as places go in this neighborhood, the house is fairly new. The estate has been in my family since the early 1800's but my grandfather, in a fit of anger, had the previous house leveled and built this one in 1930, at a cost of $1 million, a bargain even in those days. He had all the stone cut from nearby quarries in Rockport.

"In this age of supermarkets and the home shopping channel you might be surprised to know this estate is completely self-sufficient. We even have our own full-time butcher. Everything from soup to nuts is grown right here on the grounds. I take that back! We've never been able to produce a decent wine. But I do have an interest in a California vineyard that produces some excellent varietals. The champagne you're drinking is from California."

"I don't know much about wines but this ain't bad." I emptied the glass.

"I'm glad you enjoy it. Please allow me to send a case over, with my compliments, for your son's celebration. Brian has become quite a celebrity on the north shore."

"Yah, he's been like that since he was a kid. Always knew where he was headed."

"I hope you don't mind my saying so, Mac, but I really have to wonder about Cathy. I mean doing so well in law school and then throwing it all away to be a cop. I could have set her up with one of the best firms in town."

"You've caught me off guard, Phil. I didn't realize you knew that much about my kids."

"You can't rely on people if you don't know them. I know everything there is to know about all the people I rely on."

"And that includes me?"

"When I hired you, I told you, you were the best man for the job. I meant it."

"Well, right now I'm trying to get to know some people on a very short list, and one of the names on that list is yours." I decided to take this unexpected opening and go for broke.

"So you want permission to see my confidential file, right?"

"That's the way it works."

Phil sat down at his desk and quickly wrote out a note on a piece of personal stationary. He handed it to me and said, "Take this to Ralph Woodson's office on Monday and he'll supply you with what you're looking for. It won't amount to what you're hoping for, but it's easier to let you find that out for yourself.

"Now, let's see what you've brought me."

"It's a copy," I added, as I handed over the piece of paper. I studied Phil's face for any telltale signs, but there weren't any.

Phil looked up at me and said, "We obviously need to find out what this *Operation Sine Dinar* is all about. Have you told anyone about this note?"

"Only Sheila and Sunny. I asked Sid if he knew anything about that name without mentioning why I wanted to know, and he was in the dark. I also told Audrey Simone we got another note but she doesn't know the contents. Oh, yah, I mentioned to Paula that a note had come in when she gave me your home phone number."

"Mac, where in the hell's your common sense. You might as well be publishing it on the damn internet. From now on, only you and I will know a note has arrived, or its contents. Am I clear on that?"

"Crystal clear." In all the years I've known the guy I've never seen him lose his cool like that.

He must have read my mind because he quickly apologized. "I'm sorry for barking at you like that, Mac, but secrecy is so important these days. I guess I'm a little frustrated over not getting anywhere yet. The longer this goes on, the more chance there is of a leak. If that happens damage control will be extremely difficult. Mac, I need a name, and I need it now."

There was a knock on the door and the butler came in to announce a telephone call for Phil. Phil asked him to take a message, but the butler added, "It is the overseas operator, sir."

For a split second I thought I saw a flash of raw anger in Phil's eyes. Anger isn't an emotion anyone would readily associate with Philip Lord. I was ready to ignore it until I heard that smooth aristocratic voice turn icy and sharp.

"I really have to take this call, Mac. You'll have to excuse me for a moment." He turned to his butler. "Hamilton, please have a case of the California champagne brought out to Mr. MacKenzie's car."

Phil went into an adjacent room to take the call and the door remained open a crack. Curiosity got the better of me so I wandered over to eavesdrop on Phil's end of the conversation.

"I'm surprised, that's all, Henrí. I wasn't expecting to hear from you so soon ... It can't be solved over night ... I know how important the operation is ... I'll try to catch the Concorde Monday night. That should put me in Paris on Tuesday morning and at your place by noon. I'll call if I can't make connections."

When Phil returned, his familiar, disarming smile was back in place. "Forgive the interruption, Mac. I'm scheduled to attend a conference in Europe next week and I thought they might be calling to change the date on me. I hate last minute changes."

In his usual calm, collected manner he moved on to the matter at hand. "We have to get this theft business solved quickly before the wolves get the scent. Over the weekend why don't you get together with Sunny and see if the two of you can work out a list of possible suspects. First thing Monday morning give Paula a call and I'll have her squeeze you both in for a meeting before lunch. We'll go over whatever you've come up with and get started running some offense for a change." I felt Phil's hand in the small of my back giving me a signal that our meeting was over.

I knew he would extend an invitation to stay longer and socialize, but I needed some fresh air, and a chance to organize my screwed-up thoughts.

"There's nothing I'd like better than getting a little offensive, especially with Sunny." I glanced at my watch. "But right now, I'm gonna be late for my shift as chief burger-flipper if I don't get a move on. "

"I haven't even had a chance to show you around," Phil responded. "Oh well, we'll schedule a victory party after we put those crooks where they belong. Thank you so much for coming, Mac. I appreciate you taking the time to keep me informed."

As I drove down the quarter-mile long driveway to the main road, I glanced over at the case of champagne sitting on the front seat beside me. I couldn't help wonder what it all meant. Was this some kind of a down payment, a payoff for some special services I was going to be asked to perform? Or, was it an offer of friendship from someone looking for an ally who could throw a few punches when the fighting started.

Two things were real clear. Phil just lied to me about that phone call. Whoever this Henry guy was on the other end of that call, and whatever he was telling Phil about showing up in Europe on Tuesday, it wasn't something that had been planned. Phil also used the word "operation" and coincidences always got my attention.

As I walked back up Glidden Street headed to Brian's house for the second time that day, my grandson and two of his pals ambushed me. "Gramps, we need your help on something. You're the only one who won't bust us."

"I heard you're camping out at Roscoe's place," I said, putting down the case of wine and wrapping my arm around the boy's shoulder. I wished he was still young enough to be kissed. "Don't you think going for double trouble is pushing things a bit?"

"If you help us I won't get in trouble."

"You mean I'm the one who'll get blamed."

The three boys dragged me off into the shadows between two houses. Colin reached into his pocket and drew out a bright red, cherry-bomb, giving it all the care and respect such a valuable piece of contraband deserved. Private possession of fireworks is illegal in Massachusetts, so the excitement that little ball of gunpowder held for these 10-year-olds was obvious. Colin's friend, Jack, presented me with an empty coffee can, and it was clear they wanted me to supervise setting off the firecracker under the can, sending it skyward.

Getting caught with a firecracker earlier in the day had made Colin a little more cautious than usual. He was committing a serious act of trust by showing off his prize to an adult, but he knew taking me into his confidence would obligate me to help him, or risk alienating his affections. That was something I generally avoided. Besides, history was repeating itself. It wasn't too hard to recall doing the very same thing when I was his age.

"All you guys get to do is watch. Deal?" I snatched up the cherry-bomb.

"Cool," the kids answered in happy unison.

My countdown crew followed me down the block to a darkened spot, away from the lights and the people beginning to gather in the street. The explosion sent the can sailing about 10 feet in the air to the delight of Colin and his friends as they sat near-by on the curb. Colin rushed over and hugged me in gratitude then ran off with his friends after I made each of them empty their pockets so I could assure myself there were no more hidden surprises.

I watched the boys disappear into the shadows and it reminded me of how tough it was to picture Brian at that age. Too many times I hadn't been there, and when I was, I usually kept him and Cathy at arms' length. There was nothing I could do about that now, except maybe hug Colin and Maeve as often as I could. Karen would have been the one to do it if she was here.

I dropped off the champagne and drifted into the crowd collecting in the street where I ran into Sheila.

"I'm glad you finally found someone your own age to play with," she said, smiling knowingly. "Well, what did he come up with?"

I had no doubt who she was referring to.

"Nothing. The guy was a blank, just like all the rest of them."

She wasn't buying it and pressed me. "What's the sense in trying to bullshit me? I know you found out something."

"Okay, smart-ass. He got an overseas phone call and I heard him use the word "operation." Happy?"

"What's the big deal over a phone call?"

"The guy on the other end was telling him to show up in Europe on Tuesday. When he got off the line he lied to me, said it was a planned trip."

"How do you know it wasn't?"

"Because I'm a cop. Or, I used to be one. What the hell difference does it make, the guy lied to me."

"A little touchy, big boy? How did you leave things?"

I grinned at her. "He wants me to spend the weekend being offensive with Sunny. I told him it was a dirty job, but I was up to it."

"Listen, old man, you wouldn't last 2 minutes with that girl."

Twilight was settling around us and the local kids' band was warming up, nearby. The Christmas lights strung from the telephone poles were turned on, and the band, dressed in clothes from the Fifties, jumped into music from that era, which I guessed was the latest fad among teenagers.

They played "Smoke Gets In Your Eyes" and Cathy walked over and pulled me into the crowd for a dance, leaving Michael with Sheila.

"Well, what do you think?"

"I'm not the one who has to smell his breath in the morning."

"That's great fatherly advice."

"Is it serious enough that I should be giving fatherly advice?"

"He is, but I'm not sure."

"You can never be sure when it comes to people."

"Mom always said she was sure the first time she met you."

"Women like everything to be romantic, even if they have to lie about it."

"How did your meeting go?"

"Now who's butting into whose business? But I'm glad you brought that up. How come you never told me that you and Phil got together?"

"Why, what did he say?"

"Enough so that I realize you two had some contact that I never knew about."

"There wasn't anything to tell. I was in my third year of law school, working on the Law Review, and got asked to help out on an article about financial privacy in the computer age. The attorney writing the article arranged for me to interview this big wig from Europe, a guy named Henrí Bettancourt, who was in town for a conference. Phil was with him when I did the interview.

"Later, Phil took me to lunch and complimented me on the article and the way I handled myself during the interview. He asked me to look him up when I graduated. No names were mentioned but he told me there was a firm in town that needed a young lawyer in their banking department. The day I passed the bar he sent me some flowers and a note, reminding me of that conversation."

"Did you get back to him?"

"No. I'd already made up my mind to go to the academy. He's not an easy guy to turn down, so I just avoided him."

"This Henry guy, how come you interviewed him?"

"His family's big in banking; have been for generations. In Belgium I think. He travels all over the world lecturing on banking and finance.

"The attorney I was helping out heard he was going to be in Boston and got Phil to set up the interview. To tell you the truth it felt like I was talking to royalty. The guy was power personified."

I was hearing too many coincidences to overlook the possibility that I'd stumbled onto something. "While you were interviewing the guy did he happen to mention something called Operation Sine Dinar?"

"Not that I recall." She looked at me like I had just said something stupid. "That doesn't sound like something he'd likely be involved with."

"What do you mean?"

"If I remember my Latin, *sine dinar* translates into something like, "without cash." Why would a banker be interested in something that doesn't involve cash? Sounds more like government stuff to me. You know, like arms for hostages."

Cathy was too good a cop to let the subject drop. "Daddy, is something going on?"

"If there was what makes you think I'd tell you?" I started leading her back to the rest of the family, but stopped and pulled her up close to me. "For once in your life, do what your old man says. Let me know the minute Phil or this Henry guy from Belgium contacts you. Understood?"

Chapter 18

Sunday, July 5th (morning)

I called Sunny early the next morning to arrange a meeting. She came back at me with a won't-take-no-for-an-answer invitation to go sailing off Marblehead. She and Dennis showed up at my house around 8:30 a.m. and dragged me along on their way out of town. Driving past Suffolk Downs, I looked over and silently berated myself for all the bets I hadn't made since this damn case hit my desk.

From the back seat of the car, I began to think about Sheila's remarks about Dennis after reviewing his personnel file. How rich is this kid, really? Once you get past the "John Voight/Midnight Cowboy" outfit there isn't a lot of clues to follow.

I knew he was a Texan by birthright, the tall and lanky kind, with a perpetual boyish smile, and puppy-dog eyes that matched his curly brown hair. The outfit, usually jeans and a t-shirt, with Tony Lama cowboy boots, was definitely a disguise meant to throw people off guard. Like his roommate, Sunny, once you got past the attractive packaging, things just got better.

A year ago, he and I were at Jake's one night and Dennis confided to me he was the great, great, grandson of the legendary Ian Crawford, an orphan who found his way to the untamed West and helped bring Texas into the Union. In the process, old Ian managed to carve out a sizable chunk of the east Texas prairie for himself. Today, that original piece of land has grown into the largest, privately owned ranch in the world, the "Crawford Ranch."

Located in Crawfordsville, Texas, the ranch, according to Dennis, consisted of one million acres of gas and oil reserves, cattle, farming, and sundry other enterprises representing an empire so huge that it generated millions of dollars annually to every one of Ian's descendants. Every lineal descendant receives shares of stock in the family corporation. Dennis's shares make him a millionaire many times over, without ever lifting his head off the pillow.

Dennis decided his interests lay elsewhere and turned to the sea. He became a sailing enthusiast, and eventually an Olympic champion Soling racer, a difficult and extremely competitive class. That was only one of several weird things the kid did real well. The one he did best was his day job, designing and manufacturing custom motherboards for cutting edge computers.

On this holiday weekend, it was Sunny, not Dennis, who managed to borrow a fancy sailboat for a run from Marblehead to Cape Ann and back. Turned out, a while ago, while she was completing her graduate studies at MIT, Sunny got asked to help out on some computer studies being conducted by a well-known sail maker and yacht designer, Ted Hood. Her efforts were tops and Hood, along with his staff, stayed in touch with her over the years. Whenever she called looking for a favor, Ted wouldn't hesitate to lend whatever sailboat he had hanging around, especially if there was a chance of getting some feedback on one of his hot new sail designs from someone as big in the field as Dennis Crawford.

Dennis drove his Lincoln Navigator slowly through the narrow, twisting streets of Marblehead, down to the harbor, and by the time we approached the waterfront I was having second thoughts about this assignment. To me, sailboats don't look very sea-worthy. They look ready to tip over at the first gust of wind. Besides, anything that uses bed sheets and a bunch of ropes tied together doesn't inspire me with lots of confidence. Given the opportunity to make a choice, I definitely would have voted for a chair on the dock, and an afternoon of landlubber drinking.

Tourists were cramming the over-crowded streets and the locals seemed to make every effort to ignore them. Dennis worked his way inside the Hood shipyard and while he and I began unloading our supplies, Sunny took off for the office to say hello. After everything was unloaded on the wharf, Dennis drove off to find an out-of-the-way spot to park his car, and left me alone on the dock.

Ted Hood's sail loft and dock are located in the heart of Marblehead's waterfront. Marblehead harbor doesn't look like one of those marinas you see on TV with neat rows of gangways running between parallel lines of boats. It's more old-fashioned. The fleet, or what there is of it, is a jumble of sizes and shapes, moored in no particular order, in the middle of the harbor.

I stood there, alone, staring anxiously down at the long, sexy-looking boat rocking slightly in the gentle swells against the dock. My right hand reached up, unconsciously, to my empty breast pocket. Giving up smoking was a real dumb idea.

When everyone was onboard, Dennis started the engine and asked me to cast off the mooring lines. The smell of spent diesel fuel and the chugging sound of an engine helped settle me down, and as the boat moved away from the dock under power, I tried to think of it as nothing more than a funny shaped, convertible car.

Sunny handed me a beer, then moved up front to check on a few things. I sat down, took a long swallow, and stretched my legs across the wide space in front of Dennis.

Dennis was standing behind an oversized steering wheel wrapped with cord.

"You ever own one of these babies?" I asked.

"Not this big. Remember, I told you I sail Solings. They're a lot smaller. This baby was designed by Ted Hood back in the Sixties, but it's still a work of art."

"Is that old for a boat?"

"Yacht. That depends on what you're comparing it to. Ted keeps this one around to do preliminary testing on his new sails and it's great for something like that. Anything this beautiful never goes out of style."

Sunny sat down beside me. "I hope he was referring to me."

"You got that right, lady," I answered, grinning at her. "I warned you two I'm not really into sailing, but this ain't half bad. I mean I could get used to this."

"We're not even out of the harbor yet, Mac." She unzipped the light blue windbreaker she was wearing. Beneath it she had on a blue and white striped jersey and a pair of white Bermuda shorts, an outfit that made whatever age she was seem like the bloom of womanhood.

"Well, you wouldn't hurt my feelings if we just tooled around like this for the rest of the day."

Dennis laughed at me. "By the time we get you back to the dock tonight you'll think you're "Ishmael." You know, the survivor in Moby Dick."

"Just watch out for Captain Ahab!" Sunny added.

"It's getting hot," Sunny announced. "I think I'll go below and change before we clear the outer marker. I'll bring up some sunscreen for you, Mac. You don't realize how quickly you can get burned at sea."

I watched her climb down a short ladder and from where I was seated, I saw glimpses of her moving around in the main cabin. For one brief moment she passed before me completely nude and it was like seeing a centerfold come to life. Embarrassed, I quickly looked up to see if Dennis noticed anything.

"Her parents raised her in a hippie commune," he answered, without being asked. "She's never been real big on modesty."

She came back on deck wearing a bright, floral bikini and matching headband. It looked like there was more fabric in the headband than the bikini, but I wasn't complaining. Man, that was definitely one no-nonsense, all-original, drop-dead body.

My fantasy got interrupted when Dennis shouted, "All hands to the yardarms."

"That's why men should never be put in a position of power," Sunny answered. "They love being the boss. Come on, Mac, he's talking about us."

I followed her along the narrow flat deck to the mast and watched as she undid the ties holding the mainsail. She pointed to a rope wrapped around a cleat on the mast and told me, "You're going to hoist the sail by pulling on that line, while I feed the sail from here."

I did as I was told and the huge sail began rising above the water like a giant fin. Near the top, I couldn't budge it another inch, but it clearly had to go higher.

"Okay, now wrap the line clockwise around that winch and crank it until the top of the sail reaches the very top of the mast," Sunny ordered.

Dennis had us pointed directly into the wind and the engine kept us moving slowly ahead through the passing waves. Sunny showed me how to secure the main halyard, then she made her way to the front, quickly unfurled another sail attached to a wire running up to the top of the mast and fastened the bottom of that sail on the left side of the boat.

Sunny told me to take a seat on the right side of the cockpit, and just as I did, the engine conked out. Dennis spun the big wheel, making the bow swing off on what he called a "starboard tack." That's when I began to get nervous.

An incredible surge of power rushed through my body as the wind caught the sails and brought the boat to life. The deck behind my back rose up above the water as the boat began cutting through the waves like a giant sword. Chilly salt water sprayed onto my warm skin as we picked up speed. The clean, fresh, salt-air went up my nose. I looked around for something to grab onto. Yah, I was getting a little excited, too.

Dennis tossed his head back and wailed, "Christ! I love this old gal."

"Don't be such a baby, Mac," Sunny needled from behind her dark sunglasses. She slid up next to me, leaned in close, and began spreading sunscreen on my face and the back of my neck. Her silky touch and the sight of all that naked flesh so close to me, quickly took my mind off the threat of capsizing. But what came out of her mouth next had me on-guard.

"If I really wanted to dump you overboard I'd wait until we were further out to sea." She said it in a whisper, and maybe it was the touch of her hand that was making the hairs on the back of my neck stand on end.

"Why me? What did I ever do to you?" I tried making it sound like I was joking. But was she?

"To keep you from finding out about all our dark secrets during your investigation." She gave me a big smile.

S. T. MUGGLEBEE

"By now, I'm sure you've been running a very thorough check on Dennis and me."

"Technically, Sheila's doing you two. I've got The Lord and Lady Paula."

"That ought to be interesting reading."

She moved on to Dennis and spread the sunscreen on his face and arms as she continued to chatter. "Obviously, no one has stepped up to knowing anything about that code word. The one the crooks mentioned in their latest ransom note. That means you've got to check out everyone on the team. Am I right?"

There had to be a price to pay for an afternoon of watching Sunny romp around in the buff and all the free beer I could drink, but I wasn't sure I was ready to play show and tell with her. The question of why I'd been invited on this trip suddenly became more of an issue. Was she trying to get me to back off, or simply hoping I would share whatever information I'd found out so far? With Sunny Childe you never knew for sure what she was thinking.

"Once you decide the crooks aren't in it for the money it means they probably already have plenty," Dennis followed up. "The balance in my checking account puts me in that club and Sunny's doing pretty well, too. So there's not much sense in trying to make like we aren't prime suspects. Right, honey?"

Sunny sat down beside me again and began to lather cream on her own body while I made sure she didn't miss any spots.

"If we can't trust each other it makes all our jobs a whole lot harder. You're the one calling the shots, Mac, so you get to set the rules. Do we share things, or just stay in our neutral corners and prepare for the main event?"

This particular scenario wasn't something I had rehearsed, but as an ex-detective I wasn't about to let it drop. "So far, I don't see a lot to share. None of us knows what this Operation Sine Dinar is all about and that pretty much leaves us high and dry. Which is where I'd rather be right now."

"Not necessarily," she responded.

She took the helm from Dennis and he scampered forward and yelled back to me, "Unhook that line from the winch beside you, Mac." When I did so, Dennis released the smaller sail on the left side, and had me pull it in on the right side.

The maneuver went smoothly and Sunny brought us onto another tack. Dennis took back the helm, adjusted the mainsail lines, and we began picking up speed again.

After directing me to move over beside her on the left side of the cockpit, Sunny continued on from where she left off. "Just because we don't know the particulars of their operation doesn't mean we don't know anything about what they're up to. For instance, they went after a bank, not a supermarket. That tells us something right there.

"They've sent two notes, neither of which mentioned anything about money. Instead, they demanded that the bank take certain action. We still haven't figured out what kind of action they want to take, but whatever it is, it's not about stealing money. It definitely has something to do with the way Sterling does business."

"Sounds like you two are making a lot of assumptions," I argued.

"Assumptions are what computers are all about," Dennis chimed in. "The crooks set this whole thing up using computers, so they're bound to be familiar with using assumptions to reach their goals. One assumption could be that the figure $5 million is big enough to get the bank's attention, but small enough to keep it quiet, that sort of thing. Get the point?"

"Maybe I'm just a dumb ex-cop, but what I see is we're dealing with people who stick-up banks because that's where the money is, and if we don't come up with some way of stopping them they're going to take some more."

The jagged coastline of Salem and Beverly grew distant behind us as we headed north, toward Gloucester. The swells were deepening and the boat was riding up and down through the water in a relaxing rhythm. The rhythm made me less concerned about the waves and more concerned about that earlier crack Sunny had made about dumping me overboard. It struck me as an odd joke in light of her insistence that I join them on this outing.

"Think about what you just said for a moment," Sunny questioned me. "There's really only two ways to stop them. One is to figure out how they're getting into the computer and go against them there. The other is to cancel *Operation Sine Dinar,* which is what they've said they want us to do.

"We've been concentrating on trying to stop them from taking the money, but if money isn't their real objective we could be chasing our tails. Whoever is behind this game knows a lot about Sterling and how it operates. If they just dreamed up this "Sine Dinar" business, what would it get them? Someone at the bank has to know what that operation is, otherwise the message becomes a big waste of time. Trust me, *Operation Sine Dinar* is something that's a lot more important to the bank than the money."

"You two must have left me back on the dock," I laughed, trying to keep things casual. "It sounds like you know a lot more about what's going on than I do."

God, I wish I hadn't stopped smoking. Some cement under my feet would be great, too, right about now.

I looked Sunny in the eye. "What I'd really like to get are some straight answers for a change. For instance, why don't you enlighten me about that trouble you and Phil had last year, when the new system went online?"

"She's tough when it comes to truth or dare, big fella," Dennis yelled at me. "She likes to play dirty, so hold onto your shorts. Before you two get into it heavy, I'm ready to come about again. Haul your asses back up on deck and man those lines one more time."

"That's a private road, Mac," Sunny answered, as we moved to work the sails. "I assure you, traveling down it won't get you any closer to the crooks. It's strictly a personal matter, and I want to leave it that way."

My head was starting to itch and I scratched at it through the Red Sox cap I was wearing. The way she said it, the way she kept squeezing those little bunches of facts into a nice neat package and then presenting it to me like a gift, made me feel like I was being set-up. The same way I felt that first day when I started making all those calls to the banks.

I wanted to take a swing at one of the fastballs Sunny was serving up, but I couldn't figure out which direction to face. The ball just kept whizzing past me for a perfect strike.

I snapped open my fourth beer and began playing the "what if" game in my head. What if Sunny and Dennis were the ones behind all this shit. How much of what she just described, fit them? It was the same question I asked myself yesterday when I saw that case of champagne sitting on the front seat of my car. Is Sunny using this excursion to find an ally, or someone to dupe? Or am I about to have an accident at sea?

This wasn't the first time I ever had to look among my own troops for the bad guys. My old squad set up several sting operations involving dirty cops, and every time I had to face one of them in handcuffs the nauseating taste of disloyalty burned in my throat. It made me sick to my stomach. It's never good when one of your own goes bad. The line between a good cop and a bad one gets real thin sometimes, but you still have to keep it in sight.

If a member of my team at the bank was dirty, it meant that person managed to figure out a way to steal millions from the bank without getting caught, and then got hired to catch himself. Just thinking about such a fucked-up set of facts made me want to lean over the side of the boat and barf.

I looked out over the expanse of blue-green ocean and felt the heat of the sun beating down on me with relentless intensity. I hate the heat, and it doesn't take a rocket scientist to figure out I'm in very deep, shark-infested waters. Now that I think about it, I've never been much of a swimmer.

Chapter 19

Monday, July 6th (morning)

I survived the weekend boat ride, and was sitting in Phil's office at the Monday morning meeting, listening to Sunny and Phil argue. It struck me that a game of blind man's bluff was going on here, and I was the one standing in the middle, wearing the blindfold.

Sunny wrapped up her briefing on yesterday's day-long, brainstorming session at sea and the minute she repeated Cathy's translation of the code name for that secret operation, I noticed an unusual reaction on the part of my esteemed leader. I saw that same flash of anger he showed when his butler announced an overseas phone call.

Sunny and Phil were sticking it to each other all during the meeting, implying the other was holding back on something. They weren't sharing like good little boys and girls.

I wasn't ready to rule out any possibilities, and knew even Sid and Audrey could also be players in this weird game, but if they were, it was more likely as dumb foot soldiers, and not the officers. That old refrain, "You can't tell the players without a program," was ringing in my head.

A visit to Phil's office was like spending time at NASA control center. The guy's desk, a long slab of exotic wood edged in marble, had more built-in gadgets than the cockpit of a Boeing 747. Remotely controlled panels covered one whole wall, hiding a bunch of monitors that showed TV broadcasts from all around the world. Several computers were built into his desk and kept him up to date on the bank's operations and gave him instant internet access to anything he needed in the way of information.

Sunny finished voicing her theory that *Operation Sine Dinar* was some kind of arms for hostages maneuver, and Phil wasn't impressed. "Please, Sunny, this bank does not go around getting involved in paramilitary operations for the exchange of hostages." He gave her a dismissive wave of his hand. "That idea is preposterous.

"As for your other suggestion, that some mysterious organization intends to set up a cashless society, it's one of those fairy tales that's been kicking around for generations. There is no way anyone could ever pull off such a thing. To do so would require unanimous, worldwide acceptance. You can't have some countries using cash and others, not. It's an all or nothing proposition. Believe me, worldwide acceptance of anything will never occur."

She countered. "At the risk of sounding melodramatic, using a code name suggests that someone out there is trying to organize a lot of people. When the actions of many individuals are coordinated to attain a single objective I believe the military refers to it as, `objective planning.' Am I right?"

"What's your point," Phil asked. He was staring at her with an amused look on his face.

"If there was some world-wide organization whose plan was to eliminate cash, it would certainly need some form of objective planning in order to carry out such a mission. By giving that mission a name they would be following a well-established, military practice."

"You are bordering on the absurd, my charming friend." I saw a smile spread across Phil's handsome face as his eyes dropped down to the paperwork in front of him. "Banks are far too territorial to ever join forces in some kind of global union. Furthermore, if such an organization did exist and Sterling was a member, I would know about it. I can assure you that is not the case."

Phil continued signing the documents Paula set before him, then suddenly stopped what he was doing and focused his full attention on Sunny. "Besides, even if such an organization did exist, the participation of any one bank wouldn't make a difference. An organization that big and powerful surely wouldn't let a single bank stand in its way. The crooks would be wasting their time making demands on Sterling. It's only one bank."

"True enough," she responded, returning his gaze with her own steady smile, "but the message would get through."

Phil shifted his focus to me. "I was hoping to hear something much more down to earth, Mac. I told you I wanted us to go on the offensive. Tell me you've come up with something more than this nonsense about hostages and secret organizations that I can pin my hopes on."

"We're checking out every possibility, Phil. It's never easy when the other side's calling the shots. We may not be on their doorstep yet, but I think we're closing in. We need a little more time."

Phil nodded affirmatively. "Unfortunately, time is something we are running out of very quickly. I am going out of town later today and will be gone until Wednesday afternoon. Let's plan on meeting back here at six sharp, Wednesday evening. Paula will let you know if there is any change in that schedule. By then I'd like to hear something much more concrete and plausible. So please, don't disappoint me, either of you. Thank you both for coming by and keeping me informed."

I headed back to my office with a mental note that Phil had just moved out in front in the "prime suspect" race. As soon as I got there, the roller coaster I was riding took another unexpected dip. Audrey was waiting for me, and the look on her pudgy face said she was ready to go to war.

"Well, Miss Sunshine, what are you so happy about?" I walked past her and fell into my chair.

"You could lose a precious part of your anatomy real easy when I'm feeling this way." She tossed a magazine article on the desk and dumped herself into a nearby chair. "I talked to one of my profs over at NYU this morning like you told me to, and come to find out "Dennis the Menace" ain't exactly been spilling his guts to us."

I glanced at the article entitled, "LANs In Cyberspace," and noticed the author was none other than Dennis Crawford. "I take it this article says something different than what he's been telling us?"

"It turns out, a few years back, Dennis was the guru when it came to messing around with wireless LANs. That's local area networks to you. The boy was doing some rain dance about how if you matched up frequencies some way so the data could move over radio waves, or some shit like that, you could do some magic. If what he says is true, we ain't been able to find out how them hackers got in because they never laid a glove on our stuff. They probably used some screwy radio waves to pull it off and the head honcho for that kinda shit turns out to be Sunny's stud muffin. Now don't that just fry your bacon?"

"Hold on, kid. Dennis said it could work, only there has to be transmitters and receivers on both ends, and the signals have to be shielded. What's changed?"

"Oh, yeah, I forgot you don't read so good. That article says, theoretically speaking, one computer can talk to another without any modification on the server end. You've got to have a few zillion more brain cells than I do to understand what the hell he's getting at, but Dr. Hanking says the guy is no bullshitter."

"So, did he ever make it work or not?" I waited for her to deliver the punch line.

"Who the hell knows," she yelled, and threw up her hands. "Not long after he wrote that article he teamed up with Sunny and they started rigging up the new system for Sterling. Hanking says Dennis has this bitchin' lab out in California where he does all kinds of experimental shit. Only he never lets anyone in the place, so no one knows if he ever made it happen or not. The guys who used to keep track of what he was doing say that since he got hooked-up with Sunny he spends all his spare time in her pants, instead of in his lab."

"You can't blame him for that."

I began to feel like Jesus Christ standing in the Garden of Gethsemane. Even my most trustworthy apostle was beginning to sound a bit shaky.

Hell, maybe I should check out Sheila, too, while I'm at it. Maybe her and Les are in on this.

Audrey kept chomping away. "Yeah, well I ain't ready to sell Sunny down the river just because her boy-toy has shit on his boots." She leaned forward and rested her elbows on my desk. The normally dour expression on her face had grown a couple shades darker during the last few minutes. "Sunny is too smart to let some dick-head drag her into anything this dumb on purpose. Oh, sure all the computer crap is slick and clever, but big deal. Bottom line, it's still just plain old stick-em-up, gimme-the-dough, cow-pucky. My money says Dennis is behind this and he's using Sunny, and she don't even know it."

Ain't love grand.

* * *

Phil had just finished a light lunch and was packing up some papers to take with him on his hastily planned trip to Europe when his private phone rang. He answered it and the distinguished, European accent of Henrí Bettancourt came through. "Philip, I'm so glad I caught you. It became necessary for me to make a change in my plans. I've just arrived in Boston and hope that doesn't cause you too much of an inconvenience?"

"Certainly not, Henrí, it is a pleasant surprise." Phil tried to mask his instant concern. "Can I offer you some accommodations during your stay?"

"You are always so thoughtful, but that won't be necessary. I'm staying at the Four Seasons. I'm only here for a short visit, so I am hoping we might have dinner this evening. Say around, eight?"

"Of course. I'll see you then."

Henrí, never did anything unexpectedly. His schedule was tighter and more complicated than Phil's. Any change meant something extraordinary had come up. It wasn't hard for Phil to suspect what that might be. Henrí somehow had gotten wind of the second note.

Unlike most men who wield incredible power, Henrí Bettancourt liked to travel alone. He preferred to deal with important matters in a low profile manner: one-on-one. That way, if anything did go wrong, rather than worry about a string of underlings coming unraveled, he could bring the issue to a quick and final conclusion. He would simply give his word on the subject and his unassailable reputation for honesty and integrity would close out even the most intrepid investigator.

Phil called Paula into his office. "Cancel my flight to Europe. My meeting has been called off. Let Sunny and Mac know there's been a change in plans, and ask them to be in my office at 6:00 o'clock sharp this evening. You can tell them the meeting will last until 7:30."

"I've just made plans for 6 o'clock." Paula commented. She sounded confused.

Phil glanced up, briefly, and smiled at her. "How clever. I'll try to manage without you. Oh, and alert my driver that I'll be leaving at 7:45 sharp."

Chapter 20

Monday: July 6th (late afternoon)

I was standing beside Sunny in the elevator as we shot up to the 56th floor, and tried to decide whether it was some intuitive sense of style, or just that great body lying beneath her pretty summer dress that made the difference. Somehow, everything she wore always seemed like the perfect choice.

She turned to me and flashed one of her high voltage smiles. "Are we still partners?"

"You looking to borrow some money?"

"Mac, we both know you had strong doubts about Phil this morning. He was hiding something and you know it."

"I could say the same thing about you."

"Why, because I won't tell you about a personal relationship? I've assured you that it has nothing to do with what's going on now."

We stepped out of the elevator and ran into Paula rushing to catch it before it headed back down to the lobby. "Enjoy your meeting," she said with a casual wave, and backed into the vacant elevator.

What the hell's going on here? Phil suddenly changes his plans, calls a second meeting in the same day, and now Paula's running off. Things are really turning weird.

I was beginning to think the worm had finally turned in my favor. But there were still way too many suspects running around for me to get cocky.

"Thank you for coming back on such short notice," Phil apologized as we gathered in his office. "My trip was cancelled at the last moment, which is fortunate because it gives us a chance to continue on from where we left off this morning.

"Sunny, I'm afraid I wasn't giving you the proper attention you deserved on some of the points you were making earlier. Upon reflection, I realize you may be on to something. We do need to think like the crooks, even if what they are thinking is completely fanciful. Please take me back to that theory you mentioned, the one involving some worldwide plan to eliminate cash. Assuming that's what the crooks have in mind, where does it take us in our investigation?"

"Based on the messages we've received, I'd say it's pretty clear the crooks want to stop the operation before it does whatever it is supposed to do. Stealing money is only a bargaining chip, a blackmailer sending a compromising photo. The victim has to decide whether or not to do what he's told, or risk having his dirty laundry exposed.

"I think this case is moving along those lines, but it's a lot more complicated. The crooks managed to find a very quiet way of robbing a bank. Even now, weeks after the fact, very few people know that it took place. But, every time they hit us there's a chance the word will get out. Once that happens everything is up for grabs.

"Overnight they'll become the darlings of the media. Reporters will want to know how they did it, and why. The notes they've been sending to us will be dissected on talk shows and they'll have a big soapbox to stand on. Right or wrong, they're hoping whoever is behind that crazy operation stuff will agree to anything in order to avoid that kind of public exposure."

Phil was much more interested in what Sunny was saying this time around. He was even jotting down some notes, something he rarely ever did. Normally, he relied entirely on his uncanny memory.

"If you're right," he asked, "why didn't they simply go public right from the start?"

"It's an all or nothing situation. Once the citizenry knows what's going on, the organization is left with no other option but to fight. The crooks know that, and figure their best bet is to stay quiet for awhile and see if they can force the other side to go along with them."

Phil leaned back in his chair. "What made them think Sterling had anything to do with this plan, or was even a participant in it?"

"Maybe Sterling was chosen at random, but I doubt that. We have to consider the fact that Sterling is a major financial player, with ties to both domestic and foreign money markets. It's a prime example of the kind of bank that would have to get behind such a scheme in order to make things work; a worldwide consensus builder. Of course, until we know what this operation is all about, we're just speculating. My guess is Sterling has something to do with the delivery of messages to whoever is behind *Operation Sine Dinar*."

"Maybe these characters have a special connection with Sterling," I offered. "They sure don't have any trouble figuring out what's going on around here."

"Has your investigation of the personnel records produced anything worthwhile?" Phil questioned.

"Nothing I can take to the bank, pardon the pun. But, it's still early in the game. People aren't anxious to spill their secrets until they have to."

"Are you suggesting someone at this bank isn't giving you their full cooperation, Mac?"

"No, Phil," Sunny jumped in, sending a sharp look in my direction. "He's referring to my unwillingness to discuss some past differences between you and I."

Phil locked eyes with me and pointed an accusatory finger. "Don't lose focus, Mac. It is imperative that you keep your eye on the ball and not get side-tracked."

He then returned his attention to Sunny. "Do you have any idea, yet, how they are getting into our computer?"

"It would be more accurate to say I know how they aren't doing it, and that only leaves a few options open. I'd say it's looking more like an off-site operation, as unlikely as that scenario seemed to me in the beginning."

"Maybe they used radio waves," I blurted out. The minute the words left my mouth I wanted to swallow them. This wasn't the time, or the place, for me to be using any of my trump cards.

Sunny and Phil turned to me, and Sunny said, "Phil, I do believe our Scottish cop is holding out on us." There was a sly grin on her face. "Would you care to enlighten us on what it is that prompted you to come up with such an unusual suggestion."

I learned a long time ago that when you put your foot in your mouth it doesn't do any good to claim it's a banana. Someone's liable to make you eat it.

"I've been checking out every angle, technical and personal," I replied.

"But that's a pretty sophisticated comment you just made," she pressed. "You've been discussing this problem with someone outside the group and I think we deserve to know the name of that person."

"You ought to have a higher regard for your teammates," I answered. "You're overlooking the fact that I share an office with Audrey, the numbers-eating plant from

Brooklyn. So far, she's the only one who's been coming up with any answers."

"Ah, yes, Audrey Simone," Phil chimed in. "An unlikely appearing heroine but, as you say, quite effective. Has your investigation uncovered anything about her that would cause some suspicion?"

"She's *Forrest Gump* with a Brooklyn accent."

"Radio waves aren't exactly her field of expertise," Sunny continued to probe. "She must be talking to someone. Do you know who?"

"She mentioned a name but I don't recall it."

"You know my instructions about leaks," Phil reminded me.

"I'm sure no names or purpose were given out. The kid is really digging hard. She wants to keep our sticky-fingered friends from messing with her records, if you know what I mean. It's "cops and robbers" time with her, and she definitely sees herself as one of the good guys."

Phil turned to Sunny. "What about this radio wave theory. Can it work?"

"Theoretically, yes, but I'm not sure anyone has ever made it happen without transmitters and receivers on both ends. That's what Dennis says, and he's done some studies on it."

"What kind of studies?" I asked, holding back one of my trump cards.

"You'll have to ask Dennis. It's a hardware issue and I have enough trouble staying up on software."

"Assuming it can work," Phil posed, "give me an example of how it would be applied."

Sunny sat back looking like the cat who ate the canary. "Well, if I was the crook, I'd set-up a computer located somewhere, say in a nearby office building. Then I'd target a server located in this building. My computer would send out a directional beam aimed at the target server and establish a connection.

"Once the connection was made, the remote computer could do anything the server can. As long as the person operating the remote computer has a login code and password they can get access to the mainframe's data banks through that server. The flow of data would pass through the server to the remote and back again as if it was all one computer. Under those conditions, the mainframe would have no way of distinguishing between instructions coming from any of the system servers and those originating from the remote computer. In short, the system would see the remote as just another server. Our firewall protections would never come into play."

"How fascinating." Phil jotted down a note to himself. "Of course, we don't know whether any of this is real, do we? Let's get everyone together tomorrow morning at 11:00 sharp in my conference room. Please see to it that Dennis, Audrey and Sid are present. I want everyone's input at the same time.

"I apologize again for having disrupted your schedules this way, but it has turned out to be a very worthwhile meeting." He stood up and gave Sunny and me a reassuring smile. "It's been a long day and hopefully we can all get a fresh start in the morning."

Chapter 21

Monday: July 6th (evening)

Phil's driver maneuvered the limousine through the slow-moving evening traffic on Franklin Street and turned down Tremont, alongside the Commons. Phil was in the back seat concentrating on two subjects simultaneously. The first was Henrí's unusual last minute change of plans. It was so unlike him to show up unannounced in Boston. His second concern was about the information he gathered today, and whether he should pass it along to Henrí. As was often the case, the answer to the second question depended in large measure on the outcome of the first.

He settled into the soft, gray leather of the limousine's interior and, for a moment, let his thoughts drift into the past. For over 50 years he had managed to come out on top in every endeavor, largely due to an unwavering belief in one simple credo: knowledge is power. Possession of key information and knowing how to put it to good use placed him in the vanguard of the pack of baby boomers currently filling positions of power around the world. He had a very important destiny. A destiny founded partially on his birthright, but overwhelmingly on his natural ability to out-guess whomever he came up against.

For some time now Phil suspected Henrí had planted moles at each delegate's home base. His purpose in doing so would be to make sure none of those banks gained any special advantage from leaks of information about the cartel's business. It was the prudent thing to do, and quite compatible with Henrí's need to maintain tight security controls over the cartel.

If that assessment was correct, there was a high probability that Henrí already knew about the latest note, and the fact that it mentioned *Operation Sine Dina*r. Until now, Phil never thought it necessary to determine the identity or number of moles that might be operating at Sterling. He had nothing to hide so it posed little consequence to him.

Things had gotten much more complicated now. The current theft investigation had to be managed in a way that kept it out of Henrí's hands. In order to do that, Phil had to find a way of interrupting Henrí's lines of communication, at least temporarily.

Phil stepped out of the elevator on the top floor of the Four Seasons Hotel and knocked on the door of the Presidential suite. An inquisition was about to begin and even though it wasn't the first time Phil had clashed with his mentor, the stakes had never been this high.

Henrí greeted Phil warmly, offering champagne and a delicious foie gras in an effort to set a casual mood. Ever the gracious host, Henrí was completely relaxed, as if entertaining an old friend who happened to drop by for a visit. It was a good lesson from a true master; never play your hole card too early. Phil learned that particular lesson a long time ago, and had no difficulty staying focused on the issue at hand.

"I so enjoy my visits to Boston," Henrí offered, casually raising a glass of champagne in salute. "I believe it's the interesting way you Bostonians go about combining the old with the new. I find it so eclectic, so different from some of your other more garish cities like, say, Los Angeles."

"Americans consider the mixture of good and bad taste a key ingredient in what makes us such a vibrant and restless country," Phil responded, playing to Henrí's lead.

"Unlike Europeans, we never like to rest on our laurels. Even when we get it right, we start making changes."

"Yes, I agree with you in that assessment."

Two waiters arrived and rolled in a serving cart carrying the special dinner Henrí had ordered. He directed them to set-up out on the balcony, mentioning how pleasant it would be to dine in the balmy night air, overlooking the Public Gardens. The sky was clear and a slight on-shore breeze brought with it some welcomed relief from the daytime heat.

"I hope you don't mind, but to save time I took the liberty of ordering for us," Henrí said, pointing with his glass at the meal being spread out. "I know duck is one of your favorites, and I sent down a special recipe to the chef. We shall find out whether he was trained in Europe, or at one of those New Jersey soup kitchens you called a gourmet restaurant when I was here last year."

"Henrí, one of these days your Belgian snobbery is going to lead to an international incident," Phil countered, amused by Henrí's gaff. "If I'm not mistaken the head chef at this hotel is a woman, and New Jersey happens to be the home of Princeton University."

"Ah, yes, your alma mater as I recall. I've often wondered why you chose to leave your birthplace, and Harvard, to run off to some inferior university, in of all places, New Jersey? Surely, your father was not happy with that decision?"

"In those days I picked my battles carefully."

Henrí smiled briefly, as if pleased with Phil's reply. "I'm afraid this recent theft business at Sterling is not a battle any of us would have picked. Please fill me in on your progress in that matter, my friend?" His hand rested gently on Phil's shoulder as he led him out onto the balcony and dismissed the waiters.

The moment of decision had arrived for Phil. "We have been able to work out how they managed to gain access to our files and that narrows down the number of possible suspects. Unfortunately, the list includes people I work closely with, and they are quite valuable to the bank. I can't dismiss the lot of them, so I must be absolutely certain.

"Within a day or so, I expect to be able to identify the technology that was used and that will lead me to the guilty party." The look in his eyes was meant to emphasize the truthfulness of his words and gave assurance of a favorable outcome.

"Is this technology something that can be used against other banks, or is it only meant for Sterling?"

"It involves a method of communication between computers, and from that standpoint, could be applied to any system. But certain login and access codes are involved that are unique to each bank's computers." He assumed Henrí knew all of this and was merely setting things up so that Phil's own words could be used against him later in the conversation.

"Have they stolen any more funds since the initial $5 million?"

"Yes, once. Another million was taken and transferred to a new set of accounts."

"Was the money withdrawn in cash, the same as before?"

"Yes."

"What about their demands? Have these clever thieves sent any more notes?"

His question put the issue squarely on the table and Phil knew why. Henrí did know about the second letter. The news could not have reached him until sometime after the phone conversation he had with Phil on the Fourth. That would account for why Henrí initially insisted that Phil come to Belgium, and later changed his plans at the last moment.

Phil went with his instinct. "Yes, another note arrived last Wednesday. It mentioned *Operation Sine Dinar* and demanded that it be cancelled."

The implication was fully understood by both men. For the first time since its inception, the cartel's activities had somehow been compromised, whether by chance, or willfully, and its inviolate code of secrecy had been breached. Henrí would undoubtedly act swiftly to correct the situation and no doubt draw a line in the sand. The cartel would have to choose which side of that line to be on.

Phil suspected Henrí had already initiated steps to re-establish the integrity of the operation. Those steps, no doubt, included identifying whoever allowed the information to get out in the first place, and after that, deciding on how to deal with the responsible party. Everything would be handled with great expediency and the utmost finality.

"That is most unfortunate news," Henrí replied, sitting back in his chair. "As you know we were hoping none of this would involve the cartel. You assured us you were capable of handling the matter without outside intervention. Now, as you have so precisely pointed out, these thieves not only represent a threat to the cartel's plans, they are a continuing threat to every bank in the world. That is a most distressing situation indeed."

"The situation, as you call it, evaporates once the crooks are arrested."

"Au contrare, mon ami. Arrest of the thieves would only serve to compound the problem." Henrí looked at Phil the way a teacher might look at a prize pupil who has just given the wrong answer. "Do you not see the difficulty we face if these criminals are allowed to rise up in some courtroom and make scurrilous accusations in defense of their cause? The notoriety such an event would generate could easily set us back a generation. No, no, that must never be allowed to happen."

Henrí's icy, steel-gray eyes sent a cold shiver down Phil's spine, as if someone has just walked on his grave. His worst fears were beginning to materialize as he listened to what he knew was more than an idle threat from some boastful egotist. The message being delivered was ominous, and the fact that it was being said out loud, under these circumstances, meant it was already too late to alter the course of events.

The gremlins Phil had been hoping to avoid were now dancing in a circle around him. Henrí, on the cartel's behalf would do everything in his considerable power to eliminate the thieves before they ever got a chance to announce what they knew about the operation. No effort would be wasted on trying to determine whether they actually knew anything about the cartel; their fate was sealed the moment they mentioned the operation by name. Nothing Phil, or anyone else, might say or do would change Henrí's mind on that point.

The presence and identity of a mole at Sterling was now a matter of immediate importance to Phil. Every move his investigative team made, and each piece of the puzzle they uncovered, was likely being passed on to Henrí. It would be used to carry out a deadly mission. Unless Phil destroyed that line of communication and neutralized the mole, a number of people at the bank, including himself, might be in real danger.

"Aren't you jumping to conclusions, Henrí?" Phil argued, taking a sip of the excellent Poulé Fuisse to clear away some of the sour taste in his mouth. "We have no reason to suspect these thieves really know anything at all about our plans. Maybe someone simply heard the name spoken and decided to run it up the flag pole to see what kind of a reaction it got. They have said nothing to indicate they know any of the details."

"A resourceful argument," Henrí replied, and gave a dismissive wave of his hand, "but one that carries with it a certain amount of risk. As you well know, our friends are not prone to take risks when they can be avoided. I'm afraid the course is clear."

"What I know, is that Sterling Bank & Trust is my bank and, so far, this is still my problem. I will not allow my bank, or any of my people to be compromised in any way for some questionable common good, even if directed to do so by the cartel."

Phil knew his words would not sway Henri's decision. They came from somewhere deep inside him; a place he didn't often visit. His heritage at Sterling extended back for generations, and from his earliest recollections, a sense of sacred trust was passed on from his father and grandfather before him. He was weaned on that trust; his ancestors had always been the bank's protector. Now it was his turn to stand watch. He was not about to let any infidels overrun the ramparts during his watch.

"I agree the manipulation of money markets by unscrupulous politicians and schemers has been getting out of hand lately. But I've never deluded myself when it comes to the cartel's true purpose in mounting this assault on the problem. Once *Operation Sine Dinar* is fully operational the cartel will become the repository of the most extensive and invasive collection of personal information the world has ever known. Every purchase by every human being on the planet will be recorded, sorted, and analyzed by our computers. The knowledge gained from all of that information will represent incredible power, both economically and politically. With that power the cartel will have the ability to control and manipulate the spending habits of everyone on Earth.

"If the cartel is willing to gain that power through the casual destruction of would-be objectors, I am prepared to withdraw my support. I will not let Sterling be dragged into some sordid mess just to insure the cartel's plans remain undetected for a few more years."

"I must send my compliments to the chef," Henrí said, dabbing at his mouth with a napkin. "He, or should I say, she, has done an excellent job with my recipe. Don't you agree, Philip?"

It was an attempt to change the subject and allow Henrí some time to analyze and digest the excited outburst he had just heard. Phil knew Henrí was quite capable of talking about one subject while concentrating on another. Henrí did not want to over-react to Phil's challenge in any way that would make known his true intentions.

"Quite," Phil politely responded. "Can we reach some common ground on any other subject tonight?"

"You are my favorite, Philip, you've always known that." Henrí gave him a look of fatherly pride. "You deal with challenges so well that I cannot resist indulging you from time to time. I often look upon you as I would a splendid thoroughbred that must be allowed to take on a challenge every so often, just to keep that remarkable spirit alive."

Then, in the blink of an eye, the look of pride disappeared and a familiar enigmatic mask took its place. "But, you must never mistake me for Shakespeare's Richard III. A horse, in the final analysis, is still only a horse, and I would never trade a kingdom for one."

Chapter 22

Monday: July 6th (Evening)

"Daddy, where have you been?" Cathy shouted in my face, as she opened the door to her apartment. "I've been trying to reach you since 4 o'clock this afternoon. Why can't you carry a beeper like everyone else?"

"I hate those damn things," I answered, and walked past her. I made a quick check to see if she had any company and carried the 12-pack of Miller tucked under my arm, to the kitchen. It was almost 8:00 p.m. and that late meeting with Sunny and Phil had pushed me well past my usual start time.

"I want to know what's going on." Cathy pressed, trailing along behind me.

"Why were you calling?" I popped open a can, took a long pull, and shoved the rest in the fridge.

"You know damn well why. You told me to let you know if Phil Lord called and, of course, he did. I want to know how you knew he would do that, and what's really going on?"

The delicious aroma of stuffed zucchini baking in the oven filled her tiny kitchen. Cathy pulled opened the oven door to check on it, and stirred some rice boiling in an electric cooker. When she looked up there was that familiar look of determination in her eyes that meant she wasn't going to let the matter drop.

"What did Phil say to you?"

"He asked me to have breakfast with him tomorrow and specifically requested that I not mention it to you."

It pleased me to know there wasn't any hesitation on her part when it came to choosing her loyalties. But her answer put the monkey on my back for not being more open with her. Maybe the plan I was hatching would give the two of us a chance to finally be a team, instead of always going for the throat.

"That's a lot of food. You expecting `Dr. J'?"

"No, he's on duty. I always cook on my day off. If I feed you can I get some answers?" She took a bowl of tossed salad out of the refrigerator, handed it to me and, like her mother, a smile was hard to hold back.

I reached up to brush away a wisp of hair hanging down on her forehead. "Deal, only first I have to use your phone."

In the living room I dialed Sheila's home number and Les answered.

"I'm at Cathy's place. Grab your old lady and get over here."

Les was my partner for 17 years and knew better than to waste time asking questions. I heard him yell at Sheila as he hung up the phone.

Earlier, while sitting next to Sunny in Phil's office, watching them trade punches, a revelation came to me. Maybe more than one game was going on in this screwed up mess. Those two were challenging each other, all right, but not about the same thing.

Phil was worried about a lot more than just the theft of the bank's money. The fact that he'd gotten in touch with Cathy confirmed my hunch that he had some kind of problem going on with this Belgian guy, Bettancourt.

A rookie cop can't offer much help when it comes to tracking down electronic bank robbers. But some kind of secret operation stuff was something else again. Cathy could be a real asset for Phil in tracking down some organization that Bettancourt might be heading up.

As we sat down to dinner I asked Cathy to wait until Les and Sheila arrived, so I wouldn't have to repeat myself. That gave her an unexpected opportunity to interrogate me on my impressions of Dr. Mike.

"You've talked to Michael, Daddy, so what's your decision."

I tried to duck behind my usual wisecracks. "The guy definitely doesn't need to use his toes to do math. What more could a girl want? You haven't mentioned how he feels about you being a cop?"

"He's not in love with the idea, but so far he hasn't come out and asked me to quit. His folks are pretty normal, so I imagine he sees his wife as pretty much of a homebody type. You know, one that stays home and raises the kids, like Sally. Those two really hit it off at the party."

"It's hard not to. She carries on both sides of the conversation."

"You know what I'm getting at."

"Look, Honey, unless you marry a cop, they never really get used to the job. They just accept it, hold their breath until you hit retirement, and then drag you off to Florida. Every time the guy watches you strap on your weapon it'll give him a stomachache. After awhile he won't even be sure what a normal life is anymore. That's the way it was for your mother and probably will be for Dr. Mike, too, if he ever gets lucky enough to hear the word, yes, come out of your mouth."

I could feel that lobster shell around my heart starting to crack a bit as Cathy looked at me and said, "Mom always told me, you loved me more than I'll ever know."

Nine years ago, at the hospital, when I tried to find the words to explain how Karen died, I lost it, and wept unexpectedly in my daughter's arms. It was the only time in my life that happened. For days after that, I couldn't bear to have Cathy out of my sight.

"She also said you'd have a tough time giving me away."

"I never could keep secrets from your mother." I quickly finished off my third beer and got up to answer the door.

The minute Sheila got in the door she grabbed me by the front of my shirt and demanded, "You better be ready to tell this jerk behind me what's going on, before he strangles me."

I smiled at Les. "I always told you a little rough stuff would do her some good."

Cathy was clearing away the dishes and Sheila joined her. "How come there's no blood on the table? Did we get here before the main event?"

"He made me wait until you guys got here."

I got Les a beer and another one for myself. We settled down in the living room while the two women finished clearing the table.

I got right to the point. "You got any problem transferring Cathy to your squad?"

Les had taken command of my old, special ops unit right after I resigned. Many of the same detectives who worked for me, were still on the job. What I had in mind was a perfect score for that unit, and I needed people I could trust to back me up.

"She'd never buy it even if I could. You know how pissed she gets over any special treatment."

"Yah, but this time she'll go along, trust me. A big-time collar is coming down, and I think Cathy already has one foot in the door. She just doesn't know it yet.

"Things might get dicey, though, and before I bring any cops in on this I want to make sure I don't get blind-sided. I never trusted Dan McCulloch and I don't want Cathy getting involved in this while she's working for that asshole."

"You've known Duke as long as I have," Les answered, referring to our old precinct captain. "If we lay it out for him and it makes sense he ain't gonna give us a hard time. McCulloch probably won't give a shit either, as long as he gets a replacement and doesn't get wind that he's missing out on anything big."

Cathy and Sheila sat down and I began running down the whole picture of what was going on at Sterling. Les got bug-eyed when I described the thefts and the amount taken.

All of us knew how the feds liked to claim jurisdiction anytime a federally chartered bank got knocked over. The suits move in, push the local cops aside and take all the credit when the perps get nabbed. The local cops, of course, do most of the grunt work, but get none of the glory. I saw this as a chance for my old squad to work the case and get all the credit for the collar before the feds even got wind that anything was going down.

Sheila was a little upset when I mentioned the bit about Dennis being an expert in the field of radio communications between computers. She liked Dennis, and Sunny, too, for that matter, and the idea that Dennis might be using Sunny, along with the rest of us to pull off this job, left a bad taste in her mouth. I knew she had trouble trying to imagine what Dennis could possibly gain from getting involved in that kind of a mess, and so did I. He certainly didn't need the money.

By the time I finally got around to laying out the case against The Lord, Les and Sheila were squirming in their seats. They didn't need to be reminded how tough an opponent Phil Lord was, and the consequences in store for anyone who goes after him, and misses.

Cathy was having a real hard time trying to figure out where she fit in with any of this, and what Phil could possibly have in mind that involved her. It was time for me to play my ace. "I think we've got two different things going on at the same time."

"What's that mean," Les asked.

"The theft and that crazy operation," Sheila answered for me.

"Right," I agreed. "Cathy, I think that Belgian guy, Henry Bettancourt, the one you interviewed a few years ago, is involved in that secret operation. In fact I'm sure of it. Phil knows it, too. Somehow, the perps found out about whatever's going down with that action and they're blackmailing Phil. I figure the bank job is just a clever way of covering up a pay-off."

"Hold on, Sherlock." Sheila sat up straight, ready to attack. "Are you saying The Lord's letting these guys get away with robbing the bank?"

"Someone's feeding them inside dope, you've said so yourself," I answered, trying not to sound overly defensive.

"But if Phil is the one behind it, he's not going to blackmail himself."

"It's been done before. We also can't overlook one other likely scenario. You told me Sunny and Paula weren't seeing eye-to-eye. You said it might have had to do with Phil making a move on Sunny. What if it had to do with Dennis?

What if Dennis is the one running up and down Marlborough Street, playing musical beds?

"Think about it. Paula's in the best position to know what kind of shit Phil's into and could easily put the squeeze on him, big time, if she wanted to. She makes a little deal with Dennis, who doesn't give a damn about the money, but would love to get a chance to test out his new gizmo. Plus, as an added bonus, Lady Paula throws in some of the same kind of great action in the sack he's been getting from Sunny.

"I'm figuring, Phil thinks Sunny's behind the caper and Dennis is helping her. Sunny, on the other hand, thinks Phil's behind that whole secret handshake thing and is partnered up with Paula. The smart money says Paula and Dennis are the real snakes-in-the-grass.

"Phil has to keep his eye on Sunny because if she's the one behind the theft, she can make a real mess of the bank's computer system without even trying. That's probably why he brought her in, so he could keep a close watch on her."

Les was like a kid in a candy store. "Jesus, Mary, and Joseph, you're talking commendations up the "whazzoo" if even half this shit goes down. Christ, they'll be interviewing me on the six o'clock news for a month. I'm there."

I gave Cathy a sheepish grin. "That's where you come in, Honey."

"What is?"

"You're transferring to Les' unit on special assignment. A lot of juice is going to be coming down, and I'm not about to take any chances of a slip-up with you involved."

"Involved in what, Daddy? You're not making any sense."

"Look, Phil's got something in mind that involves you. I don't know exactly what it is yet, but he didn't call to ask you out on a date. Whatever it is, it's got something to do with that Bettancourt guy. The tie-in is that interview you did back in law school."

"You think he's going to ask me to do some undercover work for the bank and try to keep you from finding out? That's pretty silly. I mean he's got to know I'd tell you."

"Think about it," I argued. "You two talked before and you never mentioned it to me. Why wouldn't he think you'd go along with the same routine?"

"But if I start hanging around the bank we're bound to bump into each other."

"That's my point. He's got me working on the heist and he needs you to go after Bettancourt and whatever he's up to. That way nobody puts two and two together. All he's got to do is keep us from comparing notes."

"And you're willing to let me do that?"

"Sweetheart, I've never doubted your abilities as a cop. All right, so maybe I get carried away sometimes worrying about your safety. But as long as I know Les and the guys are backing you up, and I'm the one calling the shots, what can go wrong?"

"What about my meeting tomorrow morning?"

"We're talking a work in progress here, so I haven't gone that far down the road. Les, what do you think? Maybe she ought to carry a wire. If this thing turns out to be as big as I think it is, the D.A.'s going to want something on tape, especially against a heavy hitter like The Lord."

"Listen, you old fart," Sheila warned Les, wagging a finger under his nose, "you let Barbara do any taping on

Cathy. I don't want any of those dirty old men groping this baby while they're putting on that wire."

We all enjoyed a nervous laugh, but Cathy was still giving me a funny look. This was hard for her to swallow. Not only had I shared a moment of personal feelings with her tonight, now I was setting up a difficult assignment, one that could make the two of us partners for the first time in history.

She suddenly smiled. "Brian will never believe any of this."

Chapter 23

Tuesday: July 7th (morning)

Phil stepped into the kitchen at his Louisburg Square townhouse and instructed his driver to leave without him, at the usual time. He also told him to record on his log sheet that Phil was onboard.

As soon as the limousine drove off, Phil slipped away through the back gate, down the alley, and walked the two blocks to the plaza by the Capital Building. There was little time to waste. He quickly hailed a cab, and as he climbed into the back seat he reminded himself that now was not the time to underestimate his opponents. Anyone could be watching.

His appointment with Cathy MacKenzie was set for 8:00 a.m. and he wanted to get there ahead of her so that he could observe her arrival. Regardless of the outcome, this meeting had to remain a secret.

Cathy was the one who suggested they meet at a restaurant, "Momma's Kitchen," in Kenmore Square, not far from Fenway Park and her apartment. Phil was confident he wouldn't run into anyone he knew in that neighborhood and readily agreed.

Momma's Kitchen was a small, family-run landmark , the kind that are scattered all over Boston. It was filled with early morning regulars when Phil arrived. He had to wait a few minutes and took a seat in the first booth that became available beside a window.

An older waitress came over, set down a thick, white mug in front of him, and about to fill it with coffee when he flashed a smile at her and said, "I prefer tea, please. Earl Grey if you have it."

She grinned at him. "Mistah, the last time tea arrived in Boston, it ended up in the haabah. I'll go see if I can fish out one of them bags for you and dry it off. Trust me, coffee's a safer bet in this joint."

As soon as she walked away, Phil spotted Cathy coming down the sidewalk and waved to her. She was wearing a loose-fitting cotton shift over a white t-shirt. He knew from their past meetings, the figure moving so suggestively beneath that light material was ideal. Briefly, he wondered if she appreciated her current state of beauty. Did she realize how soon she'd have to begin the desperate battle to stay the ravages of time, like his wife Charlotte?

"Cathy, it's so good to see you again," he said rising to greet her and held out his hand. He considered kissing her on the cheek, but decided it might be inappropriate under the circumstances. "I think it's been a couple of years since we last met. You look even lovelier."

"I've been on the force for almost four years," she answered, sliding into the booth, "so it must be longer than that."

The waitress joined them with Phil's tea and put down a cup of coffee in front of Cathy. "How's the cantaloupe this morning, Marge?" Cathy asked.

"A lot better than the tea."

"Oh, don't mind my friend, here, he's a foreigner," Cathy teased. "He's from the North Shore."

"Figures. You want a bran muffin with the melon?"

Cathy nodded.

"What about you?" Marge asked, looking at Phil. "And, don't even think about any eggs benedict with a light hollandaise sauce."

"Two eggs scrambled and a side of rye toast will do fine."

He watched Marge walk away and Cathy commented, "She claims my grandfather used to come in here years ago. Says he was a real SOB. I'm not sure which part of that I care to believe."

"Well I hope you meant what you said when you told her I was a friend. I am, you know, even if you haven't let me prove it to you yet."

"Why would you want to be my friend?"

"I could say because your father is someone I respect and admire, but that would only be partially true." He looked into her eyes, trying to see as far into them as she would let him. "As a matter of fact, speaking of your grandfather, Malcolm, he once did a great service for my father and Sterling Bank."

"My grandfather?"

"The way the story was told to me, back in the Forties old Malcolm was coming around the corner of the bank one day just as two men tried to kidnap my father. Malcolm realized what was happening, rushed the men, knocked all of them to the ground, and held them at gunpoint until help arrived. My father was carrying some important bank documents at the time and if the kidnapping had been successful it would have ruined his career and possibly the bank.

"My father told me he offered to give Malcolm anything within his power, but your grandfather answered he was a cop, just doing his job. Then, and my father always said this with great flourish, `that old devil had the unmitigated cheek to ask me if I had any daughters who might like to meet his son, Duncan.' Regrettably, I was an only child. So you could say we were once close to being related."

"Phil, that's the most outrageous story I've ever heard. I don't believe a word of it."

"Ah, but you should, it's the absolute truth."

They both laughed. Their food arrived and Phil sensed the mood was right, so he broached the subject of the meeting. He looked down at his plate and began quietly. "Speaking of fathers, did you mention to Mac about us getting together?"

He didn't have any misgivings about whether Cathy would keep secrets from her father if she thought it was anything important. She had already shown herself on that score. His request that she not mention the meeting was meant as a test, to see how she responded. If she tried to convince him that she had followed his instructions without qualification, he'd know she didn't trust him.

"So far there's nothing to tell. I certainly don't make a point of telling my Dad about everyone I have breakfast with. But, if you've got something on your mind that involves him in some way, I'm sure you know I wouldn't do anything behind his back."

It was the right answer.

"I told you I respect your father. The reason behind why I asked you not to mention this meeting will become clear in a moment. First, I want to assure you I would never ask you to do anything contrary to your father's best interests."

"Then maybe you should start by explaining what this meeting is all about."

"Do you remember Henrí Bettancourt?" He looked straight into her eyes.

"The guy I interviewed when I was in law school? Sure."

"Well, I need you to conduct a very discreet investigation that involves Henrí. I have reason to believe he's a party to some corporate espionage involving confidential bank records. I can't go into all the details at this time, but I'm quite sure one of my employees is feeding him sensitive information.

"The fact that you've met him and are somewhat familiar with his background means you can appreciate the fact that he is not someone I care to publicly accuse of wrongdoing. I need you to find out who his contact is at the bank, so that I can put an end to the leak with as little notoriety as possible."

"Unless you think my father's the mole, I'm not picking up on why you're telling this to me instead of to him."

"Mac is probably the only person at the bank I'm sure is not involved. No, my reason for not going to him is simple. He is already tied up on a very complicated and important investigation. I don't want him distracted in any way from that task. Does that make sense to you?"

"Sure. But I'm still not following where I fit in."

"The last time we met I told you how impressed I was with the way you handled yourself. I meant it. You are a very bright young lady who handles herself well in delicate situations. Since then you've added the benefits of police training to your resume and have access to all kinds of investigative resources and techniques. I believe you can be of enormous assistance to me."

His smile brought to bear the full mesmerizing effect of that attribute. In spite of her best intentions to ignore any such thoughts, Cathy, for a moment, considered all of the advantages Philip Lord had to offer. A promise of life at the top, with every bit of glamour and excitement a young woman could possibly imagine.

"From my perspective you are the ideal candidate for the job I have in mind," he added. "But, most of all, and this is very important, I believe I can trust you."

"That's flattering, coming from someone like you, Phil. But I'd still like to know why you don't want my father to know we had this talk. If you know he's not involved in what's going on, and you trust him, why not at least clear all of this with him?"

"Some of the people I want you to check out work with him on a daily basis. It's very important that none of them gets wind of this investigation. Otherwise, it would get back to Henrí, and things could become very difficult. If your father knew you were involved and saw a dangerous situation developing, we both know he'd take steps to protect you and that could alert the person we're after."

"What kind of dangerous situation?"

Unfortunately, there was no way of explaining the danger to Cathy without tipping his hand. Phil simply had to do his best to stay ahead of things, on his own, and be ready to warn her, if, and when, it ever became necessary. Her police skills would provide her with some basic protection, and he let that thought ease his conscience for the moment.

Side-stepping her question, he said, "As a police officer you would know better than I, but whenever large sums of money are involved isn't there always a certain amount of danger, a danger that someone will do something unpleasant to avoid responsibility?" He studied her carefully, looking for any signs that he might have misjudged her. The hook was about to be set and he didn't want to lose her after coming so close. "We are talking about criminal activity and isn't that always fraught with danger?"

"As a cop, I like to know what's behind a door before I open it. Just what is it you have in mind?"

"I have here a list of names, addresses, and phone numbers." He slid over a sealed envelope. "I'd like you to check out each person on that list, especially their phone and travel records for the past year. I've included Henri's phone numbers and a list of cities in the U.S. where he visited during that time frame. If anything matches up, even one contact, it is very important to me. None of the people on the list have any reason to even know him.

"However, do not under any circumstances make any inquiries into Henri's records. He is extremely well connected and would be alerted by the Belgian local authorities if that occurred. It is imperative that he not get the slightest hint of any kind of investigation.

"Does any of what I've said so far create a problem for you?" he asked.

"So far, all you've asked me to do is check out some phone records and see if your employees took any trips. All of that is stuff you could easily do yourself."

"Not without drawing attention. Your father would face the same problem, by the way. That's part of the reason why I can't use him. I can feed you this kind of raw data, but any contact with other agencies must go through your regular channels and appear to be routine police business. I want to avoid raising any eyebrows."

Phil had doubts about using a police officer at all, even in such an indirect way. Doing so could easily blow-up in his face. But when Cathy MacKenzie first came to mind he saw the possibilities. She had all the right qualifications including a convenient tie-in through her prior interview with Bettancourt. What's more, she had already proven to him that she could keep things to herself.

"The truth is, I really want my cake and eat it too," Phil continued. "I want you to use the police resources and connections that you have, but without getting the police involved in any official capacity. This has to be done as an off-duty assignment. I can't afford to let you clear this with your superiors. They would be stepping all over the place in their hobnailed boots, and any hope of keeping things quiet would be lost."

Cathy laughed at his choice of metaphor. "Departmental policy requires all off-duty jobs be cleared through the squad leader. Normally, that might pose a problem, but it just so happens that I got some credit on an important collar recently and I'm being transferred to Special Ops. Sheila Woburn's husband, Les, is in charge of that unit and you probably know he was my dad's old partner.

"I know Les."

"Les is aware of how much I hate it when Dad checks up on me. Maybe I can get him to cut me some slack if I tell him I picked up some extra work but I don't want to go into any details. That way he won't have to lie when Daddy asks him what I'm doing."

"Excellent. Sounds like I'm finally going to get a chance to prove my friendship." He flashed a smile at her and held out his hand. "Do we have a deal?"

"We can give it a try and see how things develop," she said, shaking hands. "Anyway, it sounds a lot better than doing off-duty traffic control at the 'Big Dig.'"

"You will, of course, be well-compensated for your time. I hope you won't think I'm being presumptuous, but I took the liberty of bringing along a retainer." He drew another envelope from his suit pocket and handed it to her. "I don't think we need to negotiate a fee for your services.

Regardless of the results, your efforts and confidentiality will be amply rewarded. This is merely to get you started."

Cathy opened the envelope and found a thick wad of hundred dollar bills. "How much is in here?" she asked in wide-eyed surprise.

"$5,000 dollars."

Chapter 24

Tuesday: July 7th (morning)

I walked into Phil's private conference room just before 11 o'clock and thought about the last time I was in the "inner sanctum." It wasn't really that long ago, but a lot of water had passed under the bridge in the meantime. Sunny Childe was the one on the firing line that day, and this time, if things went the way I planned, it would be Dennis Crawford.

Before the meeting got underway, I got an earful of Audrey's excited plea for a chance to neuter Dennis. She was ready to slap him with the article she'd uncovered about his experiments in the field of wireless communications between computers. But things didn't go exactly the way either of us had planned.

Dennis brought up the experiments he was doing at his lab, and explained, "I wasn't able to make it work even though I still think it's theoretically possible. Maybe if I'd stayed on it and worked on the logarithms some more, the answers would have shown up. But I wasn't the only one interested in finding out if that theory could fly."

"What do you mean?" Phil asked.

"Someone broke into my lab about a year ago."

"What were they after?" I asked, straightening up at this unexpected confession.

"That's just it, nothing was taken. I figure they broke in to read my notes and examine the equipment I had set up there. I reported it to the police, but because nothing was missing, the cops just dropped it."

"What are we to make of all that?" Phil asked.

"Only that it's possible whoever broke in, took photographs of my notes so they could duplicate the set up and continue on with the experiment somewhere else.

"Look everyone," Dennis urged, searching the faces around the table, "it's like putting a puzzle together. A few years ago I published an article laying out a complete picture of what I had in mind. All anyone had to do was read that article, find the right pieces, and then figure out how to make it all fit together."

The deflated look on Audrey's face was something to behold. Maybe I should have warned her that Dennis knew a lot about taking the wind out of someone's sails.

Dennis' allegation that a "B&E" had taken place at his lab certainly opened the door to someone else being the mastermind behind the current scheme to rob the bank using remote computers. It also provided Dennis with a convenient alibi and I made a mental note to have Sheila check out that break-in, ASAP.

"When did you say that break-in took place, Denny?" I asked.

"Last year sometime, around Labor Day if I remember right."

"That's not exactly true," Sunny interrupted.

Whoa, what do we have here, a break in the ranks?

Dennis stared at her like he wanted to rip out her tongue.

"That's when Dennis discovered the break-in and reported it," she added. "No one knows when it actually occurred."

"She's absolutely right," Dennis confirmed. "I was visiting my folks at the time and hadn't been near the lab in months. I went by to check on things and that's when I found out what had happened. It could have been like that for months."

By the time the meeting adjourned the consensus of opinion was the thieves were using a remote computer to gain access to the bank's main data files. The central mainframe was located in a specially shielded, atmospherically controlled room and there was no way anyone could use radio waves to tap into it directly. Access had to come from logging onto one of the numerous servers located throughout various departments of the bank.

That also meant there was no way to shut down the crooks once they got inside the system. Dennis came to the rescue by suggesting a way of physically blocking outside signals from getting through. He could erect special shields around the servers that would deflect any outside radio waves from getting through. Phil quickly grasped the merits of that suggestion and authorized the manufacture and placement of those shields around every server in the building.

I left the meeting and went back to my office to try and match-up what I'd just heard with what I'd been listening to earlier that morning while sitting in the surveillance van parked outside Momma's Kitchen.

Phil, during his breakfast with Cathy, definitely sounded more concerned about the information getting leaked to Bettancourt. It didn't seem like Bettancourt would give a damn about some low-life stealing money from a bank in Boston. I figured he had bigger fish to fry, like maybe that operation the scumbags were trying to derail.

But if Phil was behind the thefts, why okay the placement of those shields? He'd be putting himself out of business. Suddenly things weren't adding up again.

The only thing that did make sense was my hunch that two separate groups, with two separate agendas, were attacking at the same time. One group was going after the money and issuing some strange demands. The other one was busy setting up some crazy operation to eliminate cash. And the more I thought about it, the more I could see Phil standing in between the two groups. What I couldn't see was whether Phil was trying to put out the fires, or acting as the ringmaster?

Sheila interrupted my thoughts when she walked in, shut the door and asked, "How did Cathy do this morning?"

"Smooth. Didn't miss a beat."

"Did the fish take the bait?"

"Hook, line and sinker. Cathy even got him to spill the amount of money he gave her."

"Don't even think of taking any credit."

"The trouble is, I'm not so sure The Lord's our main guy anymore. I'm starting to have second thoughts about him."

"You want to explain?"

"I can't. There is something I want you to check out. Denny just let us know his lab in Palo Alto was broken into sometime last year. Says he reported it around Labor Day. See if you can dig up a copy of that report and run down the investigating officer.

"I'm off for a sit-down with Duke Hanlon to talk him into approving Cathy's transfer. If anyone comes looking for me, make up something. Oh, and tell Audrey to get back with that professor of hers and see if he can come up with a name or two of someone other than Dennis who's been working on that radio communications crap. She'll know what I'm talking about."

* * *

Henrí Bettancourt was becoming increasingly aggravated. Those who knew him, tried hard to avoid that situation. His day started out on a bad note and became increasingly worse as time went by. A report arrived earlier notifying him that Philip Lord managed to disappear for over an hour that morning. Henrí suspected a meeting had taken place and that Phil managed to lose the tail on him in order to prevent exposing the identity of the person he was seeing.

Now, he was listening to a second piece of bad news that carried even worse implications. The prime suspect in the Sterling thefts, Dennis Crawford, had just announced that his lab had been broken into. If that information was true it certainly broadened the possibilities of who might be behind the strange thefts at Sterling.

"I need more information," Henrí replied, icily, to the person on the other end of the line. "Call me back in one hour with the details."

He put down the phone and left his hotel suite. In the lobby he walked over to one of the public phone booths, closed the door, and dialed a number from memory.

"Do you recognize my voice?" he asked when his call was answered.

"Sure."

"I am at the Four Seasons using the same name as last time. Come by at 6:00 o'clock. I have a job for you. And bring along your equipment."

* * *

Philip Lord was having a very good day. Pleased over his success in recruiting Cathy MacKensie, he walked into the special staff meeting at 11:00 a.m. with high expectations. By the end of the meeting he had received enough information so that he could move on to the next step in his plan.

As soon as the meeting adjourned, Phil left his office and went to a public phone booth where he dialed Cathy MacKensie at her home number. She was on the way out when the phone rang.

"Cathy, it's Philip Lord. I meant to pass along something else when we talked." He paused for a second to see if she had any change of heart.

"No problem, what is it?" she answered.

"The person we spoke about is staying at the Four Seasons in the Presidential suite under the name Henry Gabriel. It's highly probable he'll make some contact with the person we're looking for while he is in town. Perhaps you can check it out without drawing any attention. Just keep in mind who we are dealing with."

"I'm glad you thought of that. It's a good lead, and I'll try to follow-up on it as soon as I can."

Chapter 25

Tuesday: July 7th (afternoon)

Captain "Duke" Hanlon, like the rest of us, hadn't changed much since I worked for him. Les played the tape from Cathy's meeting with Phil Lord and any suspicions Duke might have had that I was off my rocker, were shoved aside when Cathy threw in the little goody that Bettancourt was in town.

I waited until after the tape to lay my cards on the table. "The entire operation has to be under my direction, or no deal, Duke." We were all old friends and with Les backing it, it was hard for Duke to put up any real resistance.

Duke made a call authorizing Cathy's immediate transfer, while I checked in with Sheila. "Sunny has been looking for you," Sheila informed me. "She was really digging to find out where you went."

"Did she say what she wanted?"

"No. I told her you were checking out something at the post office. Is everything set with Cathy?"

"Yah. We're on our way over to the Dump now, but I think I'll swing by the office and see what's eating the "Babe.""

Les drove Cathy to the "Dump," the name given to the headquarters for the Special Operations Unit; a cluster of offices in a grimy office building located in the North End. I headed back to the bank after promising I'd meet up with them around 3:00 p.m. to go over the arrangements for the stake-out on Bettancourt. That would give Cathy a chance to enjoy a little reunion with the guys, most of whom had known her since childhood.

I walked into Sunny's office just as Dennis was leaving.

"The price of tea just went up," he said, as he brushed past me.

"What's that supposed to mean?" I asked.

Sunny answered. "Another note came in, and this time it was sent to me." She handed me a piece of paper that read: "If you try to stop us, we'll plant a virus."

"Can they do that?"

"Probably."

"Who knows about this?" I held the note up to the light.

"Just you and Dennis. I haven't been able to reach Phil."

I felt like one of those jugglers trying to keep a dozen plates spinning on top of sticks. Every time I got one going I had to run back and re-spin the others before they all came crashing down around me.

"This is serious, right?" I asked, scratching my head.

"Very."

"Where's Denny off to?"

"To see if he can get an earlier delivery date on those shields. So far, the best he's come up with is two weeks."

"Well, I sure in hell don't know what to do." I flopped into a chair and soaked in a whiff of Sunny's perfume hanging in the air. "You're the brains in this outfit, you think of something."

"Don't you see what's happening, Mac? The crooks can communicate with us but we haven't got any way of answering them. That means they're watching us. They have some way of knowing whether this *Sine Dinar* thing is being shut down. All we can do is hope that as long as their messages are getting through, the fact that we don't understand what they're all about, doesn't really matter.

"This note is an indication that the previous ones made it through and whoever's sending them is keeping an eye on the bank to see if it takes the right action. In the meantime, they don't want us messing with their access to the computers. They're willing to wait and see what happens. I don't think they are coming back for any more money."

The more excited Sunny got, the more I got turned on. I was struggling to stay focused on the problem at hand and not let my usual fantasy get the better of me. "Christ, Sunny, you're asking for one hell-of-a leap of faith. If you're wrong we're giving those stooges an open shot at another pay day."

"They've got that shot right now and they're not taking it. Why?"

"I wish I knew. You better get this note to Phil." I handed it back. "And don't mention it to anyone else, even Paula. Phil wants everything from the crooks kept quiet. For what it's worth, you can tell him I'll sign on to your approach, at least for now."

* * *

Later on, at the Dump, it was hand-shaking, a few mock punches, and a bunch of lies with the guys. Then it was time to get down to business. Les had already briefed everyone, and Cathy explained her role and background in the matter.

"The number one target is this Bettancourt guy," I announced. "We're hoping he'll lead us to the headquarters of this Operation Sine Dinar." I felt like John Wayne breaking out of jail and climbing back on his horse. "We've got to find out what this deal is all about and who's behind it.

This guy is our only connection, so whatever you do, don't lose him."

"Do we have any idea where his home base is located?" Stan Wilkerson asked.

"Bettancourt lives in Antwerp, Belgium," Cathy answered, "but we don't know anything more than that.

"So far, we don't even know if he's the whole show or just one guy in some big-time group," I added. "Every contact the guy makes from now on goes through central ID and as long as he's in town, every call gets checked out. By tomorrow morning I want to know how long it takes this guy to piss."

It felt good to be back in my natural element. I was probably overdoing things a bit, but Les was used to it and didn't object.

"Les, can we set-up a tap on Bettancourt's hotel room?"

"Sticky, didn't you handle a deal for security at the Four Seasons last year?" Les asked the bald-headed Italian.

Frank "Sticky" Mattucci got his nickname from a passion for playing stickball as a kid. "Yah. The head of security over there is a guy named Howard something. I don't see a problem there. Moe and me can take some equipment over to the hotel and set-up in Howard's office."

"If I can make a suggestion," Cathy spoke up. "This guy's real smart and real rich. It wouldn't surprise me to find out he's got someone at the hotel on his payroll. He might even own the place. If it's at all possible, I say we set up the tap without mentioning it to anyone."

Sticky looked at Les and shrugged. "That's doable. We'll use our repairman outfits and do the fix-it routine. No big deal. But the DA won't use it unless we get permission."

I jumped in. "At this point let's not worry about the DA. We need info. We'll worry about the DA's case after we find out who's who."

Barbara Redding, one of the newer members of the squad asked, "You want me to put a bug in his room like we did over at the Copley on that bribery case?"

"What do you think, Cathy?" Les asked.

"It's not worth the risk. If he finds it we'll blow everything. Maybe we can set-up a directional mike at a nearby building."

I stood up. "Okay, now that you all realize my little girl is the best damn cop in Boston, lets get back to basics. Cathy, you've got to ID Bettancourt for us. Les, I'm thinking we should put her in the lobby with a two-way. She'll tag him and when he comes out, Stan will shoot him from the van. If he's with anyone we'll get that bird, too. Just remember Honey, don't let the guy make you."

Cathy rolled her eyes and everyone laughed.

Chapter 26

Tuesday: July 7th (evening)

The special ops squad moved in on the Four Seasons Hotel just after 5 p.m. Sticky and Moe, carrying an authentic looking work order, drove to the back service area, pulled on overalls, and headed for the telephone switching room. Stan and Les parked the surveillance van across the street from the hotel's main entrance on Boylston Street. Cathy and Barbara stepped out of the van, walked across the street, and entered the lobby. In less than ten minutes everyone was on station and checked in.

Cathy had on a blond wig and glasses. She and Barbara were dressed in conservative business suits and made themselves comfortable in the lobby midway between the registration counter and the elevators. Anyone coming off the elevators or stepping up to the registration counter had to pass by them. Barbara faced the counter and was listening for anyone who showed up and asked for Mr. Gabriel.

At 6 p.m., Sticky alerted Les, "The target's been contacted by a male in the lobby. He's on his way up."

Les relayed the information to the two women stationed in the lobby, "A guy just called on a house phone. He's heading for the elevators."

Cathy received the message in her ear, and like a rookie tried to survey everyone within her view. She coughed, bringing her hand up to cover her mouth. "Talk to me, Les. There are at least a dozen guys standing around the elevators."

"Get on one of them and see who pushes the top button."

Both women rushed to the elevators and just as the door to the one Cathy was on, closed, a man ran up and tried to catch it. He was a second too late. All she noticed was a dark blue suit and a blue and green, horizontal striped tie.

Several minutes later the two women were back in the lobby and told Les they'd come up empty. "Don't worry, it was only a shot," he said. "Get comfortable, ladies, and let's hope these guys decide to go out on the town."

Nearly an hour went by before Cathy noticed a blue and green, horizontal striped tie coming toward her. She never got a chance to look up and see the face above it because an elegantly dressed, older man stepped into her view. It was Bettancourt.

"Les, I just spotted Bettancourt," she whispered into her hand, and turned away to avoid recognition. The two men walked past her. "Bettancourt is an older man, white hair, wearing a gray silk suit and maroon tie. There's a maroon hanky sticking out of his breast pocket. He's walking with a guy in a navy suit, blue and green striped tie. I'll be right behind them so you'll know which ones I'm marking."

Cathy got up and moved in close behind the two men as they headed for the main entrance. She kept her head down, fumbling for something in her purse.

Bettancourt stepped into the revolving door and just as the stranger was about to follow him, he changed course and walked over to a side entrance. Another man came up behind Cathy and forced her to follow right behind Henri in the revolving door. She came outside standing next to Henrí on the sidewalk, beside the steady stream of taxis pulling up at the curb.

Henrí was standing next to her, and if he turned his head ever so slightly he'd be looking right at her. Cathy turned her face away and caught a glimpse of the mystery man as he disappeared down the street.

Henrí was too close to Cathy to allow her to alert Les. She knew the surveillance camera across the street was already clicking away capturing the two men on either side of her. Instead of collecting candid shots of Bettancourt and someone who might end-up being an important player, they were taking shots of Bettancourt and some salesman from Omaha. The real mystery guy had faded into the night and she never even got a good look at his face.

She turned around and went back into the hotel. "Les, I blew it," she whispered into her hand. "The white-haired guy is Bettancourt, but the guy beside him isn't the one we wanted. There was no way to warn you, it happened too fast."

Les ordered Bobby Dueschene and his partner Mike Sullivan, waiting in the tail unit, to follow the cab Bettancourt climbed into. "It happens kid," he said to Cathy, "don't worry about it. I didn't think we'd get this lucky. You and Barbara come on in."

After Henrí left, the two women walked across the street and climbed into the van. Cathy quickly yanked off her irritating wig, and began listening intently to the reports coming in from the pursuit team.

Bettancourt's cab headed north on Charles Street between the Public Gardens and the Commons, made a left turn on Beacon, and continued on in the direction of the Capital Building.

"Boss, I think we've got someone behind us," Bobby called in. "What do you want me to do?"

"Where are you?"

"We just turned onto Joy Street."

Cathy interrupted their conversation. "I think I know where Bettancourt is headed. Phil Lord has a townhouse in Louisburg Square. I'll bet he's going there."

Les decided to go with her hunch. "He's headed for Louisburg Square, Bobby. Go in off Pinckney Street and we'll get you the number. See if the tail stays with the cab when it turns off on Mt. Vernon."

Cathy called headquarters and got the address of the Lord's townhouse, and just as Bobby pulled into Louisburg Square from the north side, Bettancourt's cab arrived from the south. It stopped in front of the Lord address, and Bobby and Mike had the passenger in their sights. They watched the guy get out, walk up to the front door and stand there waiting in the shadows. A few seconds later a man in a dark business suit, carrying a briefcase, walked up and joined Bettancourt. Someone answered the door and both men stepped inside. Bobby relayed everything he saw to Les.

"Stay put," Les ordered, "we're on our way."

Stan wheeled the van around and lurched his way into the busy, nighttime traffic. "Maybe we'll get a shot of your mystery guy, after all," Les told Cathy. "Relax, honey."

Stan parked the van half a block from the townhouse at the opposite end of the street from where Bobby and Mike were set up. Both teams had their infra-red cameras ready and Les handed Cathy a pair of night-vision binoculars. Anxious to make up for her earlier blunder she began a constant vigil, waiting to see a tie with horizontal stripes come out of that townhouse so she could redeem herself.

Time dragged on and the unfamiliar tension in Cathy's body soon took its toll. Almost two hours passed before she got a sudden jolt of adrenalin. A taxi rushed past them and came to a stop in front of the townhouse. Bettancourt came out, paused in the doorway and embraced a woman, then climbed into the cab and drove away, alone.

"Bobby, pick him up and see where he goes," Les ordered. "We'll keep watch for the other guy."

As soon as Bettancourt left, the lights inside the townhouse were turned off. Boredom settled in again for the stakeout team, and Cathy started to wonder why the stranger didn't leave with Bettancourt. Was he spending the night?

They waited for another hour without any sign of the stranger, and Les finally threw in the towel. "We should have covered the alley," he murmured, more to himself than to anyone else. "Unless Bettancourt is a pimp, I don't see this mystery guy as an all-night shack-up."

"But he went in through the front door," Cathy argued. "There's no way he could have spotted us. Why would he leave through a back door?"

"That's the kind of question I never ask myself at this time of night," Les answered.

* * *

The grandmother clock in the hallway had just chimed twelve times when the woman got out of bed and walked naked across the floor to the bathroom. Without turning on any lights she took care of her business and padded back to her lover. The dampness on the sheets felt cool and clammy against her hot body.

"Still unemotional when it comes to banks?" she asked, and reached over to touch him.

"It isn't really about banks, it's about the people connected with them."

"Well banks certainly don't have any problem claiming some ephemeral corporate good whenever it suits them. Don't you feel like we've just kicked them right in their financial nuts?"

"What I feel, is we've been very lucky so far. Everything has gone according to plan."

"That's not luck, that's good planning."

"Except when it comes to number one. We may have seriously underestimated him. I get the impression he's taking this whole thing much too personally."

"I told you the guy would go off on a super power trip. We knew from the start he'd be the one fighting to hold everything together. All we have to do is stick to our plan and not deviate. He'll come around, just like the rest, when he realizes they have no alternative."

"I wish I was as confident of that as you are."

Chapter 27

Wednesday: July 8th (morning)

Audrey Simone gazed through the window of the bus she was on, down at the Charles River rushing beneath the Longfellow Bridge. She was on her way to Cambridge and stuck in the middle of early morning traffic, wondering if she had given herself enough time. Her appointment on the MIT campus with Dr. Harold Tindley, an IBM Fellow doing advanced research in computer technology, was set for 8:45 a.m. and she'd been warned not to be late.

Tindley's work centered on the development of tiny transmitters and receivers made to fit onto the already crowded motherboards of future generation computers. Professor Hanking at NYU, acting on Audrey's request, had called Tindley and convinced him to meet with Audrey and give her a few minutes of his valuable time. Hanking warned her not to expect much.

She entered the modern office tower housing the administrative offices, and the security rigors she was subjected to made her feel like she was visiting the Pentagon instead of an institution of higher learning. It served as a reminder that what was going on in the special laboratories scattered around this campus, had tremendous implications for the real world. And, like any high-stakes game, no one was fooling around.

"Hey, Dr. Tindley, I'm Audrey Simone," she announced, as his secretary ushered her into his private office. Tindley looked to be in his 50s with a full, bushy beard and a wild, rather unkempt look.

"Sure, sure, Hanking's student interested in wireless LANs. You ever take any of my classes? Sorry I don't remember you. Did you say where you work? I'm afraid I can't let you in the lab. If I did I'd have to shoot you. IBM's orders you know. Just kidding. What's on your mind?"

"First, I'm wondering if you know a guy named Dennis Crawford?"

"Sure, sure, everyone knows Dennis."

"I'm following-up on a project of his, the one where he was trying to make computers talk to each other using radio waves. He wrote an article about it a few years back."

"Sure, sure, LANs in Cyberspace. I read it, and told him it wouldn't work. It's a hell-of-a lot easier to put the transmitter and receiver on the mother boards, like we're doing."

"When's the last time you saw him?"

"I don't know, maybe two years ago. Came by to see me with Sunny Childe. You know her? They needed help with some PROMs for a new computer system they were installing at some bank in town. Don't remember which one, but that's not important, is it?"

"I'm looking to hook-up with someone who might have stayed with Dennis' idea, you know, the bit about using them radio waves. Would you happen to know anyone who's working on that kind of stuff these days?"

"Another gal came around asking that same question a while back. I'll give you the same answer I gave her. There aren't many out there who even understood what Dennis had in mind, and those who did, agree with me; it can't be done. So the answer is, no."

"You remember the name of that woman?"

"Hell, no. Wait a minute. Maybe. I remember she was a real looker, dark-haired, young, sharp dresser."

"What about a name, professor."

"Sure, sure. I'm thinking. It was real simple, like Susan, or Sally, or something."

"Paula?"

"That's it, Paula Harding. I remember now because it was the same name as that skater who got in all that trouble a while back. You better check it out though, maybe I'm wrong on the skater's name. Big news story. Sorry, but I'm due at the lab."

He started stuffing papers and books in his briefcase while he was talking, and headed for the door. "Don't waste your time on that radio wave gorp. Even Dennis gave up on it."

"What makes you think so?" she asked, still standing beside his desk.

Tindley was halfway out the door. "Because he gave me some test results I needed."

"I don't get it, Doc," she shouted after him.

Tindley came to a stop and looked back at Audrey as if he just realized she was suffering from some rare, incurable disease. "To get those test results he had to be using one of my designs."

* * *

I stopped off at the Dump on my way to the office this morning to get a quick briefing on last night's stakeout. I looked through the pictures taken outside the Four Seasons and picked-up Cathy's report. It sounded like they had a real productive night in spite of not being able to get a make on the mystery guy.

I made a mental note to give Cathy a call and a few, well-deserved strokes. Knowing her, she was probably beating herself up over not getting a good look at the stranger.

What had me bothered was that late night visit Bettancourt made to Phil's place. If Phil was so worried about information being leaked to Bettancourt, why meet with the joker? And what role did the guy with the tie play? Just when it looked like things might be getting a little clearer, in rolled another fog bank.

By the time I got to my office, things were definitely on the downhill slope. Sheila let me know that she'd made contact with a couple of college kids who were used during the second heist. The perps followed the same procedure as last time, but the kids were directed to send their cash to P.O. boxes in Denver and Memphis; there was no mention of Chicago.

"Maybe they didn't know you were in Chicago when the second hit went down," Sheila said, trying to make me feel better. "It sounds like they planned to use a different collection point each time they hit us, just to be safe."

I groaned, "Sunny thinks they're sitting back watching to see what happens on that *Sine Dinar* crap. She's planning to ask The Lord to hold off installing those computer shields Dennis has been trying to get built."

"That would account for the message she left you yesterday afternoon. She said to tell you, we're on hold."

I nodded, "Any luck running down that report on the break-in at Denny's lab?"

"A copy of the report came through and it confirmed what you already knew, except for one difference. Dennis made the decision to drop the investigation after he found nothing was missing. I'm still waiting for a call-back from the investigating officer."

"Does the report describe the place, you know, the equipment he had set-up?"

"No. Don't worry, I'll stay on it." Sheila smiled at me and got up to leave. "You are going to call and congratulate her, right?"

I nodded again, picked up the phone, and dialed Cathy's number. She was still asleep and her machine picked up before she came on the line.

"One night out on point and you're sleeping in," I growled at her. "Les and I spent years doing that and I still got up and made every one of your school plays."

"I was never in a school play, Daddy," she answered.

"Well, if you had been I would have been there. I read the report. You did your old man proud last night."

"I blew it," she snapped back. "The guy walked right past me and the only thing I noticed was his tie."

"Listen, Honey," I said, trying to be reassuring, "if the guy is in on something he'll show up again. Who knows, maybe the tie will turn out to be his signature."

"What's Les saying?"

"Haven't talked to him yet. That meeting at the boss's place late last night has me guessing. I'd sure like to get some answers on that. Have you got any way of making contact?"

"No. He said he'd contact me every couple of days."

"When he does, play it cool. I don't want him to know we've got a tail on. See if he brings up that meeting. If not, do some hinting.

"Daddy, you sound like someone who's talking on a bugged line."

"Baby, when the mucky-mucks get involved you can't afford to overlook things. Money's no object with them. They can afford the best and the best don't always wear blue uniforms. Remember that."

* * *

An hour later, I got one of my hunches and as usual there was nothing logical about it. I barged into Ralph Sansone's office on the first level of the underground parking garage at Sterling Tower. Ralph is in charge of all the maintenance and assignment of vehicles for the bank's fleet of cars and trucks.

"Ralphy, you ready to bring back the Rocket? Martinez smelled like low tide at Revere Beach, Monday night."

"Don't get me started, Mac. I'm still thinking of putting out a contract on the Yawkeys for letting "Big C,"go."

Both of us laughed, and the phone rang. Ralph took the call, and I casually stepped over to the log sheets hanging on the wall and pulled down the clipboard for Phil's limo.

When a chauffeured car is permanently assigned to one of the bank's officers, travel records get filled out on a daily basis by the driver. The driver records the date, time, destination, and mileage of every trip, along with the names of any passengers onboard during the trip.

The top sheet on the clipboard showed yesterday's activity and for once my hunch paid off. I knew Phil had a meeting with Cathy yesterday morning in Kenmore Square, but according to the log sheet he got picked up at his townhouse at 7:30 a.m. and was driven straight to the bank. Why the lie?

Another entry also caught my attention, the one for last night. The record showed Phil left the bank at 8:00 o'clock, with Paula as a passenger. They were dropped off at her apartment on Marlborough Street fifteen minutes later, and the driver came straight back to the bank. The car wasn't checked out again for the rest of the night.

That doesn't make sense. If Phil spent the night at Paula's apartment, what's Bettancourt doing at Phil's place?

"So, what's the scoop, Mac?" Ralph asked. "And don't give me any of that hush-hush, horse shit." Ralph was a frustrated wanna-be-cop, who loved listening to tales from the good old days.

"You know how it works. If I tell you, I have to kill you," I answered, with a grin. "Where's Jelani hanging out?"

Ralph saw me put back the driver records for Phil's car. "Shit, if you're messing with The Lord I don't want to know about it. I think Jelani ran up to the cafeteria. You want I should call him?"

"No, I'm headed that way myself. I'll catch you later."

I found Jelani Trammell, Phil's regular driver, enjoying coffee and danish in the public cafeteria located on the second floor of the building. He was sitting with Yasmine Brown, a cute little secretary who worked for Paula Harding.

Maybe Lady Paula left a pair of her expensive panties in the back seat of Phil's car last night.

"Hi kids," I said, taking a seat without waiting for an invitation. "Mind if I join you?" They looked at me, and then each other with frowns.

"Say, Mac, what's up," Jelani answered, cautiously.

"I don't want to interrupt anything. It's just that I've got to pick out a wedding gift for a young couple about the same age as you two, and I was hoping you might have some suggestions." I smiled at them, hoping my ruse wasn't too transparent.

Yasmine brightened up, giving me an indication of where she was at on the subject, and quickly started running down a well-thought out list. Jelani turned away and shifted around in his chair like he was getting ready to take off.

I thanked Yasmine and turned to Jelani. "What do young guys like to do at bachelor parties these days, Jelani?" I asked, hoping Yasmine would take that as a cue to leave, and she didn't disappoint me.

"You best take your time answerin' the man's question, cause there ain't no good answer," she declared defiantly to Jelani and stood up to leave. Jelani just grunted and waved at her.

As soon as Yasmine walked off, Jelani leaned in close to me and asked, "We talkin' brothers, man?"

I clamped my hand down on top of both of Jenlani's. "Look, kid, I need some straight answers and I'm not talking about weddings or stag parties." I gave the young black man a bad-assed stare. "This is between you and me. You follow?"

Jelani looked away and asked, "Am I in some kind of shit, Mac?"

"None whatsoever, as long as you give it to me straight."

"Hey, ain't nobody payin' me to do otherwise. What you want to know?"

"You reported picking up the boss at his townhouse yesterday morning and taking him directly to the bank. Is that what happened?"

Jelani leaned forward again and this time spoke in an excited whisper. "Yeah, man, I been wantin' to know, what's that all about? I show up and pulls in the garage at his place like regular. I mean the guy operates like a Rolex. You know what I'm saying? Everything's got to be right on the sharp. Only this time when I step inside his kitchen for my usual cup of Joe, the dude's waitin' for me. Says he wants me to leave at exactly 7:30, drive to the bank without him, and write on the report he's onboard. I'm cool, you know, and do like the man says. But I've been drivin' the dude around for almost two years now and this is the first time he's gone wiggy on me."

"What about last night?" I asked.

"What about it?"

"You reported driving him and Paula Harding to her apartment, dropping them off and coming straight back to the bank."

"So?"

"I don't care about them shacking up together, but I do need to know if he spent the night there."

"Hey, look man, I ain't exactly givin' no exclusive when I say it was definitely business as usual from where I'm sitting. You know what I'm saying? I drop them off, the man says, come back at the usual time in the a.m., and that's what I done: Over and out. What the dude done between the time I dropped him off and picked him up ain't none of my damn business."

"When you dropped him off did he say he wasn't going out again?"

"You got that right, Jack. That's how come I took the limo back and split for my pad."

I sat there for a minute trying to fit all the pieces together. "There's only two people at this table, Jelani. So don't let me find out someone else knows what we just talked about."

"Shit, that ain't gonna happen. Even I don't know what we just talked about."

When I got back to my office Audrey was there, pacing back and forth like a mechanical bear. I couldn't remember the last instructions I'd given her and hoped she wasn't going to point a finger at someone new like, say, Sid Moore. I definitely didn't need any more surprises this morning.

"I just had a meeting with a computer nut over at MIT and guess whose dainty little footsteps I ended up steppin' on?" she announced, as soon as I got in the door. "Shit, you'll never figure this one out in a million years. Lady Paula, her "royal" self. Is this gettin' weird, or what?"

"What in the hell are you talking about?" I demanded, and fell into my chair. Christ, I felt like I'd just celebrated my hundredth birthday.

"I did like you said and called Hanking at NYU. He gives me the name of this guy at MIT, Harold Tindley. Tindley knows everything there is about wireless communications between computers. So I meet with him and he tells me he knows about Dennis' work and he ain't giving it a passing grade. Says Dennis went back to putting transmitters and receivers on both ends of the connection.

"When I asked Tindley if anyone else tried doing things Dennis' way, he lays on me that our very own Lady Paula dropped by asking the same questions."

I snapped to attention. "How long ago?"

"He couldn't remember."

"Was anyone with her?"

"He didn't say."

I hit the intercom button for Sheila. "Have you heard from the Palo Alto P.D., yet?"

She came in and took a seat next to Audrey. "Yah, he called about an hour ago. He remembered the investigation because Dennis had all this strange high tech looking equipment around, and acted real nervous when they answered the call. He said Dennis wanted to make a big deal of it, but when they checked everything and found nothing

187

missing, he couldn't get them out of there fast enough. The cop says he had some doubts about the whole thing."

"Like what kind of doubts?"

"Like, maybe it was phony, an insurance scam or something. I asked him if he could describe the set-up for me, but he couldn't.

"He did say he asked Dennis what he was doing with all that crap and Dennis did a little demonstration. Somehow he managed to control the computer in the cops' patrol car. The guy said it was real spooky."

Audrey interrupted, "That don't match with what Tindley just told me. He said Dennis' stuff wasn't going anywhere."

I started to scratch my head. "You're right, it doesn't make sense. Dennis gets his mouse trap to work, and Paula starts running around trying to find out who else is working on the same stuff."

What I needed to do was tie all of it in with the strange events of last night, but nothing fit. The fact that Phil was shacked up at Paula's apartment while Bettancourt and some mystery guy were at Phil's townhouse was really odd.

All of a sudden, Sheila popped up with a winner. "It sounds to me like Dennis and Paula have different agendas. I know you've been hoping those two were playing footsie, but it looks like you're wrong. Maybe Dennis came up with something worth millions, Paula found out about it and has been trying to get in on the action so she can dump the Lord."

"That works for me," I answered. "It leaves Sunny and Dennis as the prime suspects working the scam on the bank, with Paula going after Bettancourt and that secret operation crap, through Phil.

"Hold on. That still doesn't make everything come out right. What the hell was going on at Phil's place last night?

Chapter 28

Wednesday: July 8th (afternoon)

I sent Audrey back to her old desk in Operations with a new assignment. I wanted her to check out every new account opened during the last six months. Her search was limited to any large deposits coming in on a regular basis from the Isle of Mann, or some other offshore location. The cash from the last hit was last seen headed for a bank on the Isle of Mann, so I figured the pay-offs might come from there.

After hearing Sunny's rendition of what the perps were up to, I was ready to accept the fact that someone was watching the bank. Whoever the plant was, they needed to get paid and the easiest way to do that was to have the money deposited into an account at Sterling. That's the way I'd do it.

I would set up a series of accounts so I could pass the dough from one account to the next. All of the accounts would be set up under fake names, to make it tough to track down the identity of the true owner. Bank investigations always bog down when they get stuck in a maize. Audrey was the perfect candidate for this kind of job and I armed her with some inside info that only Sunny and I knew about.

Every time a computer terminal in the bank's system was used to input data setting up a new account, a hidden code became part of the account file. It was one of the few security measures I asked Sunny to implement in the new computer software program and she obliged without telling anyone.

If Audrey found an account that was receiving regular deposits from overseas, she was instructed to type in a special command. The background data attached to the file for that account would then be displayed on her monitor. Included in that information was the number of the terminal that was used to set up the account. A special index kept in my office identified the specific desk that terminal sat on. Sunny told me it was like having an electronic signature of the person who set up the account.

* * *

Sid stepped out of his office and noticed Audrey working at her old station. He walked over to find out what she was up to. "You come by to do your laundry?" he asked, coming up behind her and stealing a glance at the computer screen in front of her.

"Geez, Sid, you scared the shit outta me." She glanced at him, and continued on with her work.

"Don't let me interrupt you," he said, sarcastically. He leaned over her shoulder to take a closer look.

"Don't mess with Mozart when she's composing," Audrey warned.

"It looks like you're running a search of our main data files. What the hell is that all about?"

"Check with the cop. It's his idea."

The computer suddenly found a match with the search criteria Audrey had set up and all the data for that account appeared on the screen. She entered the command to display the imbedded technical information for that file and a stream of information flashed into view. She quickly checked the index beside her and determined the terminal that was used to open that account was sitting on the desk of the new accounts clerk at the bank's branch in Lincoln, Mass. She canceled the entry and resumed her search.

"What the hell did you just do?" Sid asked.

Audrey turned around to explain her mission just as Sid's secretary called out to him. "Sid, Paula Harding is on the line." Sid hustled off, leaving Audrey to her madness.

* * *

It was 3:00 p.m. when I stopped by to check on how Audrey was doing. "Hear any new notes yet, kid?"

"Nothing worth dancing to."

"Maybe we need to expand the time frame? What we're looking for might have been set up further back."

"Don't get touchy, but I set it up to check every account opened during the last year. I figured six months was kinda lame, if you know what I mean." She grinned without looking away from her monitor.

"You find that account and we'll let you become a real citizen." I watched as the information streamed by on her screen. "Is Sid around?"

"Paula called him about an hour ago. I think he's still in his office."

I walked over to Sid's office and stuck my head in the door. "Take your thumb out of your mouth, and tell me what's going on, Chief."

"Get your ass in here, Mac, and tell me what the hell you're up to. And don't give me any bullshit. Nobody tells me anything, anymore."

"Aren't you the guy who always says he's got too much shit in his own yard to step in anyone else's?" I flopped into a chair, grabbed a report off his desk, and started flipping through it. "Looks like the paper zombies are winning."

Sid pointed with his finger. "I look out there and see my best analyst back at her old desk, so naturally I'm thinking, maybe now I can get some of my own work done for a change. But when I check with her, she says she's following your screwy orders, running some crazy search of our main data files. What the hell are you after, Mac?"

"Simple. The bad guys are getting inside dope. That means they've got someone on the inside keeping an eye on things."

"What's that got to do with customer accounts?"

"Whoever's keeping watch needs to get paid, right. I'm betting they set-up an account here that's getting deposits from an off-shore bank." I smiled at Sid.

"You're losing your fucking marbles along with your hair. No one's dumb enough to have an account in their own name if that's what they're up to.

"Ah, but I've got a secret weapon, "Super Sleuth" Simone. She's on the trail, and if that account is here she'll find it." I threw the papers back on his desk and stood up. "I hear the boss called you. Save me a trip up there and clue me in on what he's up to today."

"Says he's going out of town for a meeting. Paula mentioned something about Toronto. He wanted the latest figures on the thefts."

What kind of meeting could be so important that Phil would leave town in the middle of this mess? Outside of Paula, the only person I could think of who might have an answer to that question was my daughter.

I headed back to my office and called Cathy at the Dump. "Hey, kid, heard from your number one client lately?"

"No, Daddy, not a word. Why, what's up?"

"What's the latest on our foreign friend? Still got your ears on?"

"He flew the coop this morning, probably back to Transylvania. All my playmates have gone home, too." She couldn't hold back a giggle. "This is really silly. If anyone is listening in, they probably figured out who we're talking about long ago."

"Don't get cute, and don't forget who's in charge. I want you to check something out and get right back to me. Top Dog is supposed to be on a plane to Toronto. Is the bad guy headed in the same direction?"

Within a few minutes Cathy returned my call. "They're not partying together. The bad guy was on a flight to Amsterdam. Anything else I can get for you, boss?"

"Then what's our man Flint doing in Toronto?" I asked out loud. "Good work, rookie."

Chapter 29

Thursday: July 9th (morning)

I decided to go with another one of my hunches. I drove over to Phil's townhouse knowing Phil was in Toronto, and hoping his wife was still in town. I thought this would be a perfect time to renew my acquaintance with the lovely Mrs. Lord.

Birds were chirping away in the trees lined-up along the old cobblestone sidewalks of Louisburg Square. As I walked beside the neat row of overpriced town homes, the taps on my shoes made a clicking sound on the uneven stones.

I needed a plan, but all that came to mind was a sketchy idea. My hunch was, Charlotte Lord might be in on the visit Bettancourt paid to this neighborhood two nights ago. One of the photographs taken by Les' team showed Bettancourt putting a lip-lock on some woman in the doorway. I figured it had to be Charlotte. Even if it wasn't, my guess was she knew what was going on in there that night.

I rang the doorbell and the maid answered. She quickly told me Phil wasn't in and went to get Charlotte. Christ! I do believe I'm on a roll; my hunches have been paying off lately. I should be at the track.

"Mac, what an unexpected and pleasant surprise," Charlotte said, coming down the wide hallway wearing a smile and not much else. She was dressed in a short silk robe that floated over her body. She took me by the hand and lead me back down the hallway, through the living room, and outside to a small patio and garden in the back yard. It looked like something out of a Fred Astaire movie.

"Phil is out of town, so I have you all to myself," she said with a not so subtle smile.

"Well, aren't I the dummy," I answered. "Sorry for the intrusion. I must have gotten my wires crossed. I could have sworn Paula said Phil was at the townhouse."

"I'm sure she knows exactly where he is, she always does." Charlotte reached across the table and poured me a cup of coffee. Her robe fell open, revealing the fact that she had nothing on beneath it. The exposure of her breasts didn't bother her, and she carried on without correcting the situation. "Why are you looking for him?"

"We've been messing around with a little problem at the bank, and I needed to ask him some questions."

"Maybe Paula got her townhouses mixed up," she laughed, and gave me a knowing smile.

"That's probably none of my business," I answered. Her comment had cleared up one question I had on the way in: Phil's relationship with Paula Harding was certainly no mystery to his wife.

"You're so right, Mac." Her voice was low, and she laid a soft, smooth hand on top on mine. "What Phil does is his business, and what I do is mine. That's the way we operate."

"It was probably my mistake. The last time I spoke to Phil he mentioned there was going to be a meeting here on Tuesday night, so I assumed he was still in town."

Charlotte took the bait. She pulled back her hand and adjusted her robe. "There was no meeting here Tuesday night. I came into town on Tuesday afternoon, and Phil hasn't been around since I arrived. I was in all night. You got your townhouses mixed up."

I looked away and focused my attention on one of the robins playing in a nearby tree. It didn't bother me to hear that she and Phil liked to jump in the sack with other people. That was life. And even Charlotte's rather obvious invitation for a romp in the boss' bed, was only mildly aggravating. What made me sick was the fact that she had just lied to me; that meant she was selling out her husband. The "why" didn't matter. She was plotting with Bettancourt, against Phil, and that kind of disloyalty was something I can't stomach.

Some of the other pieces of the puzzle were also falling into place. Bettancourt had come by to see Charlotte that night, not Phil. It was Charlotte putting the make on Bettancourt in the doorway. How that arrangement got set up and the purpose of their get-together on that particular evening still wasn't clear, but I was beginning to get a pretty good idea of what they were up to.

The mystery guy was probably there to plant some bugs so Bettancourt could keep an ear on whatever Phil was up to. That way, even if Cathy fingered the spy at the bank, Bettancourt would still have Phil covered in the one place Phil was most likely to drop his guard.

I resisted Charlotte's invitation to stay longer and headed straight back to the office. Someone was playing with that damn remote again.

* * *

By the time the anxious caller reached Henrí Bettancourt, the eight-hour time difference put it late in the day in Belgium. Bettancourt picked up the receiver and immediately put the caller on the defensive. "I assume you have a very urgent problem, and have taken all necessary precautions?"

"Yah, on both counts. Something unexpected popped up and I thought you ought to know about it right away. The investigation has taken a crazy turn. Somehow they're onto my deal with you and they're checking out deposits from overseas banks. They haven't found my account yet, but the way they're putting two and two together it's only a matter of time."

"That is unfortunate. When you say `they,' to whom are you referring?"

"The gal tracking down the account is an analyst named Audrey Simone, but she takes her orders from Mac MacKenzie, the bank's security chief."

"Ah, yes. If I'm not mistaken Audrey Simone was the one who first uncovered the theft. She has turned out to be a most resourceful young lady."

"Well, what do we do?"

"The first thing you should do is not over react." His voice was calm, almost sympathetic. "Do you have Ms. Simone's home address available. Perhaps we can get her to put her talents to a different use."

"You're barking up the wrong tree there. She's red, white, and blue, if you know what I mean."

"I can be quite persuasive. Leave the matter in my hands and, in the meantime, do what you can to cover-up your own vulnerability. I'm sure you must have taken some precautions to prevent discovery of your secret wealth."

The numbers and locations of every secret account the caller had set up to hide his funds, were well known to Henrí, including the one in the Caymans where the bulk of those funds landed. Bettancourt was able to have them traced because the caller never thought to take the money out of the system, in the form of cash, before re-depositing it.

Henrí carefully screened all of the people he used on special assignments and, so far, the cartel never had any reason to question his judgment. He was secure in the loyalty of his underlings because he knew he could make a single phone call, and every dollar they had on deposit, anywhere in the world, would be frozen. It was a devotion based on greed.

Chapter 30

Thursday: July 9th (evening)

I stopped my car in front of Brian's house and shut off the engine. The muggy air closed in around me like a steam bath. It was 7:00 p.m. and the daytime humidity was still high. I wondered how the mosquitoes and fireflies buzzing around managed to fly in such wet conditions.

Sally called me, bitching over the fact that I'd spent so little time with the family on the Fourth. She insisted that I show up for dinner tonight. I knew the main course was going to be a grilling on what I was up to with Cathy. But she was right, I did need to spend more time with my family.

I played with my grandkids before dinner, listening to all the stuff they had stored up for me, and joked a bit with Brian. But in the back of my mind I was still struggling with the best way to let Phil know what his wife was up to. He needed to know there were probably phone taps scattered all over his townhouse.

When I sat Maeve down in her highchair, she patted me on my head and popped out with one of those zingers little kids are so good at. "Grampy, how come your head's so shiny on top?"

"Sweetie pie, I'm so old, my hair's wearing off just like your Pooh bear." I kissed her on the top of her head and sat down beside Colin.

I nudged my grandson with an elbow and said, "Don't get old kid. Live hard, die young, and leave a good-looking corpse."

"Dad," Sally howled from the kitchen, "I heard that. You know he thinks everything you say is gospel. He already has so many demerits from listening to you, that he'll have to carry them over into his next life."

I grabbed the kid by the back of his neck and growled at him. "I take back what I just said. I want you to be a lazy good-for-nothing, grow old, and die all shriveled up with no hair on your head, like me."

Colin started laughing, which made his sister bang away with her spoon on the tray, adding to the commotion. Sally made a pass at trying to look upset, as she shoved a bowl of potato salad at me.

"Cathy's having a hard time over Dr. Mike," she added, as she prepared a plate for Maeve. "I know you never like getting involved in that kind of stuff, but maybe this time you could let her know how you feel. It would mean the world to her. Of course, I'm assuming you like the guy; we certainly do. He seems so down to earth. He's really smitten with her."

"Smitten? What the hell kind of a word is smitten? Brian, your wife's been going to one of them female consciousness raising groups, again."

"Give me a break, Dad," Brian answered, grabbing me by the shoulders. "Just tell us what you think of him. And while you're at it, what's up with this new-found partnership between you and my sister?"

"What did she say?"

"Not much." Brian went to the kitchen to grab a beer for me. "Something about the mountain finally coming to Mohammed."

Sally took a bite of food and quickly jumped back into the conversation. "You may not realize it, Dad, but you've created a big dilemma for her. This exciting guy shows up in her life and before she can decide what to do with him, you're putting a whole bunch of other choices in front of her."

"She's on a special assignment, not the damn dating game," I shouted in defense.

"Oh, sure. You surround her with all these attractive, big-time hitters, including The Lord and her own father, who Arnold Schwarzenegger would have trouble competing with, and then expect her not to notice anything. Old Doctor Mike has to try and score against the rest of you guys and he can't even throw a forward pass. No wonder she's having doubts."

Mac smiled at her. "You've been hanging around football coaches too much, Honey." Shifting to a serious note, I added, "Cathy better not be letting any of this romantic crap interfere with her job, or her judgment."

"You're missing the point, Dad," Brian argued. He handed me a beer and poured a glass of wine for Sally. "When you decided to let her get involved in whatever it is you've got going, you made her biggest dream come true. She gets to play in the super bowl with the real pros. All she wants to do now is make good in your eyes. You took on a big responsibility, and between you and me, your track record on meeting responsibilities ain't been too good lately."

The conversation was interrupted by the telephone, and Brian went to answer it. "It's for you, Dad, it's Audrey."

"Yah, kid, what's up?"

"Sorry about calling like this," she whispered. "Sheila told me where you were and said it'd be okay to call."

"Sure. What's on your mind?"

"I've been tracking down them accounts you wanted and I found something. And just to be sure, I re-checked everything a couple times. I'm still at the office."

"Speak up, kid, I can hardly hear you."

"Can you meet me at my place? I don't want to talk about this over the phone, if you catch my drift. I'll bring the stuff with me so's nothing happens to it."

"I think you've been at it too long. Take a break."

"This ain't my fucking imagination, Mac," she snapped. "You're gonna have a hard time keeping from dropping a Lincoln Log yourself when you see what I found."

I could tell she had her teeth into something and wasn't going to let it go. "Okay, it's 7:30 now and I'll be at your place by 9:00 o'clock. Gimme the address."

"What was that all about?" Brian asked when I returned to the dinner table.

"I'm not sure. Just something she wants me to check out. Might be nothing at all."

"She sounded too upset for it to be nothing. You want me to tag along with you?"

In total shock, I looked over at my son. "All of a sudden you want to play cop? What is it with you guys? You think the old man can't handle the job anymore just because his hair's getting a little thin?"

* * *

I turned off the Fitzgerald Expressway and made my way onto Endicott Street in the middle of the North End. This was my turf. I knew every inch of it like the back of my hand. The two-story, clapboard-sided house on Hull Street where my kids grew up was only a few blocks away. Karen caught the bus at a stop, one block away.

I pulled into an empty spot on the narrow street in front of Audrey's apartment building, stepped out of my car, and looked up and down the street. There were at least a dozen families on this street who owed me a favor going back more than one generation. That's the way things were around here.

A young couple was coming through the small vestibule inside the front door of Audrey's building just as I climbed the stoop. I grabbed the inner door before it closed and went inside. The building was a three-story walk-up, and had the same stale odor in the dingy hallways that all these buildings had in common.

As I climbed the stairs to the third floor, the worn, wooden, stair treads creaked like the whole building might come tumbling down at any minute. I couldn't count how many times over the years I had to sneak up stairs like these to make a bust.

When I got to Audrey's apartment and knocked on the door it swung open. I figured she'd left it open for me, but the place was dark and there was no sound.

"What the hell?" The light from the hallway cast a shadow into the room and I saw some broken and overturned furniture. That's when it hit me. "Ah, shit!"

I stepped inside and my right hand automatically reached for the non-existent gun under my left shoulder. "Hey, Audrey, it's Mac. You okay? You need to get a maid." I kept an eye out for any sudden movements as I glanced around.

No weapon, no back-up, and no idea of what's going on. This is a dumb move. The book says wait for back-up.

Just as I was about to call out again I noticed a Nike clad foot sticking out from behind the sofa. I ran over and knelt down beside Audrey's unconscious body. My breath caught in my throat and I bit into the knuckle of my clenched fist as I looked down at her bloodied face. "Son-of-a-bitch!"

A floorboard creaked. I looked up in time to see a shadow move across the dimly lit kitchen. My heart skipped a beat, and I jumped to my feet and pressed myself flat against the dark wall.

The air in the apartment was stifling and there wasn't much of it. The wallpaper behind me felt damp, and then I realized the wetness was coming from my body. My pulse was racing like a rookie on his first bust.

Everything felt wrong. This was the way things go down when you bite the big one. None of it made any sense.

Is this just a fucked-up burglary? Did I end up in the wrong place at the wrong time? Why doesn't this shithead just blow me away and get it over?

Rule number one: burglars carry guns. I looked down at Audrey's bloody face right below me and could see she'd been beaten with a fist. For some reason this fucker didn't want to shoot her. Why?

I need a weapon. A broken chair leg was lying near my foot and I reached down and picked it up. As I slid along the wall toward the doorway to the kitchen I called out, "Listen up, punk, I'm a cop and I'm armed. My partner's covering the fire escape, so you ain't going nowhere. Just put down your weapon and come out with your hands on your head."

"Okay. I didn't do anything, so don't be getting all crazy on me. I came in to help out. I'm unarmed and I'll be walkin' out with me hands up."

I grabbed the chair leg with both hands, like a baseball bat. When I saw his foot come across the threshold, I swung the bat, head high, into the empty doorway.

The perp had outsmarted me. He came through the doorway in a crouched position and I realized too late the mistake I'd made. His fist shot up into my balls and the instant jolt of excruciating pain made my upper body jackknife and I fell to the floor. My brain instantly prepared itself for the kick to the chin I knew was coming. Instead, the scumbag pushed past me and ran out the door. I listened as his footsteps moved down the hallway.

Ignoring the pain in my groin, I dragged myself over to Audrey. I pressed a finger against her carotid artery, and found a faint pulse. "You're alive kid," I yelled at her bloody face, "don't give up on me."

My eyes searched through the darkness for a phone and I spotted one on the kitchen wall. Holding onto my groin, I pushed myself up the wall and staggered into the kitchen trying to find enough air to breathe. When I reached the phone it came to me why the shithead beat Audrey unconscious, and didn't bother to finish me off on his way out.

All the windows in the apartment were shut in spite of the fact that it was such a hot, humid night. A slight hissing sound was coming from the stove, and it was that sound that registered in my brain. My pain was replaced by instant panic. I quickly shut off all the gas burners and bent over to look inside the open oven. A small gadget was lying on the rack and I reached in and grabbed it, breaking off a wooden match just as a striker snapped against my thumb. Shit, another second and Audrey and I would have been toast.

I wiped away the sweat dripping off my forehead, pushed open a window behind the sink, and gasped for air. Next, I dialed 911, ordered an ambulance, and then dragged myself back to Audrey. Using a dish towel, I wiped away some of the blood smeared on her face and tried to make some sense out of what had just taken place.

This kind of live-action stuff used to be what I lived for. A real threat of violence or death was mother's milk to me. An incident like this would have given me a high for a week.

But a quick reality check confirmed that I was a bloated old man, with shaking hands and sweat pouring off him, contaminated with fear, sitting on the floor of that small apartment with Audrey in my arms, struggling with all my regrets. A voice deep inside was crying out, "Please, just hold on, Honey." My eyes were darting furiously back and forth in the dark trying to spot some place that I could go to, to pay the price for all my past mistakes: a place where I could buy redemption for the innocent body in my arms.

* * *

The EMTs arrived and took Audrey to Mass. General. I followed along and as they wheeled her into the emergency trauma center, I spotted Michael. I pulled him aside and quickly clued him in on what had happened.

"Mike, I've got a big favor to ask. The kid's been worked over by a pro. He meant to kill her in an explosion and by now he knows it didn't go off. I need you to do everything you can for her, but, at the same time, you have to keep all of this quiet. I'll make sure she gets some protection, but, for the time being, I don't want anyone to know her identity, or the condition she's in. Are you following me?"

"Not exactly, Mr. Mackenzie. What do you mean, keep things quiet?"

"No names, no reports, and no one that you can't personally vouch for gets anywhere near Audrey. I'll be right here in case you have any questions." I pushed him toward the sliding doors and added, "Just make sure she stays alive, Mike."

Ignoring the angry protests from a nurse, I picked up the phone on her desk and called Les. "Les, grab a couple of the guys and meet me in emergency at Mass General. The table stakes just went up."

Chapter 31

Friday: July 10th (early morning)

Les arrived 20 minutes later with Sticky and Moe. As soon as I filled them in on the details, Les ordered his two detectives back to Audrey's apartment to dig up whatever evidence they could find. I told them to look for a dark blue, canvas knapsack that Audrey always dragged around. The attacker took off empty-handed, so I figured it was still there. Hopefully, it contained some answers.

A half hour later, Michael came out and said, "We've got her vital signs stabilized, but she's in a coma. She took a blow to the head. Until the swelling on her brain goes down we won't know if she suffered any permanent damage, or when she might regain consciousness. Her nose is broken too, and she's got several bruised ribs. That's one beat up girl. I hope you get the guy who did it."

The image of Audrey's battered face was fresh in my mind, and I felt the heat boiling inside me. Every time I closed my eyes I saw that poor kid lying on the floor, bloody and beaten. I had to find some way to make it up to her. Paybacks are hell, and I intended to make sure whoever did this paid big time.

Les agreed with me the attack was carried out under a professional contract. Someone had gotten word of what she was up to and put out a call to have her hit. She was smart enough to get me over to her apartment rather than discuss things over the phone, but, unfortunately, the hitman was already onto her.

The guy waited until Audrey felt safe inside her apartment before making his move; the sign of a real pro.

He knocked her unconscious so that even if her body was recovered after the explosion and fire, there wouldn't be any evidence that someone had taken her out. The whole thing would end up looking like some dumb accident.

From the shape her apartment was in, Audrey must have put up a damn good fight and that threw off the scumbag's timing. I showed up just after the guy set up his little gizmo, and that's why he was anxious to get out of there. There was no need to finish me off because once the ashes cooled down, I'd be one more pile of cooked meat in the burned-out ruins of that apartment building. Lucky for me, all I ended up with were some sore nuts.

While we were standing around, Les happened to mentioned that Cathy checked out the phone records for Bettancourt's suite at the Four Seasons and came up with two incoming calls. Both calls originated from phones inside Sterling Tower. One was made from Phil Lord's private line and the other came from one of the public phones located somewhere inside the building. They came in before the squad set up taps on the phone lines so there was no way of knowing the nature of the calls.

Audrey was still on my mind and the significance of what Les was saying didn't register at first. Then it hit me, I had a much bigger problem on my hands: one that needed attention, fast.

I grabbed Les by the arm. "Do you know what Cathy was going to do with that information on those phone calls?"

"I guess she was gonna shove it in front of Lord and see what he had to say. Why?"

"Damn it. I've got to stop her."

I grabbed a nearby phone and dialed Cathy's number. She was asleep and as soon as she picked up the receiver, I yelled at her, "Did you call Phil yesterday?"

"I tried, but he wasn't home," she answered, groggily. "I got his machine. What's got you so upset?"

"Did you leave a message?"

"Yah. Why? You're making me nervous, Daddy. What's this all about?" She sounded wide awake by then.

"I'm sorry, Honey, I should have gotten to you sooner. It's my own damn fault. A lot went down tonight. I'm on my way over to your place, and I'll fill you in on everything when I get there. In the meantime, don't let anyone in, and if Phil calls don't say anything to him. There's a bug on his phone."

"Should I call Les?"

"No need to, he's standing next to me. I'll be there in 15 minutes."

* * *

Paula Harding was standing just around the corner and out of sight, listening to Mac's conversation with his daughter. She kept her presence a secret while she tried to decide what to do about the unexpected events that had occurred that night.

Less than an hour ago she had received an unexpected phone call from Henri Bettancourt directing her to go to Mass. General and find out the present condition of Audrey Simone. The news that Audrey had been hurt came as a shock to her, and Paula had to fight back an urge to scream at Henri. He ordered Paula to report back to him as soon as she had the information.

Having overheard Mac's conversation with Les Woburn about the attack and bugs being planted at Phil's townhouse, she decided to remain out of sight until both men left the area. When she came around the corner she saw a policeman standing guard at the entrance to the ICU. Mac had mentioned the doctor's name who was treating Audrey and Paula walked up to the cop and said, "Officer, I need to talk to Dr. Michael Jordan. It's very important."

"Go ahead," he answered, and pointed, "That's him standing right over there."

Paula walked up to the tall, handsome young doctor, and turned her feminine charm up a few watts. She stepped purposely close to him, and whispered in a quiet, seductive voice, "Dr. Jordan, my name is Paula Harding. I'm the executive assistant to Philip Lord, the CEO at Sterling Bank & Trust. Mac MacKenzie called me with the awful news that one of our employees, Audrey Simone, was brought in tonight after being attacked."

Michael interrupted her. "I just saw Mac a minute ago making a phone call." He stepped around the corner with Paula in tow, but Mac was gone. "You must have just missed him."

"Have you discussed Audrey's condition with him?" she asked. "I mean I don't want to bother you, doctor, if Mac already knows all the particulars."

"At this point there isn't much to know. She's in a coma and we simply have no way of knowing when or if she'll come out of it. I don't quite understand why Mr. MacKenzie would want you to come down here?"

"Mr. Lord is out of town and Mac knew he'd want me to find out, first-hand, what happened and what's being done for Audrey in his absence. He's very particular about that sort of thing. I can say with certainty, he will insist that she be given the very best care.

"As you probably know, Mr. Lord is a trustee of this hospital, so I'm sure you understand my position, doctor."

She stood close enough to him that he could feel the heat from her breath on his face.

"Well, uh, you know everything Mr. MacKenzie knows," he stammered, stepping back to widen the space between them, "and we're doing everything possible. So if you'll excuse me, I'll be getting back to my patient." He backed up a few steps, keeping his eyes on Paula, then turned and walked into the ICU.

"Thank you, doctor," she whispered under her breath, and headed for the exit. "You've been very helpful." She had a very important call to make, and it wasn't to Henri Bettancourt.

Chapter 32

Friday: July 10th (morning)

Henrí was in a very bad mood. "You are wasting my time bringing me excuses. Why you failed is of no consequence. I wanted the job done. If you can't fulfill your obligations, I will find someone who can." The abrupt finality of his statement was no idle threat.

"You're over-reacting. I said I'd take care of things, now didn't I? I was just lettin' you know my schedule got thrown off a little, that's all."

Henrí's bad mood began an hour ago when he received a call from Charlotte Lord letting him know that a woman named Cathy had called Phil and left a message. It was a new name, one Henrí wasn't familiar with, and that concerned him. He doubted Philip would start a new affair at a time like this. That would be so out of character for him. There had to be another explanation.

While he listened to his present caller's explanation of the circumstances leading up to his bungled mission, it brought to mind that secret meeting Philip held a few days ago. This new woman, Cathy, could have been the one Philip was meeting with that morning. If so, why would he go to such lengths to keep it a secret, then allow her to call his home?

The caller's mention of a man arriving unexpectedly at the Simone apartment and interrupting his plans provided an answer. The pieces started to click into place. From the description the caller gave, the man who disrupted things was Duncan MacKenzie, and if memory served him, Mr. MacKenzie had a daughter named Cathy.

Henrí quickly reviewed his brief encounter with Cathy MacKenzie. She was the bright young lady who interviewed him several years ago and later became a policewoman. It made wonderful sense.

If she was the same woman who called Philip it meant his star pupil was in fact operating true to form. He probably hired the young policewoman to join forces with her father, in an effort to ferret out the people Henrí had planted inside Sterling Bank & Trust. It would be a very smart move indeed.

"I have another task that also needs some attention," Henrí said, casually interrupting his caller, "but I hesitate to bring it up in light of your past difficulties." He knew the ambitious young man on the other end of the line would jump at a chance to exonerate himself. He might even offer a rare bargain in return.

"My target's in a coma, under 24-hour guard, so there's gonna be a bit of delay until I can conclude that matter. In the meantime, I could take care of your other problem at, say, half my usual rate. Just to make up for any inconvenience I might have caused."

"Do we understand each other on the consequences of any further disappointments?"

"Don't be worrying none about that. There won't be any mistakes."

"Your instructions and the information you need will be delivered tomorrow in the usual manner."

* * *

The Air Canada flight from Toronto touched down at Logan Airport just before 9:00 a.m., and Phil spotted his driver, Jelani, waiting for him as he came through customs.

"Bet things was a whole lot cooler up there in Canada, huh, Mr. Lord," Jelani commented, taking the bags and following Phil to the car parked at the curb. "It's been sweatin' time around here.

"The more I travel, Jelani, the more I appreciate coming home."

"Ain't that the truth."

"I want you to stop at my townhouse," Phil instructed.

The gray limousine weaved its way slowly through the traffic surrounding the terminal, then headed into the Sumner Tunnel on the way into the city. Phil knew Charlotte was planning on coming into town while he was away, and he thought it might be wise to stop and check on things before going to the office.

In the foyer of his townhouse, he stopped to shuffle through the collection of mail piled on the front console and glanced up when he saw Charlotte coming slowly down the staircase. Her short, silk robe was hanging half-open, as usual, and revealed much of her well-tanned body.

"Good morning, dear," he said, sending her a pleasant smile. "Anything interesting going on in your life?"

"No. Too bad I can't say the same for you." She blew him a kiss in the air, and turned down the hallway, on her way to the back garden. "Cathy called."

Charlotte had her back to him and didn't see the momentary look of surprise on his face. Cathy MacKenzie knew better than to make contact in such an indiscreet manner, Phil thought to himself. What now? He pushed open the double doors to the library, went to his desk, and played back the brief message. "It's Cathy. Please call."

Phil dialed her number and as soon as she answered, identified himself.

Her response was terse. "Don't say anything. Same place in 45 minutes." There was a click, and the line went dead.

How very odd, he thought. Whatever was going on had to be terribly important for her to act so abruptly. Then it came to him, her warning could only mean one thing; someone's phone was tapped. A small knot started to twist in his stomach. Things were moving much too fast.

He walked out to the back garden and sat down at the glass-top table, across from his wife. The small patch of grass surrounding the brick patio had been trimmed early that morning, and the clippings gave the tiny oasis a clean, fresh smell. He glanced around to see if the gardener was tending to things properly, and when he looked back, Charlotte had absent-mindedly poured him a cup of coffee.

"To what do I owe this new-found interest in my activities?" he asked, looking at her and reaching for the tea pot. "Jealousy has never been one of your sins."

"Who says I'm jealous?"

"When you start implying that I'm sleeping with my tailor's secretary, it sounds a little bit like jealousy." She would check, of course, and by coincidence his tailor at Louis, Boston did have an assistant named Cathy. He made a mental note to place a call to Howard later that morning and make sure he confirmed that his gal had called to inform Phil that the latest fabrics from Italy had arrived.

Charlotte stared back at her husband. Part of their ritual was that neither of them told the truth. She assumed he was telling a lie, and it amused her to think he had grown tired of Paula Harding. She knew at least two people who wouldn't be very happy to hear that news. But she was also a little concerned. If he was telling the truth, she would appear the fool for having passed along such insignificant news.

Chapter 33

Friday: July 10th (late morning)

My temperature was rising faster than the thermometer hanging outside the window at *Momma's Kitchen*. Cathy and I sat there, waiting for Phil to show up. Cathy hadn't voiced any concerns about her personal safety, but I knew it was on her mind. A lot depended on whether Charlotte Lord had picked up the message and passed it on to Bettancourt. I kept turning the coffee mug around and around in nervous anticipation of finding out the answer to that goddamn question.

Phil arrived just after 10:00 a.m. and looked as polished as ever. As if nothing grubby or undignified, not even Audrey's blood-smeared face, could ever touch his privileged way of life. I felt like giving him a smack in the mouth for putting Cathy in the way of creeps who could do something like that.

"A gathering of the clan MacKenzie," Phil joked. "How unexpected."

Madge came over and stuck a cup of hot water and a tea bag in front of Phil. "I saved it for you, from last time." She nodded at me and Cathy, and added, "Them two have been staring at each other like two Brits at an Irish wake, so I ain't even going to ask if anyone wants something to eat."

As soon as she walked away, I said, "You're in deep shit, Phil, and we don't have time to fuck around. Have you talked to Charlotte this morning?"

"Yes. Why do you ask?"

"Did she mention Cathy's call?"

Phil wasn't keeping up with the line of questioning and reacted out of habit. "Don't forget who you are talking to, Mac. Something is obviously going on here, and I'm in the dark." He turned to Cathy. "What happened that made you violate our agreement this way?"

My hand clamped down on Phil's and I began to squeeze. "I asked you a question and I want an answer."

Phil looked more surprised than frightened. "Yes."

That answer only boosted my anger. I leaned forward, looking him in the eye, and snarled, "If anyone touches a hair on my daughter's head, I'm gonna squash you like a bug."

"That's enough, Daddy. You're out of line." Cathy grabbed me and pushed me back in the seat. "Phil, a lot happened since we talked, and Dad's right, you're in trouble. You haven't been straight with him or me, and maybe you've got a good reason. But things have gotten way too serious to mess around anymore. Someone tried to kill Audrey Simone last night."

Phil stared at her, as if he didn't understand the words she used. His eyes shifted to me, then back to Cathy and back again to me. His mouth was moving but no words were coming out. Finally, he managed to say, "I thought I had more time."

I heard a different message. I heard the whine of a member of the privileged class complaining because things weren't going exactly the way he wanted them. "I guess you ain't so smart after all."

"Time to do what?" Cathy asked.

"For you to find the person we were looking for at Sterling. I thought if I could keep that person from finding out who the crooks were, I could keep anyone from getting hurt. But I don't understand why anyone would go after

Audrey? She wasn't important. It just doesn't make any sense."

Cathy continued filling him on the details. "We think Audrey figured out who the mole was. Whoever's in charge somehow got wind of what she was doing and put the word out. Now she's in a coma and all we've got to go on are a bunch of account numbers she took home to show Dad."

Phil looked at me with a whipped-dog expression. "Trust me Mac, we are on the same side. Please tell me why you asked about Char. Do you know something about her that I should know?"

As mad as I was at this guy, sticking him with the cuckold's horns wasn't my idea of revenge. I had no way of knowing whether he and Charlotte still cared for each other in spite of their sick lifestyle. If there was any connection left between them it was about to end.

"She sold you out to your friend Bettancourt," I answered, abruptly. "He and another guy were at your place, Tuesday night, while you were with Paula. My guess is the mystery guy was there to plant some bugs. Yesterday, I went by your place saying I was looking for you. I wanted to find out what Charlotte knew about that meeting. She said she came into town on Tuesday and no one came by Tuesday night.

"If she brought up Cathy's call to you this morning, it means she listened to the message, figured Cathy for some new playmate, and probably contacted Bettancourt to let him know what was going on. We figure Bettancourt's the one who called for the hit on Audrey. If he figures out who Cathy is, she could be next on his list."

Phil tried to pick up his cup of tea, but his hand was shaking too much. He reached over and touched Cathy's hand. "You've got to explain things to your father. Make him realize who we are dealing with. You know Henrí and what he's capable of. Tell him."

"I don't know, Phil," she answered softly, "not really. Do you know what that Operation Sine Dinar is all about?"

Phil looked down at his cup. "I know Henrí Bettancourt is out to silence the crooks, permanently. He wants to keep them from ever telling anyone what they know about that Operation. It doesn't matter whether the crooks really know something, or not. They'll be silenced just to make sure they don't talk, along with anyone else who gets in his way."

"Why didn't you tell me that before?" I asked.

"There are complexities to this whole mess that are not easy to explain. I thought I could keep things under control. My focus has been on apprehending the crooks, not eliminating them."

Cathy interrupted him. "Phil, do you have any idea who Henrí might have gotten in touch with while he was in town? The guy he was seen with the other night was average height and build, sandy hair, dressed in a business suit and wearing a horizontal striped tie."

"No, he always deals with sensitive matters on a one-on-one basis, so people won't be able to answer those kinds of questions."

"Why did you call him on Monday?"

"I didn't," Phil responded with a look of surprise. "What makes you ask?"

"I found a record of a call to Henrí, at his hotel on Monday morning. It was made on your private line." Cathy pulled out a copy of the telephone log. Two calls on the list were highlighted.

Phil studied the sheet for a moment, then looked up at her. "He called me that morning. I didn't even know he was coming to town. He turned to me. "Remember the call I took on the Fourth while you were at my place in Wenham. It was Henrí. He wanted me to come to Europe to meet with him. On Monday morning I was packing up to leave. I can't explain this other call.

Cathy helped him out. "We think it was Paula who made that call. Do you know if she has ever been in touch with Bettancourt?"

"All I know is, ever since he found out the thieves had used that code name, Henrí has been trying to learn their identity, along with the name of whoever divulged the information to the thieves."

"Was it you?" Cathy asked, almost in a whisper.

"No," Phil answered, without hesitation. "But that's not the point. In Henrí's mind I'm a very likely suspect, and for that reason a possible target for elimination. Henri doesn't believe in taking risks. He'd much rather eliminate a problem than deal with it."

"Am I supposed to get out my violin," I snarled at him. My fists were clenched like two sledge-hammers. "Audrey almost got killed and she wasn't even a part of your game. Now you've dragged my daughter into this mess and didn't bother to warn her about what she could be facing."

"From where I'm sitting, Mac, it looks like you are the one who dragged Cathy into much deeper water than I ever had in mind."

We stared at each other, without wavering.

Cathy spoke up. "That's enough, you two. Daddy, fill him in on what you know about Paula."

I relaxed a little and threw a loaded question at him. "Did you send Paula out to question some computer professor at MIT on the work Dennis Crawford was doing?"

"Why would I do such a thing? I can assure you that Paula does not spend her time checking out computer theories."

"Well, she did, and the only question is, who's her dancing partner? She ran some kind of an investigation and I'd like to know why." Mentioning her name brought to mind Audrey's favorite saying, "things were getting juicy."

Cathy glanced out the window and suddenly turned toward me and shoved me with both hands. "Move, damn it!" I stood up and she jumped to her feet and ran out of the diner.

I didn't have a clue on what she was after and let my instincts take the upper hand. I ran after her. As I dodged pedestrians and tried to stay close enough to cover her back I could see she was trying to catch up with someone. Who? I scanned the sea of faces ahead of us, but nothing registered.

* * *

Phil sat there watching the two MacKenzies run down the street, numbed by the news of an attack on Audrey, the revelation that his wife had deceived him, and now this inexplicable turn of events. He was uncharacteristically confused. He didn't have enough information to make any sense out of it and was hesitant to leave without getting a better idea of exactly what he was up against. Above all, he needed more information.

Marge came over and said, "That routine of theirs works every time. I guess you're stuck with the bill, Daddy Warbucks."

"This should cover it," he said, handing her a fifty dollar bill. "Is there a phone I can use?"

She directed him around the counter, by the men's room. After finding out there were bugs planted in his home,

223

he didn't trust the phone in his limousine parked out front. He had made at least one mistake that needed to be corrected immediately, and he dialed a private number.

* * *

I finally caught up with Cathy at a crosswalk. She was standing there, turning around in circles, having lost sight of whoever she was chasing.

"What's this all about, Honey?" I asked, trying to catch my breath.

"I think I just saw him."

"Saw, who?"

"That mystery guy from the other night."

"I thought you never got a look at him?"

"I didn't, not really. But subconsciously his face must have registered because I noticed this guy standing on the sidewalk outside the restaurant, and I swear he was watching us. Then it clicked. I knew it was the same guy. He's about six foot, slender, maybe in his late 30s, wearing a blue ball cap. Don't ask me why, but I think he's Irish, or maybe English."

Her last comment triggered a replay of the scene in Audrey's apartment last night. When I called out to the guy to give himself up and he answered me, there was a definite Irish accent to his voice. Why in the hell hadn't I remembered such an important piece of evidence. Maybe I am losing it?

In the old days I wouldn't have missed something that big. Maybe I'm not capable of protecting Cathy, or anyone else close to me. Maybe my only daughter is going to end up dying in my arms like her mother because of some stupid mistake on my part?

I let Cathy know Audrey's attacker had an Irish accent, and while we walked back to the restaurant I suggested she get with a police sketch artist and do a drawing. After that she could go through central intelligence files for known IRA operatives in the area.

We stopped and watched Phil's limousine dart off into the heavy, morning traffic. "I'll catch up with that prick later," I said, "but first I'll drop you off at the Dump. It's time I had a little `come-to-Jesus' meeting with Sunday's Childe."

Chapter 34

Friday: July 10th (afternoon)

"I hate stupidity," Sunny screamed at me. A yellow and black marker pen flew past my head like a bullet, and I had to duck to avoid getting hit. It was a little stronger reaction than I thought I'd get when I walked into her office to let her know what happened to Audrey last night.

"Hey, lady, I'm here to get answers, not your opinion of my intelligence," I yelled back at her.

"Oh, for Christ sake Mac, don't go getting paranoid on me, not now. Don't you get it?"

"I guess not. Why don't you fill me in".

"Audrey's the only one in this whole screwed-up mess who's an unknown. The rest of us probably have dossiers an inch-thick, telling both sides everything they need to know about us. Audrey was a wild card. There is no way anyone could have predicted she'd be involved. Since they didn't know anything about her, they wouldn't have had any reason to think she might tip off someone, somehow."

"Would that someone be you?"

"What do I have to do, draw you a picture? It doesn't matter who. Both sides already know most of the facts. That's why the messages have been so obtuse. What they don't want is for the other side to find out what they don't know. It's cat and mouse."

I stepped forward, placed both hands flat on her desk and leaned toward her, close enough so that I could smell the sultry fragrance of her perfume. "You're running me around in circles again, and I don't like it. I'm about to ring that pretty little neck of yours unless I get a straight answer. Did Audrey find something out about you, or didn't she?"

Sunny glared back at me. "There's nothing to find. You still don't understand what's going on here. Hasn't it dawned on you, you were hand-picked for this job. You are the bait. This isn't a game of hide and seek, it's seek and destroy. You're here to draw fire.

"You're an expendable pawn. Every move you make is being choreographed by one side or the other. Something big is going on, bigger than you, bigger than me, and probably bigger than Sterling. To use one of your dumb sports metaphors, when the varsity game gets under way, they'll send you to the bench with all the other second-stringers."

Her words held a hard truth and their sting felt like a slap in the face. I'd been trying to hide from that truth long before she came along. She was talking about a truth that had stared back at me in the mirror every day, and left me sweating and shaken in Audrey's apartment last night. Over the past nine years I'd become nothing more than a cardboard cop; window dressing for an egomaniac. The right stuff just wasn't there anymore, and they all knew it.

I eased my emasculated bulk down into a chair. The hard-assed, ex-cop routine wasn't fooling anyone. Everyone knew I'd lost my nerve the day Karen died in that grocery store.

"Goddamn it, Mac, don't quit on me now," Sunny yelled again. "Stick to your job. Who cares what they think, it doesn't mean they're right. I say we can still beat them, you and me together. You owe it to Audrey."

I stared back at her. Those gorgeous green eyes held the same kind of determination I saw that night we shared drinks at Jake's. I used to see that look in Karen's eyes when

I'd come home after some slimy collar had laughed at me on his way out of the courtroom after getting off on a stupid technicality. I'd bitch about it to Karen and she'd yell back at me, "Do your job, the rest don't matter."

If only I'd kept my gun in it's holster that day, if only. That was my job. But I couldn't bring Karen back, and there's no way to make up for that mistake. What I didn't want to do now was make another mistake, one that might put my only daughter in danger.

"You keep saying they. How do I know they aren't you?" I mumbled.

"You don't, you big jerk. You'll just have to take my word for it. I'm not the one going around putting people in the hospital."

"Then drop the cheerleader act and start telling me what's really going down here." Anger began to replace the doubts that had been filling my head.

She had a sly grin on her face. "Don't you ever wonder about all that personal information the banks get their hands on every time you use a credit card?" Dennis' warning to me about playing truth or dare with her, came to mind.

"What do you think they do with all that information? Surely, you've seen someone's life laid out on some sterile credit report. Do you think they're collecting all that stuff just for the fun of it?"

My cop instincts started to kick in. "Are you saying the perps came up with a way of stealing money from banks so they could blackmail the banks into not collecting information about some asshole's grocery bills?"

"It's more complicated than that. Operation Sine Dinar could be a set-up that allows banks to take over economic control of this whole planet. If that's true, and the crooks are standing in their way, things are definitely going to get a lot hotter than they are right now." Her eyes were flashing with excitement and for a moment I thought she might be on the verge of making a major confession.

"If cash were eliminated completely, as a trading commodity, every single transaction, no matter how big or small, would end up being recorded and documented by some bank. Think about it. Just imagine the power and control they would have through knowing everyone's spending habits. Once that information gets passed along and stored away in some central data file it will be all over. We'd be living in a world where Big Brother turns out to be a bank?"

"Is that why you did it?" I felt the truth was finally at hand.

This time it was a pencil that came whipping by my head. "Stop trying to play games with me," she yelled. "You're never going to know who's telling the truth. Everyone lies. You're dealing with the best liars in the world. Trying to figure out who's telling the truth is thinking like a cop, and that's what they want you to do. You have to concentrate on what these people are doing, what their next move is going to be, not worrying about getting some stupid confession."

She hesitated. "Do you remember Phil spouting some reason why the idea of a global cashless society would never work?"

"Something about all or nothing?"

"Right. What he said was, no one on the planet would be allowed to use cash; it would have to be eliminated completely. If large amounts of cash were still circulating it would become a form of contraband. Clever people would hold onto the cash and try to create a black market for the stuff. If enough of it stayed around it might even prevent their operation from becoming a reality."

"How much cash would it take to screw up a deal like that?"

The corners of her lush red lips turned upward. "That's an interesting question. If the currency was, let's say, in dollars, who knows, maybe only five or six million."

"I'm surprised you keep me around to carry the water bucket." Obviously, she'd been way ahead of me right from the start.

I was also hearing way more than just an educated guess. Sunny had just identified a real motive behind the thefts and there was no doubt in my mind that she was talking with first-hand knowledge. It was another one of those neat little packages she liked to serve up, just like that day on the sailboat. I finally got what she had in mind that time she asked me if I was ready to work with her, instead of staying in my own little corner.

She needed me to get at Bettancourt. He was the real danger, and the only way to prevent any further attacks was for me to get to him first. Everything else could wait until later.

Sunny was standing behind her desk, hands on her hips. "Now it's your turn to ante up. I want to know what Audrey told you when she called. Maybe I can use it to figure out their next move."

Maybe I will have to arrest Sunny for the bank heist tomorrow, but today I'm not going to worry about that. Today I'm glad she's on my side. The bad guy is Bettancourt and that hit-man he hired to take out Audrey, I'm certain of that. And they're the ones I need to punish.

I stood up, pushed my shoulders back to their normal upright position, and stuck out my hand. "Okay, we're still partners. So, do we get to kiss and make-up?"

Sunny laughed, came around the desk, and hugged me. Her body rested against mine with no sign of stiffness and it felt every bit as good as I dreamed it would.

She looked up at me. "Mac, I've always appreciated the fact that you never had any problem thinking a woman could be behind this whole thing. But I have to tell you, right now I hope whoever's calling the shots on the other side doesn't have such a high regard for female intelligence." Then she kissed me full on the lips.

We headed back to my office to go over the stuff in Audrey's knapsack. Sunny mentioned that Dennis had just taken off for the West Coast. The Palo Alto police had called him again to let him know there was another break-in at his lab. This time, a real estate agent, mining for business, noticed the rear door had been jimmied and called the police.

I left Sunny with Sheila so the two of them could start foraging through the printouts Audrey had made, and headed for Mass General to check on Audrey's condition. Along the way I decided to stop at my house on Hull Street, not far from the Old North Church.

Eight years ago, when I turned in my badge, drinking had become my nighttime ritual. There were plenty of middle-of-the-night episodes, when, my body drenched in sweat and my hands shaking uncontrollably, I reached into the draw beside my bed and pulled out my old Smith & Wesson. I'd hold it in my hand and the feel of the hard metal triggered a sound in my whiskey-soaked brain, the sound of the explosion launching a bullet on its deadly path. The terror-stricken expression on Karen's face would light up the darkest recesses of my soul.

In those moments of delirium, I would scream at the night over and over again, "You asshole, why did you draw? You made it all happen. You've got to make things right. Go ahead, pull the damn trigger one more time, you fat fuck!"

The words spewing from my mouth would turn me nauseous and I often vomited. Afterwards, I'd sit there on the edge of the bed rocking back and forth, staring at the short thick barrel, as if it was a cancerous tumor that had just been cut out of my body. Why hadn't I cut that sickness out of my life sooner, before it spread to Karen? Why were some mistakes so impossible to correct?

Today, stone-cold sober, and for the first time in eight years, I strapped on the black leather shoulder holster and pushed my old semi-automatic into it. It was time to face my demons, at least long enough to get done what had to be done. A professional killer was on the loose and Cathy might well be his next target. I couldn't afford any more mistakes.

The two punks who shot and killed Karen were scared rabbits and probably weren't planning to shoot anyone. Everything went wrong for them that day, and they panicked. This was different. This time I'd be facing a professional assassin and letting him make the first move would be the biggest mistake of all.

When the time came, I had to be ready to draw my weapon without hesitation, before it was too late. There wouldn't be time to argue. My brain had to be ready to tell my hand to squeeze the damn trigger. Could I do it? "God, I hope so."

I walked out of my house armed for the first time in years, and it felt awkward. I carried that weapon for years, and yet, now, it felt so heavy; much heavier than I remembered. I tried to ignore the sour taste that was climbing up my throat.

At the hospital I ran into Phil. He told me there was no change in Audrey's condition. "I've made arrangements for the top specialists in town to consult on her case, and assured Dr. Jordan no word of her condition would get out. He told me you instructed him to make sure of that, and seemed especially anxious to follow your orders."

"He's Cathy's boyfriend."

"Ah, yes, that would account for his loyalty. Mac, we need to clear up a few things from this morning. It won't do either of us any good to be working at odds with one another."

"I guess that depends on which side you're on."

"I'm on the same side as you. I always have been. I haven't lied to you. You'll have to take my word on that, but it's the truth."

Phil dragged me by the arm, down the hall, to a vacant office. As one of the trustees for the hospital's Foundation, he was well-known to the staff and a nurse ran ahead of us and unlocked the door. As soon as we stepped inside, Phil locked the door from the inside and turned to me. "Mac, under no circumstances are you to catch the crooks."

Chapter 35

Friday: July 10th (evening)

Phil walked into the dining room at his townhouse. Charlotte was seated at the table, toying nervously with a gin and tonic. She was wearing a peach-colored, sleeveless, chiffon dress that favored her skin tone and helped create a carefully planned aura of genteel innocence.

That morning, when he called her from *Momma's Kitchen*, Phil suggested they share a quiet dinner together. He knew she'd accept, given the circumstances of their earlier conversation in the garden. The match wasn't over and no one had won, yet.

"Good evening, darling," he said. "You really do look lovely tonight. That color suits you perfectly."

"And you, my dear husband, were designed for a tux," she answered, saluting him with her glass.

Phil sat down at the magnificent dining table, large enough to accommodate 12, and placed the damask napkin in his lap, as Hamilton poured him a glass of champagne. People who live with wealth for generations, treat dinner as an elegant affair, even for two. Trying to compare this evening's repast with the most expensive meal served at the finest restaurant in town, would do the Lord family a disservice. This was truly the lap of luxury.

Every bit of the decor, the crystal, the china, even the silverware, was genuine museum quality. The exquisite chandelier, casting its gem-like sparkle around the room, was recovered from the Marquis de Montagne's chateau in Lyons, France in the 1930's. The antique mahogany, dining suite they were seated at had been commissioned by one of Phil's ancestors from the Scottish-born cabinet maker, Duncan Phyfe, during the height of that craftsman's popularity. Today, that suite was generally considered to be one of Mr. Phyfe's finest works, easily worth a king's ransom.

Many would also consider the exquisite Persian rug, covering the polished oak flooring beneath their feet, much too valuable to be subjected to the risk of damage from a spilt glass of wine, let alone walked on.

Of course, none of those material objects were on the mind of either Phil or Charlotte, as they sipped their perfectly chilled gazpacho, served to them as a refreshing appetizer on this warm summer evening. The trappings of wealth and power were merely a background against which they lived out their privileged lives. They never consciously thought about any of it; the same way a woman doesn't think about the diamond ring on her finger until it's suddenly missing.

"When did you arrive in town," Phil inquired, casually.

"Tuesday. I told you I had a hair appointment."

"So you did. I forgot. Did you catch the new play at the Shubert?" Going through the mail he noticed their series tickets for Tuesday night's performance were still lying on the front hall console, unopened. Charlotte hated to miss an opening night.

"No. I was feeling tired and went to bed early."

"Then who entertained your guests?" he asked, allowing a slight grin to expose his amusement.

Charlotte gave a sudden look of surprise. "Now who's sounding jealous. It doesn't become you, Phil. I went to bed alone."

"Then you must have waited until your guests departed."

"What in the world are you talking about?"

"Come, come, my dear, it's not like you to keep playing after the point's been lost. Oh, did I forget to tell you? I've been having some problems at the bank, so I put the house under surveillance. The pictures really don't do you justice."

Charlotte struggled to keep her composure. She couldn't decide whether to laugh or yell. "You're bluffing. You would never let anyone take pictures of me. You'd be too worried about being blackmailed."

"I don't think Henrí Bettancourt is in a position to blackmail anyone. After all, arriving with another man at my house at 8 p.m., while I'm out of town, and being welcomed by my wife in her negligé, might be a little difficult to explain, almost as difficult as explaining this." Phil withdrew a tiny microphone from the pocket of his white dinner jacket and slid it across the table.

"What is that?" she asked, staring at the object like it might explode.

"It's what they call a "bug," and I just removed it from the phone in my bedroom. Would you like me to take another one out of the phone over there and show it to you?"

They both fell silent as Hamilton entered the room and quietly served the main course. He deftly placed several thin slivers of baby veal, sauteed in a light sherry and cream sauce, onto their plates, then laid several spears of blanched asparagus beside the meat and carefully spooned some of the cooking sauce over both items. He then poured a sampling of California chardonnay in a wine glass for Phil.

In a gesture intended to establish the sincerity of his comments, and to make it clear to Charlotte that he'd won the match, Phil sampled the wine and said, "This is really excellent, darling. You must try some."

Charlotte stared back at him, ignoring the delicious meal and the glass of golden wine being poured for her. It was the first time either of them had so conclusively won or lost one of their intimate games, and she was unsure of just what the penalty was for not having scored a single point.

After what seemed an interminable pause, Phil added, "I believe you owe me an explanation."

The angry expression on Charlotte's face quickly transformed into an attractive smile, and she gave him a dismissive wave of her hand. "Why not. It won't change anything. Henrí says you've burned your bridges with him, and I know that can't be good. I may not be able to hurt you, but he certainly can, and that's all I ever wanted to see happen."

"Why would you want to hurt me, Char?" He was genuinely surprised at the vindictive tone in her voice.

"Because no one ever has. You've lived your entire life without ever once getting kicked in the balls. I want to see you cry out in pain. I want to see you fall on the ground and grovel like every other human being has to do some time in their life. Maybe then you'll begin to appreciate the price the rest of us mere mortals have to pay in order to share an existence with Philip Cabot Lord III.

"The trouble is, my darling husband, you don't even realize what a bastard you are. How could you? Every time you look in the mirror things only get better, never worse. Sometimes I want to scream it's so damn unfair. All I ever had going for me was my looks, and now, even that is being taken away from me, wrinkle by goddamn wrinkle." Her voice rose to the level of her frustration and she started spewing words like an erupting volcano.

"But, not Philip Cabot Lord III. No, for The Lord life only gets better and better. He gets to take his choice of the brightest and prettiest; the tightest asses; the biggest tits. He can demand the best and second best never even comes into the picture. Well, who the hell made you a god? There's never any fucking justice around when you need it?"

He had never heard his wife swear like that for as long as he'd known her. And she hadn't been this animated over anything in years. Neither one of them had planned on this particular battle being so decisive, but it was obviously a watershed in their on-going war.

"It wasn't easy," she continued, "but I found someone who has more power than you and in my book that makes him a lot sexier. Power is what drew me to you in the first place. Did you know that? Don't they always say in the old westerns, someone comes along with a bigger gun. Well, Henrí Bettancourt has a bigger gun than you and that makes him a better man. And he wants me."

Phil smiled at her. "Don't be absurd. He's only using you to get at me. Any man who goes around screwing a married woman is really only trying to get at her husband. Whether consciously or not, it's always there in the back of the man's mind. Henrí has no real interest in you, and you know it."

"Tell it to someone who cares. I don't. Years ago I cared. Years ago I even had dreams. I dreamed of being a mother. Just because I couldn't have kids, you decided to go out and anoint every slut in town with your precious cum, so they would worship at your feet. Hoping that you would some day let them share your throne. Well, fuck you, mister lord and holy master, your fucking luck's run out."

Fifteen years ago the subject of children had come up in their lives and nothing was the same after one fateful day. The doctor told them Charlotte would never be able to conceive. Phil and Charlotte assured each other of their undying love, and that children didn't really matter, but that was the first of many lies to follow. They quickly buried their true feelings and the subject was never mentioned again. Only a vague ache lingered behind, a constant reminder of how their lives had taken a sharp turn and never got back on track.

"I accept the fact that you no longer care about me," Phil said to her, "but I cannot believe you would go out of your way to hurt innocent people. I am going to ask you a question and you must tell me the absolute truth. Did you tell Henrí that I received a call from someone named Cathy?"

"I'll answer that question if you tell me who she is, and why she called."

"I can't, it would place the young woman in too much danger. I assume you are only interested in proving that I lied to you this morning. I did. However, she is not someone I am sleeping with. That's the truth, whether you care to believe it or not."

Charlotte studied her husband's handsome face and carefully considered his words. "Yes. I called him before you came in this morning."

"God, you have no idea how much harm you've caused." He walked over to her and placed one hand gently on her shoulder. He could feel the heat coming off her normally cool, smooth skin. "I really am sorry about the way things turned out."

He left the room and went to his library to make a call.

Chapter 36

Sunday: July 12th (morning)

Thick cumulus clouds drifted across the sky, and it smelled like rain was on the way. Boston needs a good rain to cool things off. I'm driving south on the Fitzgerald Expressway, on my way to what I know will be a very shitty deal. The events of yesterday were lined up in my head, one behind the other, like a row of stalled cars with everyone leaning on their horns and shouting out the window in the goddamn summer heat.

Yesterday morning started off with a call from Sheila, letting me know she'd made contact with the Palo Alto Police Department. The same investigator she talked to earlier, called again to say Dennis' lab had been broken into again.

What came as a surprise was the cop's comment that this time the place was almost empty. All of Dennis' equipment was gone and like the last time, no one was exactly sure when the break-in took place.

Two hours later I got a second call, this time from Sunny. She wanted me to come to her office and see for myself what she and Sheila dug out of Audrey's backpack. I was a little touchy about that kind of call and wasn't about to take it lightly. "You call down to Sheila and tell her I want a uniform posted outside your office, and I mean right now. I'll be there in 15 minutes."

Audrey had begun her search by checking out every account that received any deposits from an overseas bank. Every one she checked looked legit.

Anyone else probably would have cashed in and gone home at that point, but not Audrey. She continued slogging through those files until her infallible ear picked up a new note.

A Belgian bank was making deposits into a certain account on a monthly basis. That fact alone wasn't too unusual, but the sum, $9,900 every month, stuck in her head. It was a figure that was just below the amount that had to be reported. The account had been set-up by a new-accounts clerk and on the surface there was nothing to set it apart from thousands of other similar accounts at the bank.

Acting on a hunch, Audrey decided to move in for a closer look. She checked out the account activity and found payments arrived every month and, within a day, were transferred to another Sterling account. The second account had also been set-up by a new-accounts clerk at one of the branch offices and in both instances the clerk noted the accounts were being opened as "auxiliary" accounts. That meant they were being set-up for an existing customer. For efficiency purposes the detailed customer information was kept in the originating account.

Once the money was transferred into the second account, it was immediately moved again into a third account. That was when she knew she was onto something. She managed to call up the file information for that third account and hit pay dirt.

From the third account, the one that was serving as the originating account in the maze, the money was being transferred to an offshore bank in the Cayman Islands, thereby eliminating any further traceability. On the surface, this simple movement of money through three separate accounts might appear to be rather obvious in its purpose.

But, in fact, there were a number of built-in safeguards that made it an almost untraceable series of transactions.

Only someone with access to Sterling's customer files and the imbedded codes would have ever been able to establish the connection from one account to the next. But the even tougher part was being able to determine who actually set up each account. The originating account was opened in the name of Esther Russell and, despite the fact that it showed the name of one of the new-accounts clerks as the person who set it up, the tell-tale, hidden marker revealed the terminal used was not on that person's desk. That tell-tale marker turned out to be a "smoking gun".

A trap had been set and the guilty party couldn't avoid it because he didn't even know it existed. The Esther Russell account was set up by Sid Moore.

Operationally, all queries on customer accounts automatically got reported to Sid, as Chief of Operations. That placed him in the perfect position to control any investigation of his accounts, should that situation ever arise. It also gave him notice if someone was looking around and the opportunity to take some evasive action.

Sid had set up the three accounts several years ago, long before the recent thefts, so what he was doing didn't tie him to the heist. What they did tie him to was that Belgian bank, and marked him as one of the foot-soldiers in this strange war that was now going on. It turned out, Sid was taking orders from a Belgian general named Bettancourt.

Sunny did some checking and confirmed that the Belgian bank making those monthly payments to Sid was, in fact, owned by Henri Bettancourt. I supplied the final missing piece when I told her Esther Russell was the name of Maryanne Moore's deceased mother.

Based on the monthly deposits Sid had been receiving, Audrey calculated close to $400,000 had flowed into Sid's Cayman account over the years. If he was, in fact, the owner of all that money, his retirement fund was a whole lot bigger than mine.

All of Audrey's info was running through my head as I pulled off the Expressway and drove through the outskirts of Quincy. The joke I'd made about Sid not being smart enough to be a good crook came to mind. It turned out I was the dummy. That didn't make things any easier, though. Sid was like a brother to me, and I felt like I'd been kicked in the nuts, again.

It was nearly noon when I walked across the wide front porch at Sid's house and knocked on the screen door. His sturdy, well-maintained two-story, wood frame house on Standish Avenue looked like all the rest of the houses lined up in that working-class neighborhood. The tree-lined streets, narrow sidewalks, and manicured front lawns weren't nearly as attractive as, say, Beverly or Wenham, but there was that same sense of permanency and security that always made me feel uncomfortable.

There was, however, one big difference between Quincy and Beverly. Sid and Maryanne were now one of the few Caucasian families left in the area. Sid liked to claim he was the last holdout.

Maryanne came to the door. "Mac, what a great surprise. Give me a hug you big galoot. I hope you've come to take me away from all this mess." A wave of her hand took in the Sunday paper spread across the living room floor, two girls shouting at one another upstairs, and several radios, set to different stations, competing for attention in the background.

"I've got two tickets to Paris right here in my pocket," I answered.

Maryanne giggled, and yelled upstairs, "Sid, Mac is here." She grabbed me by the hand and dragged me into the kitchen so she could finish packing food in a cooler. "We're on our way to Sid's folks for a barbecue. Why don't you come along? You know everyone, and they always ask about you. How's Sally and Brian, and the kids? I hear Cathy's dating a doctor. Isn't that great?"

In a lot of ways Maryanne was like Sally, and I felt like a heel when I gave her that kiss on the cheek. As a cop I was always embarrassed going into someone's house to make an arrest. Thankfully, those days were behind me now, or so I thought until today.

Sid walked into his large kitchen pulling on a polo shirt. The instant his eyes meet mine I could tell he knew something was wrong. He nervously glanced at Maryanne, then back at me. "Grab a couple beers from the frig," he said, and ducked out the back door, headed to the garage.

I could feel the wetness on my back being absorbed by my t-shirt and followed him to the open garage. Christ, I hate this summer heat. Both of us stared at each other for a few minutes chugging our beers without saying anything. Finally, Sid spoke up, "You're making me nervous, asshole. You gonna say something, or what?"

"What's there to say when you find out your best friend is a lying sack of shit."

Sid's body stiffened. "Hey, who are you to come into my house, in front of my family, and pass judgment on me? How many times have I pulled your sorry ass out of the fire?"

"Not enough to cover you on this one. You fucked-up big time, Sid. Audrey's in the hospital, in a coma. The guy who put her there tried to waste her."

"What!" The bottle slipped from Sid's grasp and shattered on the concrete at his feet. He jumped back against his car and almost lost his balance. "You can't possibly think I would have anything to do with that?" I saw panic in his eyes.

I turned away to avoid the expression on his face. "She found out about your accounts and the pay-offs from Bettancourt. Someone put out a contract on her to keep her quiet." Then I faced him straight on. "So from where I'm standing, your name's right at the top of my shit list."

"I swear to you, Mac, he said he was going to talk to her, and try to buy her off. That's all!" His head was swinging from side to side as if to emphasize his denial of guilt. His whole body was twitching like one, big, nervous tick. "I can't believe that shit head would go and do a thing like that!"

"So you're saying it was Bettancourt?"

"I don't know what else to think. I swear to you, I don't even know what this whole thing is all about."

"How come you got involved with Bettancourt in the first place?" I studied Sid's body language, looking for any clues.

"I met the guy several years ago at a conference. He's some kind of royalty, you know, smooth as glass. Could sell snowballs to fucking Eskimos. Hell, he makes The Lord look like a country bumpkin.

"All he wanted was to be kept informed of anything unusual that popped up at the bank. Nothing specific, just anything I thought he might be interested in. Until this latest shit started going down, months went by and there wasn't anything to tell him. The guy just kept right on paying whether I said anything or not."

"What was the attraction?"

"I told you, I don't really know. He never talked about it. I knew he and Phil were real tight, so I figured he was maybe trying to keep tabs on him. You know, keep him from screwing-up, or something."

"You don't pay ten grand a month to keep tabs on someone."

"The hell you don't. That's petty cash for guys like him. You have no idea how wealthy a guy like that can be. For all I know he owns Sterling and maybe a hundred other banks just like it."

"What about Operation Sine Dinar?"

Sid's youngest daughter, Debby, came outside and interrupted our conversation. "Hi, Mac. What's new?" She jumped up on me and gave me a kiss, then said to her father, "Mom wants you to be sure and pack the beach chairs."

"Okay, Honey. Go tell your mother I'll be there in a few minutes, after I finish talking to Mac."

Debby turned back to me. "Did Cathy tell you she's going to take me on patrol with her one night?"

"I said go tell your mother I'll be there in a minute, damn it," Sid yelled.

"Geez, Dad, chill out," Debby answered and ran back in the house.

As soon as she was out of earshot, Sid, in an exaggerated whisper said, "What's going on with all this *Sine Dinar* bullshit? You asked me about that the other day, and I told you I never heard of it. What's it got to do with anything?"

"Bettancourt never mentioned it to you?"

"No. I told you, I tell him things. He never tells me anything."

"What did you tell him about Audrey?" I was beginning to get the picture. Sid had been kept in the dark. Sunny was right, we were all expendable little pawns in some fucking game.

"Only that I thought you and her were onto my accounts. Last month I told him she was the one who figured out how the money got stolen, but I had the impression he already knew it."

"Didn't it ever occur to you, you might not be his only stoolie at Sterling?"

"A minute ago you were telling me no one's stupid enough to pay good money to keep tabs on The Lord. Now you're saying he was doubling up? If there was someone else, Bettancourt never even hinted at it."

Maryanne yelled to us from the back door, "Sid, we need to get going. Throw Mac in the back seat. You two can finish talking on the way."

"We'll be in, in a minute," he yelled back.

"She doesn't know anything about this. What am I going to say to her, Mac? How am I going to face her and the kids if I lose my job over this stupid mess?"

I avoided Sid's questions. This whole thing was so fucked-up that I didn't have any ready answers. "You're not telling me what I want to know. Give me something I can pin on that Belgian turd."

"Forget it, the guy never makes mistakes. You think Clinton's slick, wait until you try to pin something on Bettancourt. If you're even thinking about going after him, drop it. He'll flick you off like a fly."

"It's nice to know everyone's got such high praise for my abilities these days."

247

Sid kept pressing. "How much does Phil know? Has he got any idea I've been taking money from Bettancourt? What's he's going to do, Mac?"

"Phil's got bigger problems than you to worry about. You're only one of several leaks. Right now, your biggest problem is with me."

Sid grabbed my arm. "Tell me, what can I do to make amends, buddy. Give me some help, here. Christ, I know I did wrong, but try to look at it from my side. I was staring at a retirement that offered nothing but crackers and tuna fish. There was no way of ever getting ahead. You've got to believe me, in my wildest imagination, I never thought anyone could ever get hurt. It was just a chance to get some easy money, that's all."

"You know what they say, easy come, easy go. When's the last time you checked your little nest egg?"

Sid's face turned white as a ghost. "No way! Bettancourt can't possibly find that account."

"Audrey did. If he's as smart as you say he is, he'll find a way."

"Christ, you've got to be wrong." Sid ran inside the house and I followed along. In the living room, he yanked open a cabinet, sat down in front of his personal computer, and began frantically entering a string of codes, trying to connect with his bank in the Caymans.

Maryanne came into the room. "What's going on, guys?"

Sid ignored her. The modem connection with the bank went through and Sid entered his private account number and password. He waited nervously for a few seconds, praying he would see the familiar data appear on the screen. Instead, a message flashed before him, "Access denied."

"Shit, it's got to be a fucking mistake." Sid quickly went through the whole procedure again, but the results were the same.

"Sid, what is going on?" Maryanne asked again. She moved closer and I could tell how upset she was over her husband's strange antics.

"Don't bother me now, Maryanne," Sid snarled at her. He grabbed his briefcase and dug out his personal phone book. He dialed an overseas number to the Caymans and got the solicitor on the line who helped him set up the account, and ordered him to ring up one of the officers at the bank. He waited online for the connection.

I only heard one side of the conversation, but the sick look on Sid's face made it clear he was getting a run-around. His money was gone and there wasn't a thing he could do about it. Bettancourt wasn't so free with his dough after all. It was an important lesson: one that gave me a new appreciation for who I was up against.

This was the second time in a week that I'd had to witness a family on the verge of destruction. In Phil's case, I didn't have much invested and couldn't feel that sorry for him, or Charlotte. They were willing participants in this high stakes game and knew all the rules. What's more, they could pay the price of admission and, in the end, would move on with only a few added scars to show for their battles. There wouldn't be any real changes in their extravagant lives.

Sid and Maryanne wouldn't be so lucky. They had no idea they were betting their whole future on a game of chance. It's always "Joe Schmuck" who ends up losing. The rich never let anyone but their own kind get in the winner's circle, never. Sid never stood a chance of coming out a winner.

But he wasn't the real enemy, he was just another one of the casualties. He'd backed the wrong horse. I put my hand on his shoulder and bent over to whisper in his ear. "I want Bettancourt kept in the dark for now. Play it like business as usual, and don't say anything to anyone. It ain't over yet."

Sid spotted the bulge under my sport coat and looked up at me. "You said you'd never carry again."

"Whoever put Audrey in the hospital is after Cathy."

"Cathy! What in the hell has she got do with this?" I saw a look of sudden desperation in his eyes as he realized, for the first time, what might happen to his own family.

"The less you know about that, the better," I told him. "Just keep me informed. And by the way, don't do anything stupid."

I wanted to offer something more, but there wasn't really anything I could say. I turned and walked past Maryanne who reached out to me and cringed when I didn't stop.

I threw my jacket on the front seat of the car, climbed in, and slammed the door shut. How can one lousy goddamn bank job get so fucked-up. Is this the way things are going to be from now on? Anonymous assholes, using computers play games and get to walk away with the money, while innocent schmucks like Sid get stuck holding the bag?

Phil once gave me some good advice. "Keep your eye on the ball." Maybe this isn't so much a new kind of game as just a whole new set of rules to play by. The tough part is trying to figure out who the real target was meant to be.

When this mess started I saw my job as trying to figure out who was behind the heist. Now I knew that was only the first step. The guy I was really after was the one trying to steal people's lives, not the bank's money. Sunny was wrong when she said it wasn't about the money; it was. It was about all the goddamn money in the world.

Chapter 37

Sunday: July 12th (afternoon)

Phil was ready to take the final step in his plan to outflank Henrí. Everything was in place and all he needed to do was set the trap. He delivered messages to each of the cartel delegates, arranging an emergency meeting in Boston, on July 16th at 8:00 p.m. Calling a meeting was a calculated and unprecedented maneuver that could easily backfire on him. He saved Henrí for last.

"Henrí, it's Philip. I'm making a secure call."

Henrí quickly changed phones and, as usual, tried to establish a friendly atmosphere. "Philip, I'm so pleased to hear from you. Although the meal was superb, and your company as enjoyable as always, I felt we parted on rather unpleasant terms the other night. My duties prevented me from calling you back so we could clear the air, as you like to say."

"I thought you might be harboring some bad feelings, especially since I didn't hear from you again before you left town."

"Be assured it was only the press of business and your own sudden departure that prevented me from doing so," Phil replied.

A smile appeared on Phil's face. Henrí had just made a rare *faux pas*. He alluded to Phil's trip to Toronto, and there was no legitimate way he could have come by that information. Phil had gone to Toronto to attend a meeting of the cartel's North American Group, and Henrí would not have been notified because regional groups never apprised him of their activities. Each region left it up to their delegate to keep the regional and global interests coordinated. It served as an added security measure, and along with maintaining the secrecy of their membership rosters, provided sufficient independence and a sort of checks and balance system.

"Please forgive my break in protocol," Phil continued, amused over Henrí's blunder, "but I've taken the liberty of calling a conference in Boston this Thursday. I have excellent news to report regarding the Sterling matter. In light of our disagreement the other night, I was concerned that you might not feel comfortable endorsing any further discussion on that subject, so I took it upon myself to arrange the meeting. My staff has come up with some answers, and I believe we are ready to put the entire unfortunate episode behind us and move on."

"You know my only interest is to see our plans brought to fruition. If you have successfully identified those thieves, nothing would please me more." As usual, the tone in Henrí's voice gave away nothing.

So far, all of Henrí's efforts to identify the thieves had failed, and Henrí was reduced to ordering the elimination of anyone who even looked like a possible suspect. That created an untidy situation. Anything messy added a considerable risk that something might go wrong. Even his recent attempt to find out whether Dennis Crawford had been able to refine his technology to the point of being operational, proved to be a wasted effort. The operative who broke into Crawford's laboratory in California found the vital equipment had already vanished.

Phil knew Henrí planned to eliminate the thieves as soon as possible. Once the name of the guilty party was divulged at the conference, Henrí would immediately order that person kidnapped before any local authorities could move in and place him or her under arrest. After that person confessed and revealed the name of the person who had broken their pledge of secrecy, the problem would indeed go away, permanently.

"I promised you I would take care of things without involving the cartel," Phil offered, trying to sound reassuring. "Trust me, Henrí, the delegates will feel much more secure once they hear the good news." It was a careful choice of words, and Phil hoped he hadn't over-played his hand.

"You certainly have peaked my interest. I will be looking forward to your pronouncement," Henrí answered. "You may count on my support and presence."

Chapter 38

Sunday: July 12th (afternoon)

I left Quincy and drove to Boston, still pissed over Bettancourt's self-anointed invulnerability. I wanted to go *mano-a-mano* with him, at least once, before this thing was over.

I headed straight to the Dump to catch up with Cathy. I knew she was scheduled to be on duty that afternoon and was anxious to find out whether she had any luck running down the Irish guy.

When I got there the squad room was empty, so I stuck my head in the door of my old office. Les looked up, "You just missed them."

"Them who?"

"Cathy and Sunny Childe. How come you never said anything about Sunny being a walking wet dream?"

"What the hell was she doing here?"

"Sheila brought her over with a bunch of paperwork and the three of them made like sorority sisters for about an hour. Then Sheila took off for the bank to get something, and a few minutes ago Cathy said she and Sunny were heading over to Sunny's place."

I felt old, and fell into a nearby chair. The handle of my pistol stuck out from beneath my sport coat and Les spotted it.

"Jesus Christ, Mac, what the hell are you doing packing again? Give me that damn thing before you hurt yourself." He'd taken that gun away from me so many times over the past eight years that the words came out in one long gush.

"I know what I'm doing this time," I said, and covered the handle. "The other night at Audrey's, I swear to you, I reached for it just like nothing ever happened. You hear what I'm saying, I reached for the damn thing."

Les stared at me like I was nuts and put out his hand. "Yah, and I hear amputees scratch their missing foot. It still ain't the same as using it."

I could tell he was angry and upset at the same time. We both knew what happens when a cop pulls his weapon and then can't use it. That's why I gave up my badge.

Eight years ago, I confided my little secret to Les, and he convinced me, as my partner, that he was the one who would likely end up getting shot. The truth of the matter was, I couldn't bring myself to draw my piece without seeing Karen's blood all over the floor of that grocery store. On the job, even a momentary hesitation and someone takes a slug. I had to retire. A desk job at department headquarters was never an option.

The phone rang, interrupting our conversation. Whatever Les was hearing on the other end of the line was a lot bigger problem than me carrying a gun. He forgot all about my piece.

"Get in there and find out what he's up to," Les yelled. "I don't give a shit. ... I'll get one if we need it. Just do it, and call me as soon as you find anything."

"What the hell's going on?" I asked.

"I haven't had a chance to tell you. We ID'd that guy Cathy made the other day. His name is Sean Feigen. The sheet says he's IRA, from Belfast. One of them Irish nuts who started throwing bombs at the age of 12 and has been whacking people ever since. He spent some time in the can over there, but nothing big. Arrived on our doorstep about two years ago. The Brits think he's over here picking up dough for the cause. They say he's definitely a contract shooter."

I tasted the same kind of sick feeling that swept over me that night at Audrey's when I spotted that shadow moving across her kitchen. Sooner or later, me and that Irish prick were going to cross paths again, and when we did, I needed to be ready.

"I sent Bobby and Mike to stake out the guy, but he gave them the slip. You heard me tell them to get inside his place and find out whatever they could that might give us a lead on who, or what, he's after."

I jumped to my feet and pounded my fist on the desk. "Why the hell didn't you pull the asshole in when you had the chance? He's after Cathy. Is there any doubt about that?"

"Yah, there's doubt," he shouted back at me. "There were three people sitting in that booth when Cathy spotted him. He could have been scoping out Phil Lord, or even your sorry ass, for that matter."

It never even dawned on me that I might be the next target for elimination. What was it Sunny said the other day: no one expected me to catch anyone. I'd bought into their game plan without even realizing it. I ignored my own vulnerability because I didn't see myself playing a significant enough role to warrant getting hit.

Maybe I was getting a lot closer to the truth than I thought. Things were definitely turning ugly, and it looked like whoever was calling the shots was getting desperate.

Sid told Bettancourt that me and Audrey were onto Sid's accounts, and right after that Audrey lands in the hospital. Did Feigen's contract have a second page with my name on it, or Cathy's?

The phone rang again. This time Les stared at me while he listened silently to Bobby Duschene. "Get your asses over to Mac's house and keep your eyes open," he ordered, and slammed down the phone. "They found pictures of you and Cathy, with your addresses written on the back. It looks like he's packing, too. They found an empty box of 9mm shells. Bobby and Mike are on their way to cover your place, and I'll get some uniforms over to cover Cathy's apartment."

"You said she was on her way to Sunny's place."

"Shit, that's right. Do you know her address?"

"How were they getting there, Les? You said Sheila brought them over here."

"Christ, I never gave that a thought."

"Knowing Cathy, she probably took the goddamn subway," I added, getting to my feet. "Sunny lives on Marlborough, a few blocks off the Commons. The green line stops at Arlington, so that's probably what they're on. We need to get on that train." I jumped up and ran out the door, shouting over my shoulder, "Get me a picture of Feigen."

Les grabbed the file on Sean Feigen off Cathy's desk and handed it to me as we climbed into his unmarked police car.

"They left about ten minutes ago," Les said, switching on his siren and speeding off through the narrow city streets, "so I figure our best bet is to pick them up at the Government Center station."

I nodded in agreement while I studied a photograph of what looked like an ordinary guy staring back at me from the folder in my lap. I couldn't help think about the past. Two young punks stumbled into my path one afternoon in a grocery store and came to a tragic end when I made the costliest mistake of my life. Was I about to make another one?

The face of this wiry looking, sandy-haired man with dead eyes burned itself into my memory, right alongside Audrey's battered face and Karen's blood-soaked body. This was the face of the enemy. Not just this prick, personally, but every killer like him, who goes out on a mission to destroy the lives of innocent people.

"What's our move when we get there?" Les asked.

It had been a long time since the two of us went out on the chase together. The fact that Cathy was the one in danger only boosted my nervousness.

"First, we make sure Cathy's safe. Then, if Feigen shows, we nail him. First clear shot takes him out. No fucking around." I gave Les a look that left no doubt as to what I was saying.

"Hey, the scumbag might not be armed?"

"That rat bastard is going down, Les. You know and I know there's no other way."

"Those days are over, Mac. It carries too much heat. Besides, you're blowing smoke. No matter how bad you might want to do it, you'll never pull that goddamn trigger and you know it." He looked sideways at me. "Just let me handle things and you play back-up."

"Promise me you'll take him if the shot's there and I freeze. I don't want this asshole getting any second chances."

"I say we use the old drunk routine," Les answered, ignoring my request. He swerved to miss a truck that suddenly pulled in front of us. "The guy knows what you look like, so I'll take the point. You cover the girls from the back door. And for Christ's sake, don't take him on. That Irish prick probably knows how to whack someone by just spitting on them."

The tires skidded as Les jammed on the brakes and came to a halt in front of the entrance to the Government Center subway station. I jumped out and raced down the stairs to the south-bound, green line platform, while Les opened the trunk of his car and fished out a filthy, torn overcoat and rotten looking ball cap.

I watched Les as he slowly made his way down the stairs and began staggering when he reached the bottom step. He was sweating from the heat and had managed to wipe a little grease and dirt off one of his hubcaps onto his hands and face to lend a little more authenticity to his imitation of a homeless drunk. He leaned against a pillar, and from his coat pocket, pulled out an empty whiskey bottle wrapped in a paper bag and made like he was taking a swig, all the while arguing loudly with some nonexistent friend.

I was stationed about a car's length away and both of us were carefully searching every face on that platform as we waited for the incoming train. The guy we were after was a pro, and that meant he could appear disguised as either sex, young or old, even black. Anything he thought might get him closer to his target without raising attention.

Spotting a guy like that generally came down to keeping an eye out for some small detail. An inappropriate piece of clothing, exaggerated make-up, an oversized bag, anything that just didn't seem to fit. It was strictly a guessing game and the only thing Les and I had to rely on was our experience.

Fortunately, on a hot day like this, 90% of the population is sitting in their backyards, or laying around at the beach trying to enjoy the heat. The kind of Sunday afternoon that lulls people into closing their eyes and feeling secure. Nothing important was going to happen until Monday morning. Defenses were shut down and the antennae people usually use to warn them of impending danger are turned off.

"Hey, buddy," Les shouted at me in a slurred voice, "can you spare some change for a fella down on his luck?"

"Get lost," I answered, and turned away with a disgusted look on my face. He was telling me that he hadn't spotted the perp. That meant we could concentrate our attention on the train pulling into the station. I moved into position so that I could see into each car and tell whether Cathy and Sunny were onboard.

There weren't that many passengers onboard as the cars slid by me, gradually slowed down, and finally came to a halt. My knowledge of Cathy's habits was right on the money. I spotted her and Sunny sitting together in the third car. Their backs were to me, just inside the forward doors. I nodded slightly in the direction of that car when it stopped a few feet south of where I was standing. Les raised his bottle in a drunken salute to the train, which meant he saw them too.

He weaved his way onto the train at the front of the car, and began making as much noise and commotion as he could to draw everyone's attention. I slipped through the rear doors while everyone was watching Les. I quickly scanned the passengers and got that familiar knot in my stomach when I spotted Feigen sitting alone. He was on the opposite side of the car from Cathy, halfway between her and where I was standing. His attention was on Les.

The guy wasn't wearing a disguise, just sun glasses, which was enough that Cathy hadn't spotted him. He was casually dressed in a light sport jacket, reading a magazine. Sometimes that's the best disguise of all because he looked perfectly harmless.

This was a real, live killer, ready to strike at any moment, and he looked like he wouldn't hurt a fly. Any doubts I might have had as to whom his next target was going to be, ended the minute I spotted him on that train.

Les lurched toward Sunny and Cathy. Sunny, who had just met him for the first time an hour ago, recognized him. She probably thought he was playing some kind of elaborate prank for her benefit. I heard her start laughing and knew she was about to call out his name when Cathy jumped to her feet.

Cathy knew this wasn't a game. She was familiar with this old routine and figured I was nearby, even though she hadn't spotted me yet. Before Sunny could say a word, she shouted angrily at Les, "Get out of here you lousy old drunk," and pushed him.

Les looked over her shoulder and saw Feigen sitting halfway down the car. He also spotted me moving into position behind the killer. Angles are real important in this kind of deal. We had to stay out of each other's line of fire, in case the perp panicked and started shooting.

Les staggered forward, awkwardly grabbed Cathy and pulled her down with him as he fell drunkenly into Sunny's lap. "Feigen's behind you," he whispered in Cathy's ear and reached inside his coat for his gun.

Feigen had Les in his sights and was watching carefully during all the commotion. Guys like him have been in situations like this many times, the slightest unexpected disturbance put him on edge. When I saw Feigen's eyes drop down to Les' shoes, I knew it was time to act. The muscles along Feigen's jaw tightened and his right hand reached inside his sport jacket.

Suddenly, everything in my world slowed down. As I reached for my gun I could feel each bead of sweat as it dripped down my back. My trembling fingers took forever to wrap around the butt of the pistol.

Don't fucking do this to me! My teeth clenched and I tried to will myself into ignoring the familiar image of Karen's face that was forming in my brain. I've got to shoot this bastard. Feigen's hand was coming out of the jacket with something black in it. Shoot him, you son-of-a-bitch!

Instead of releasing its grip on my right hand, my brain short-circuited and a time shift sent me spinning into the past. I saw myself following Karen around the corner of the aisle in Marinelli's grocery store. The two punks pulled their guns on the owner, and I could see the fear and panic in their pimply faces as they stood there, unaware of the disaster that was about to overtake them.

My first two shots took down the closest one, but in the fraction of a second before the third bullet reached the second kid, a short burst from the uzi he was carrying sprayed the whole area, shattering bottles, boxes, cans, my knee, and Karen's chest and stomach.

My brain suddenly shifted again and dumped me back in the subway car. Feigen was rising from his seat in slow motion, facing Les and Cathy. I saw the 9mm Beretta in Feigen's right hand and watched as it moved in slow motion into firing position behind the magazine he was holding. Every muscle in my body strained in an effort to pull my gun out of its holster.

The dark hair and shining face I saw turning toward me just beyond Feigen was Karen's, not Cathy's. Oh, my God, Karen is still alive. I'm being offered a chance to correct my mistake. If I draw my gun she'll die forever, just like she has every night for the last nine years. I can't do it anymore.

I let go of the coarse grip in my hand and a sudden clarity of purpose swept over me like a bucket of fresh spring water. I knew the sacrifice I had to make. I'd been anointed and finally cast in the light of everlasting redemption. Charging forward, I bellowed at the top of my lungs, "Feigen, you asshole!"

Feigen, caught completely by surprise, made a quick decision. He spun around, fired one shot at me, then tried to turn back in time to finish off Les and Cathy. It was a fatal mistake. He was a second too late. Les' first shot shattered Feigen's right shoulder and the next three slugs caught him square in the chest. Some mistakes can never be corrected.

The bullet he fired at me tore through the flesh on my upper left arm at the same moment I heard Cathy scream, "Daadddy!" The slug didn't hit any bone and ripped through the back of my arm, allowing my momentum to continue forward. I crashed into Feigen, wrapped my right arm around his chest and pulled him down onto the dirty vinyl floor.

Feigen managed to keep hold of his piece and like a pro, made one final effort to complete his contract. Cathy was scrambling across the floor to get to me, and Feigen raised his gun up, but my right hand clamped down on it and yanked it away before he could squeeze the trigger.

"Who hired you?" I snarled in the punk's ear.

I felt Cathy's hands clutching me and could hear her voice crying, but it sounded distant and hollow. A red stain was spreading out beneath me onto the gray floor and I heard a final gurgle of blood spew from Feigen's mouth.

The doors of the train silently closed and the clacking sound of the iron wheels started up as the train moved slowly out of the station. The last sound I heard before darkness closed in was my name.

Chapter 39

Monday: July 13th (morning)

Cathy was hovering over me and the pain-killer the nurse had given me an hour ago was starting to wear off. Almost 14 hours had slipped by since the shooting, and I felt stupid being the only one in that room lying in bed.

"I still say, letting you come along was a bonehead move on my part," Les repeated, with that dumb grin on his face.

"My grandmother draws faster than you do, and she's dead." I threw back at him.

Cathy had already filled me in on the details of what happen after I passed out. By the time the "T" pulled into Park Street station, the cops had been notified and EMT's were waiting at the scene. They ran me over to Mass. General with Les using his belt as a tourniquet to stop the heavy bleeding until the medics took over. My arm got stitched up, but now the doctors wanted me to stay over for another day to make sure the stitches didn't rupture, and to keep me off my feet.

"Both of you old farts ought to be put away for your own good," Cathy said, pushing a pillow down behind my back and adjusting the sling wrapped around my heavily bandaged left arm. "I can't believe you tried a stunt like that. I hope you realize how close you came to ending up with a total disaster on your hands."

"Now who's sounding like a 'Wanda-Worry-Wart?'" I grumbled, and covered her hand with mine.

Sunny was part of the small crowd gathered in my room and she still looked pretty shaken-up by the whole mess. Everything happened so fast, just a few seconds, and I guessed she was having a hard time getting over the shock. Street action can do that to you.

Cathy's crack was echoed by Sheila. "I want everyone in this room to know, Butch and Sundance's careers are over for good. And if you, you big gas bag, ever so much as smell that old holster of yours," she warned me, "I'll kick your south end all over the North End.

"As for you, Lt. Smartass," she added, turning to her husband, "you've got two choices. Boston P. D. makes you a captain and puts you behind a desk, or you retire. Make up your mind. You certainly proved you're stupid enough to qualify for either post."

"Obviously, even retirement doesn't count for much with these two bozos," Brian added. Cathy had called him from the Park Street station and he made it to the hospital just before they wheeled me out of surgery. He was leaning against the wall next to Les and I could tell from his body language he was relieved. He had one arm wrapped tightly around Les' shoulder.

When Brian was a kid, he and Les got real tight. I'm sure he got a lot more advice from Les than he ever did from me. Knowing the kid the way I do, he was probably wondering how two old farts pulled off such an incredibly dangerous and tricky play. Maybe now he'll have some renewed respect for the old man's skill and training.

Everyone in the hospital could hear that booming voice coming down the hallway. "Where the hell is that Scottish son-of-a-bitch?" Duke Hanlon burst into the room with several uniforms right behind him. "Mac, if there was any possible way of my doing so, I'd fire your ass, right after I shot it off." He walked up to me and stood next to Cathy.

"I should have my head examined, letting you and that idiot ex-partner of yours get back together. A quiet, little investigation, my ass. I've got a girl in a coma upstairs, two attempted assassinations, a wounded ex-cop, and I emphasize ex-cop, plus a dead IRA prick on my hands. And it's been less than a goddamn week."

I saw him grab Cathy's hand and squeeze it while he was going through his little tirade. This visit was as much about family, as it was about business.

"Now I'm stuck with a pack of reporters outside who want to know what the hell is going on. Either one of you two knuckleheads care to enlighten me on what I should tell them?"

He turned to face Les and spotted Brian. "Hey, Brian, give me a hug. Sally and the kids okay?"

"You bet, Duke," Brian answered. He hadn't seen Duke since Maeve was born.

Still holding the floor, Duke walked over to Sheila and hugged her with a smirk on his face. "Lady, would you mind explaining to me what that jackass of a husband of yours was thinking? I'm getting too old for this kind of shit. It would serve him right if I just quit and let the commissioner make him take over."

Sheila grabbed Duke's face in both hands and planted a smacker right on his lips. "That's the ticket, Duke," she said laughing.

"Who's this?" he asked, and stepped up to Sunny without waiting for an answer.

"My name's Sunny Childe. I work with Mac."

"Oh, yah. You're the one who was with Cathy when this mess went down. Well, the official story is, it was an attempted hold-up and Les and Mac just happened to be on the train at the time. You and Cathy weren't even there. You got any problem with that?"

"None whatsoever," she answered, smiling at him. "I'm sure Mr. Lord at Sterling Bank will appreciate anything you can do to keep things as quiet as possible."

"What the Christ is going on, Mac?" Duke barked. "This gal almost gets whacked and now she's worrying about the guy you and Cathy are trying to nail. Am I missing something here?"

"I know it sounds confusing, Duke," I answered, "but we're getting close to making a collar. Just give us a little more time."

He took another hard look at Sunny, then turned back to me. "I see another dead body around this town it better be yours. Les, you show up at IA this afternoon for the shooting inquiry. I'll cover you on this one, and thank God that idiot lying there never got off any rounds, or we'd all be in deep shit. Cathy, I'm counting on you to keep your old man strapped down for a month. That's an order."

He stormed out of the room the same way he arrived, leaving behind two patrol officers to keep watch over me.

"What did he mean about nailing Phil?" Sunny asked.

"Ask me again when this is all over," I answered. "I want to know what you two girls were up to yesterday afternoon."

"That can wait," Cathy interrupted. "Tell me what you found out from Sid?"

"Sid," Brian shouted, "don't tell me he's somehow mixed up in this."

"He doesn't know squat," I answered. "Bettancourt played him for a sap just like the rest of us. While I was there he found out his big retirement account got flushed down the toilet. That Belgian prick had him by the balls all along."

"What about Maryanne, Daddy? Does she know what's going on?"

"She was starting to get the picture when I left. It looked like things were going to get pretty rough between them. I told Sid to play dumb with Bettancourt and go on operating as usual for now. I didn't know what to say to Maryanne."

"I can't believe you could be that cold. How could you walk away and leave her like that?"

"What was I supposed to do? He played on both sides of the line and got caught. I don't make the rules."

"Here comes the Lord, and Lady Paula's with him," Sheila announced.

Phil and Paula walked into the room. "Good morning, everyone," Phil said, sounding in charge as usual, and dressed like Cary Grant on holiday. "I've had a quick chat with the doctor and unless Mac bowls left-handed, the word is he should be back to normal in a few weeks."

Not the least bit uncomfortable about interrupting whatever was going on, he stepped up to me and asked quietly, "Have you mentioned our talk to anyone?"

"No." I answered.

"Good, then we need to go over a few things, privately." Phil glanced around the room and said, "Everyone, if you don't mind, I need to have a word alone with Mac. I know it seems rude and presumptuous of me, rushing in like this and asking you to step outside, but I'm afraid it can't be helped. We'll only be a moment, and it is very important."

As soon as everyone left, Phil pulled a chair over close to the bed. "I have excellent news. All the arrangements we discussed have been made, and based on Henri's reaction I'd say he hasn't been doing much in the way of long-range planning. I still find it hard to believe that he would send some Irish hit-man after Audrey and Cathy."

"I was on that list, too."

"We'll never know how many others were, as well. If that killer was ordered to eliminate all three of you, I'm sure he was the only one Henri hired for the job. Normally, he's more careful about putting all his eggs in one basket. He probably didn't have enough time to get anyone else lined up. In any event, he has given a commitment to show up at the conference on Thursday. That should keep us all safe, at least until after he's left town."

"Have you changed your mind about being wired for that meeting?"

"No. I told you it's too risky and, besides, I'm not ready to participate in that kind of treachery. Even sharing as much as I have with you makes me uncomfortable. We must do this my way. I'm sure it will work out." He sounded calm and smug.

"You better know what the hell you're doing. Playing the game your way puts my ass on the line, not to mention your own."

"Trust me, after Thursday night there will be a lot more answers available and we will all be able to take a deep breath." He got up and left, stopping to apologize to everyone outside, and took Paula with him.

"What was that all about?" Cathy asked as the group shuffled back in.

"He wants me to be on his polo team."

"You tell one more lie and your nose is going to stick out further than your gut," Brian laughed.

Sunny came up to me and said, "I have to go, too. Dennis is flying in and you know him. When he hears how he missed all the excitement there will be hell to pay." She bent down and kissed me lightly on the lips, and whispered, "Thanks for being my hero. I owe you."

As soon as Sunny left, Sheila quipped, "You can forget that fantasy, it ain't never gonna happen."

"Les, tell your old lady to stay the hell out of my dreams," I yelled.

"No wonder Sally's been striking out every time she tries to fix you up, Pop." Brian was standing behind his sister with his arms around her waist, grinning over my obvious embarrassment.

"I can see he's not going to get any rest with all of you making fun of him," Cathy complained. She stepped away from Brian and said, "It's time to clear out before they kick us out. I'm going to stay behind for a little while until Michael gets off."

"I'll call Sally and tell her you're on your way," I mumbled to Brian when he leaned down to kiss me on the top of my head.

After the crowd was gone, Cathy came over and sat down beside the bed and laid her head down on my chest. I gently caressed her hair with my one good hand and after a moment of silence, began to feel some wetness as my fingers brush across her cheek.

"Honey, you're crying. What's the matter?"

My question only made things worse. Her body started to shake and I could hear her sobbing. It was one of those times when I felt like a complete ass.

Several minutes went by before she could speak. In a stammering voice she said, "I was sooo scared, Daddy. I heard your voice and when I looked up all I saw was you getting hit. Then you were on the floor and there was all that blood. I—I thought you were dead." She sat up, her pretty face flush and streaked with wet lines. "All the pain I felt when Mama died came back. Only this time it was much worse. It made me realize what you must have felt every time I went on duty."

The big lump in my throat made it difficult for me to respond. "You remind me so much ..." I reached out and touched her face. "When I lost your mother I tried to rip out everything inside me to stop the pain. You remember that picture of me in my patrol blues, the one you had blown-up and stuck to cardboard for my retirement? Well that's what I wanted to be; a cardboard cop. I turned myself into an empty shell. Now you've filled it back up, baby. The big guy gave me another chance down there in that stinking subway, and I plan on staying partners with you for a long, long time."

I pulled her close, and kissed her wet face. She wrapped her arms around my neck.

Chapter 40

Wednesday: July 15th (evening)

I took a long pull on the cold beer in my hand and continued staring vacantly at the T-bone steaks grilling on the barbecue. I was standing in my neglected backyard trying to ignore the stitches in my arm that were beginning to itch like hell. Not that I needed any reminders of my little near-death experience. A lot of guys don't get a chance to walk away from that kind of shit; it makes you wonder.

Tomorrow will be my first day back at the office and I know it's going to be a long one. The plan Phil laid out to me depended a lot on how well he managed to handle Bettancourt at some secret meeting scheduled for tomorrow night. He refused to tell me the location, or the time, figuring I'd get antsy and bust in on them. He was right about that. So, I have to wait for him to call me after the whole thing is over.

I looked up and saw Cathy through the kitchen window. She had temporarily moved back home to look after me, and was in there fixing potato salad and steamers.

Since the shooting I haven't had anymore mind switching episodes. I guess my moment of redemption in that lousy subway car chased away all my demons. For the first time in years I was enjoying looking at my daughter's beautiful face. No recriminations. No regrets.

I heard the phone ring in the background and Cathy moved out of view to answer it. A minute later she was standing at the back door calling to me. "Daddy, hurry, it's Michael. Audrey's out of her coma."

"Mike, is she okay?"

"So far, so good. Her vital signs are steady and there doesn't appear to be any brain damage. She's still pretty weak, though, so we're trying to take things slow."

"Look Mike, I know Phil Lord gave you instructions to notify him the minute her condition changed, but I need you to give me a little lead time on this. Cathy and I are on our way over, and I'd appreciate it if you didn't let on about Audrey's condition to anyone else."

"I understand, Mac. Keep in mind, I can't guarantee how responsive she'll be. I don't want her put through any unnecessary stress."

"Thanks, Mike. We'll be there in 15 minutes."

By the time I hung up the phone, Cathy had already shut off the steamers and stuffed the salad in the refrigerator. We were out the door and half way down the block when I remembered I left the steaks on the grill. It wasn't the first time either of us had thrown away a good meal for a chance to question a witness. We looked at each other and laughed, almost like partners.

"Hey, Mac," Audrey called out weakly, with a smile, as I walked into her hospital room, "been catching any bad guys lately? Hi, Cathy, you keeping the old man straight?"

"You finished goofing off?" I answered.

"Nah, I ain't been treated this good since my first communion. Maybe I'll take up laying around as a new profession."

At least her Brooklyn attitude hadn't gone south. Hopefully, her memory was still in tact, too. I needed answers and she was the only one who could supply them.

Cathy beat me to the punch. While I was dragging a couple of chairs over beside the bed, she asked, "If you feel up to it, Audrey, we'd like to ask you some questions. You know, to see how much you can remember. You've been out for a week."

"Yeah, tell me about it. One minute it's Thursday night and I'm walking into my apartment, and the next thing I know it's a week later and I'm laying in this hospital bed."

"What's the last thing you can remember, kid?" I asked.

"Walking into my place and turning around. This fucker's standing right there. I don't know how the hell he got in, but he was waiting for me. Bam! He sucker punches me, but I don't go down. Shit, I've been hit harder by girls."

"Did you get a look at him?" Cathy interrupted.

"Sure. I guess he was surprised I was still on my feet cause he hesitated long enough for me to lay one back on him, right on the button." She sat up in bed and smacked her fist into her open hand to demonstrate her point.

"We don't want you to push this too fast," Cathy urged. "Try and relax."

Cathy pulled out a photo of Feigen and showed it to Audrey. "Hey, that's the shithead. You get him? I'd sure like a chance to crack his nuts."

I ran down what happened at her apartment and the shoot-out later on the subway. While I was describing Fcigen's attempt to blow up her place and getting her to the hospital, the "Brooklyn Bomber" did something I wasn't expecting. Tears started to spill out of the corners of her eyes and she reached for a Kleenex.

"I guess I owe you one, big guy," she said, wiping away the wetness.

"This must be my week for I-owe-you's," I answered, thinking back to Sunny's comment when I was the one laying in bed.

"Daddy came through for a lot of us," Cathy added. "We need to verify the information we pulled out of your backpack. That night, were you all excited because you found out Bettancourt was paying off Sid Moore to feed him information on what was going on at the bank?"

"You got that right. Who would have thought good old Sid was playing spook. Kinda makes you wonder about John Wayne, don't it?"

"One more question, kid." I had to smile at her last remark. "Did you find anything on Paula; was she getting a payoff too?"

Audrey looked away before she answered. "Nah. You know, Mac, if I was you, I'd be lookin' in places where you wouldn't expect to find answers."

"What the hell's that supposed to mean?"

"I think you were right, Cathy," she added, dodging my question and refusing to look me in the eye. "I'm still feeling a little punk. Maybe we ought to do this another time." She leaned back against the pillows and closed her eyes.

"Sure," Cathy said, and looked at me with a puzzled expression. We were both taken by surprise at Audrey's strange reaction to such a simple question.

Chapter 41

Thursday: July 17th (morning)

I was on the way to my office when Sheila came running up to me. "I don't know how, or when it got there. Marilyn saw it when she brought in the mail this morning."

I stared at her for a second and then my brain translated the message. "From the perps?"

"I don't think so. It wasn't mailed."

I ran to my desk and saw it laying there, an ordinary white, no.10 envelope with my name printed on it. I stared at it without moving or saying a word.

"Don't be such a baby," Sheila scolded. "We aren't going to know what's in it unless you open the goddamn thing."

Inside the envelope was a single sheet of paper with an address printed on it. "580 Congress St., Rm. 1212." Neither of us said anything and just stared at each other.

Then it hit me. I grabbed the phone and dialed Cathy at the Dump. "Get Les to make out a search warrant for room 1212 at the Singleton Building, 580 Congress Street, and meet me there as soon as you get it signed".

I turned to Sheila. "Audrey made a weird crack last night about looking in places where you wouldn't figure to find answers. While I'm gone, see if you can run down Dennis' last trip. He was supposed to be out on the West Coast. I want to know if that's where he went."

"What the hell does an address on Congress Street have to do with Dennis going to California?"

"I don't know yet, but it's the last thing in the world I would think to check out right now. I also need copies of Sunny and Paula's ID photos, right away."

"Boy, you aren't making any sense at all. Maybe they should have kept you in the hospital a little longer."

I decided to walk the three blocks to the Singleton Building and halfway there I realized it was a big mistake. The life-sucking humidity was draining all my nervous energy. By the time I arrived and stepped inside the lobby I was sweating like a pig.

The Singleton Building was one of the oldest skyscrapers in Boston and, at one time, the tallest tower in the financial district. Several decent businesses still occupied a few of the upper floors, but, for the most part, the big hitters had moved on to newer, taller buildings. Now it served as a temporary way-station for a lot of small service-related businesses that took care of all the behind-the-scenes needs that come with a major financial district.

I didn't want to screw up the search warrant Les was bringing over by breaking in too soon and decided to check with the building manager to get some basic information. On the marquee I noticed "Jane's Secretarial Service" was listed in Room 1212. That name didn't ring a bell, so I dug out my little notepad to look up the notes I'd made during the interview I had with that college kid in Minnesota, Brad Holtzman. The kid said a woman hired him but he wasn't sure of her name.

Jesse Steiner, the building manager, came up with a bunch of wisecracks and some silly ass reasons why he wasn't going to cooperate with me. I was about to grab the little prick by the throat, when Cathy and Les showed up. Their badges and the search warrant made a difference with the officious little toad and he brought along a file on Jane's Secretarial Service as he lead us to the 12th floor.

When Maurice opened the door to Room 1212 it wasn't what I expected. The small outer office had a few pieces of rental furniture: a desk, several chairs, an empty bookcase and a clothes tree. No pictures or personal belongings of any kind, and the only piece of equipment was an old IBM electric typewriter sitting on the desk. I knew without checking, the place had been wiped clean of finger-prints.

I pushed open the door to the large inner office and swore out loud in frustration, "Shit, she's already pulled out." The room was completely bare except for several large, rubber mats spread across the carpet.

This particular office was situated at the southwest corner of the building, and the south and west walls of the inner office were glass. In the middle of that room, lying on the floor, were two Polaroid snapshots. They'd obviously been left there on purpose. Cathy picked them up and Les and I huddled around her to have a look.

The photos showed the same room filled with equipment. A bunch of computers and several large monitors were installed against the inner wall. Some kind of strange directional antenna was stuck up against the glass, pointed due west, and several large black boxes were stacked up beside the antenna.

"You said, `she left,' Daddy. She, who?"

"What's this all about, Mac?" Les asked.

I ignored their questions for the moment. "Jesse, when was this place rented?"

He checked his file. "Well, the lease started in February, but I remember she was real particular that it had to be this particular office. So she actually reserved it last year."

"You remember the woman who leased the place?"

"Sure, I always remember someone who pays for a whole year in advance. That's why I didn't ask for any references." He looked around and added, "Looks like she's pulled out, like you said. I hope she doesn't expect a refund. We never give refunds."

I pulled out the photos of Sunny and Paula, and showed them to Maurice. "Which one of these two gals was it?"

"Are you kidding," he laughed. "I would have paid either one of them to move in. Nah, we're talking a short, heavy-set, Italian-looking woman, talked with a Brooklyn accent.

"Audrey?" the three of us shouted in surprised unison.

I turned to Cathy. "You got that portable telephone on you?" She handed it over and I called Audrey's hospital room. The phone rang but no one answered. Finally the operator came back on the line and said there was no patient in that room.

I tried to stay calm, and had the operator page Dr. Michael Jordan. When he came on the line, I asked, "What the hell happened to Audrey? She's not in her room."

"I know, she disappeared. When the night nurse went in to check on her, she was gone. You didn't want any records kept, so she was never officially here. There's nothing I can do. The last person seen visiting her was a woman named Paula Harding."

"Paula?" I bellowed. "Jesus Christ, is there anyone who isn't a part of this fucked-up mess?" I turned to Les and Cathy. "Paula took Audrey out of the hospital last night."

I handed the phone back to Cathy, but as soon as she got rid of Mike, I took it back and called Sheila. "I want you to find Sunny and sit on her. Have you seen Paula today?"

"No," she answered. "The Lord called you a little while ago and when I told him you were out, he said he'd catch up with you later. How come you knew Dennis didn't go to California?"

"I didn't. Where did he go?"

"Amsterdam. You gonna tell me what that's all about?"

"I would if I knew. All I know is everyone's taking a powder. Just find Sunny."

I hung up and walked across the room to the west window. The forest of tall buildings surrounding me was just that, a forest. What went on inside this room, and why did it have to be this particular office? I looked down at the photo in my hand, and notice that it was taken from an angle looking out through that same window. It took me several up and down looks before it finally dawned on me. The antenna in the picture was pointed straight at Sterling Tower.

"Les, I want an APB put out on Audrey, Paula, Sunny and Dennis. I haven't figure out the connection yet, but those four are in this together, and we have to grab them before they get out of town. If we don't they'll disappear just like the dough. And Phil may be walking into a trap." I looked at the photos one more time and added, "It looks like some of my IOU's just got paid off."

Les took off for the Dump to coordinate setting up check-points on all the exit routes out of town. Cathy drove me over to Audrey's apartment. By the time we got there the place had been cleaned up and every bit of her personal belongings were gone; clothes, photographs, even her toothbrush.

"Looks like she's planning on being gone awhile," Cathy commented.

"Yah, like forever."

We stopped at the super's apartment and he told us a guy came by late yesterday afternoon and left with a large suitcase. He described the guy as tall, wearing a t-shirt, jeans and cowboy boots.

Talk about your odd couple. What could possibly make Dennis hook-up with Audrey?

"How long is the rent paid for on that apartment?" I asked.

The super checked his records and told me, "She paid two years in advance, as of last January."

We then drove over to Paula's apartment and found the same thing. A cleaning woman was there and said Paula paid her for two years in advance to come in twice a week and clean.

"This is a goddamn set-up, so we can't say for sure they've left town," I yelled, banging my fist on the wall. "And that means they've already gone."

On the way down the block to Sunny and Dennis' place, I told Cathy to call Les and get him to send some of his people over to Audrey and Paula's apartments to check for any clues as to where they might have gone.

Sunny's pad was just like the other two: the furniture was in place, but not a single personal item anywhere. "Hey, Honey, check this out. There's a note stuck to the face of this grandfather clock."

The note read, "Have a drink on me."

"It's a grandmother clock."

"What?"

"It's smaller than a grandfather, so they call it a grandmother."

"Christ, you females are something. Always got to get in on everything."

I was at a dead-end. Nothing matched up with what I knew Phil had planned for that evening. Sunny, Dennis, Paula, and Audrey taking off together was something I never figured on. Phil set up his meeting with Bettancourt and a bunch of banker types who he claimed were involved in Operation *Sine Dinar*. He never said where it was taking place, only that if everything went well, by the end of the evening Bettancourt would no longer be a threat to Cathy, or anyone else.

How in the hell did the disappearance of that foursome tie in with Phil's meeting? Clearly every impression I'd formed so far was off the mark. I might as well have stayed home. I now realize every one of them was playing a role, right from the beginning, including Audrey. Like I said, she turned out to be the best damn actress I'd ever seen.

Sunny was giving me a clue when she said I shouldn't be concerned about who was telling the truth; everyone was lying. I was too damn busy worrying about being played for a patsy to pick up on what she was getting at. Now it seems I was the reliable lead dog, sniffing his way down the path, just like she said.

"To tell you the truth, Daddy, I thought Phil was behind the thefts when he made that comment about having more time," Cathy offered. "It sounded like he was the one running the show. But I still don't understand what's in it for any of them? What's this thing really all about?"

"Money, sweetheart, and not just some money. Control of all the money in the world. The four of them pulled off the thefts to put the screws to Bettancourt.

They're probably black-mailing him, big time, and Phil's going to get cut down in the crossfire. If they can get out of this alive, they'll disappear so Bettancourt can't put them on ice. Then, if the cartel doesn't keep paying, they'll simply tap into another bank.

"A special meeting is going on tonight, and we've got to find out where. Phil may be in a lot more danger than he thinks. I doubt he knows Sunny and the rest are ready to jack up the stakes."

Chapter 42

Thursday: July 17th (evening)

Phil had decided to hold the special global conference at the Federal Reserve Bank building on Atlantic Avenue for very specific reasons. It was not the first time the cartel had gathered in Boston, and the landmark building served as an ideal location for such a sensitive and private event. The monitored, subterranean entrance allowed the delegates to enter and leave without public display, and the unique conference room was certified "bug-free" and secure from any outside eavesdropping.

Bettancourt would take control of the proceedings once it got under way, and Phil planned to use that to his advantage. The meeting was scheduled to begin at 8:00 p.m. and delegates started arriving, under the cover of darkness, shortly before the top of the hour. Henrí was there to greet them in an effort to assure everyone he was still very much in charge. Phil took the high road, and appeared somewhat vulnerable to attack.

By 8:10 everyone was in place, and Henrí stood up to give his opening toast. Phil rose with the rest, smiling nervously at the other delegates gathered around the table. He gave the appearance of a man who was unsure of himself.

Henrí lifted his glass and intoned his ritual greeting. "As chairman of this conference I salute all of you and wish you inspiration and good fortune as you carry out your responsibilities. To God and to our mutual good fortune."

"To God and to our mutual good fortune," came the familiar retort.

The delegates took their seats and all eyes turned to Henrí who wasted no time shifting the glare of the spotlight onto Phil. "It is my pleasant duty to report to all of you," he began, "that a rather unfortunate and alarming turn of events took place in regard to that unusual theft at Sterling Bank & Trust of Boston. After our last meeting, the thieves stole another $1 million using the same electronic procedure and sent a second note. That note identified Operation *Sine Dinar* by name." He paused for maximum effect. The delegates, except for Phil, glanced at one another with expressions of surprise and concern.

"What might have turned into a disaster fortunately has been averted by our stalwart colleague, Philip, who, true to his word, tracked down the guilty party for us. Now we can take appropriate action before these criminals manage to cause us any further embarrassment."

Henrí's enigmatic mask dropped momentarily as he smiled proudly at Phil. "Philip, I'm sure the delegates are most anxious to hear all the details and don't be modest when it comes to your own extraordinary efforts to ferret out these devils."

If this were a game of pool, one might say Henrí had just buried the cue ball. Phil, it appeared, was left with practically no open shot on the table. But Phil was up to the challenge, and pool happened to be a game he excelled at. He was prepared for this moment and executed his first shot perfectly.

"When I spoke with each of you recently I promised that I would have some exciting news to convey, and I do. As Henrí so succinctly stated, another $1 million was taken from Sterling bringing the total to $6 million, in cash. I would like you to keep that figure, $6 million in cash, in the forefront of your minds as you listen to the rest of what I have to explain.

"The second note from the thieves was actually quite a bit more specific than just mentioning Operation *Sine Dinar* by name. It demanded the operation be cancelled." The group wasted no time expressing their concerns.

"I hear a threat in those words," Joaquin Montenegro, the delegate from South America, shouted. "Are we to understand that these thieves are holding Sterling hostage, as some sort of price to force us to cancel our plans?"

"With all due respect my good man, you can't possibly imagine for one moment that Sterling Bank is that important to us," Sir Edward chimed in. "Why, the complete demise of your bank wouldn't amount to a farthing against our global objectives."

Phil caught the slightest hint of a smile on Henrí's face. It certainly appeared that Phil's coffin was being nailed shut much quicker than even Henrí planned.

"All of us are clear on that point, Sir Edward," Phil answered calmly, "and I take no offense at your words because they state a fact, a fact that we must assume the thieves know full well, and can also appreciate. Therefore, we must reach a conclusion, Joaquin, that they are not interested in holding Sterling hostage."

"Then what is their purpose?" Robert Amm, the African delegate, questioned.

"I, for one, would like to get past all of this subtlety about motive and purpose and hear directly the results of your investigation?" Mai Wu Chang interrupted.

"Yes, yes," several others joined in, enthusiastically.

"Excellent." Phil responded, showing no sign of discomfort over this brief exchange. He nodded respectfully to Mai Wu. "First, allow me go back to Henrí's opening remarks about the thefts. It is important that you understand how they managed to steal the money, in order to fully appreciate where we now stand.

"A new technology has been developed allowing one computer to communicate with another, using radio waves. Conceptually that may not seem like such a remarkable feat, but applied in this instance, it becomes extraordinary. A remote computer managed to merge with a randomly selected server at my bank in a way that masked its connection. You might think of it as a kind of stealth computer, no one knew it was there until it was gone.

"Once this computer connected to our system, any information, in any file, was accessible, and the customer's accounts could be electronically emptied in the blink of an eye. The truly amazing part, though, is we don't have any way of stopping them once they are online, short of shutting down a bank's entire computer operations."

He paused for a moment and casually took a sip of champagne, allowing the delegates a brief moment to create in their minds, personal scenarios based on what he had just described. "I, therefore, put it to you, my fellow delegates, that Sterling is not being held hostage by these thieves, but rather is being used as a live demonstration: a performance, if you will, letting each of you know what is in store if their demands are not met.

"This time it was Sterling, the next time it could be any one of you, even *Banque Du Monsart*." He looked directly at Henrí and when their eyes met the message came through loud and clear.

"How dare you threaten me," Henrí exclaimed, in an unusual display of temperament.

"I threaten no one, Henrí. I am merely explaining the circumstances as they appear before us."

Henrí quickly regained his composure and now that he recognized what Phil was up to, he made an expansive gesture with his hand. "Then along with these questionable facts you have been delivering, I'm sure the delegates would like to know your personal views on how to deal with this omniscient menace." It was an attempt on his part to cut Philip off from securing the high ground.

The delegate from Southeast Asia, Luc Do Than, interrupted their sparing. "Before you get into that, Philip, I would like to ask, can this new technology be used to gain access to the data files we are planning to maintain once *Sine Dinar* becomes operational?"

Phil's comments had found their mark. The delegates understood the seriousness of what had taken place and the implications those acts would have on their future plans. The outcome of this crucial debate now rested upon Phil's ability to withstand the onslaught of Henrí's ire, which was sure to follow.

"To give you a simple answer, Luc Do, I must say, yes. Armed with the proper codes, I believe any computer system can be invaded. Once online, the information being stored in the cartel's main data files could easily be accessed. So you see, the message demanding the cancellation of Operation *Sine Dinar*, however arrogant it may sound, carries with it a very large stick.

"I'm sure no one in this room holds any delusions about the real benefit *Sine Dinar* is meant to bestow on the cartel. The successful implementation of that operation will bring about world domination. For the first time in history, an invasion will take place without a single soldier firing a shot, or a single bomb being exploded. By the time the invasion is over every citizen on the planet will be subject to the cartel's will and manipulation.

"Total domination can only be achieved, however, if we alone have the knowledge gained from that incredibly vast amount of data we intend to collect. If some competing interest were able to acquire the same knowledge, the power inherent in it would dissipate like sand through a sieve."

Henrí then delivered what he intended to be his *coup de grace*. "How well put, Philip. You must agree then, it is of the utmost importance that we act quickly to eliminate this threat, and insure there will be no such competing interests. After all, everyone here agrees the cartel, which has been serving the needs of the worldwide financial community for generations, is the only organization capable of handling such awesome responsibility."

Phil had led him to the water and now it was time to get him to drink. "We are all familiar with the old adage, `power corrupts and absolute power corrupts, absolutely.' In this instance, I see the issue not as whether the cartel is the right organization to control such remarkable knowledge, but whether any organization should ever have exclusive control of such a mighty weapon."

"Are you suggesting we share our responsibilities with these common criminals, who acquired their knowledge through blackmail and treachery?" Henrí challenged.

"Our skirts are not so clean that we can go around castigating the methods used by others, who may also seek the same objective. Are we not using similar tactics as an integral part of Operation *Sine Dinar*? Is there anyone in this room who doesn't think we are having this debate simply because an outsider uncovered what we intended to keep secret?" He searched the faces around the table and tried to discern their reactions.

"Who are these outsiders that you would have us join with in partnership?" Henrí demanded. "I believe Mai Wu's earlier question has not been answered. Have you identified the thieves?"

"Yes, I know precisely who is behind the thefts, and the notes sent to Sterling. But you, Henrí, are the one who has created a heavy burden for me in regard to what I should do with that information."

Phil rose to his feet. "You see, my friends, Henrí has advised me that he intends to eliminate the thieves before they can inform anyone of what they know. I simply cannot allow that to happen."

Sir Edward, who was clearly confused over what was going on, argued, "My dear boy, your refusal to divulge the information may well jeopardize our schedule. A rather good deal of time and money has been invested to bring off this bloody operation. We need to know straight away who is interfering with our plans."

"Bloody operation is right, Sir Edward," Phil responded. He walked behind Sir Edward, placed both hands on his colleague's shoulders, and said, "Are you, are any of you, prepared to commit murder in order to eliminate the opposition? Are any of you willing to get blood on your hands in order to see these plans carried out?"

"I find that remark outrageous," Robert Amm shouted. "We are not a pack of thugs, nor for that matter are we power hungry invaders out to dominate the world, as you charged earlier."

"With all due respect, Robert, I submit that you are both if one takes into account the actions taken recently by our chairman, in the name of the cartel. For instance, are any of you aware of the fact that Henrí gave an order to have a young woman, an employee at Sterling, attacked and almost beaten to death because she found out the identity of a spy he had planted at my bank. The young woman is presently in a coma from the beating she took at the hands of Henrí's hired assassin.

The same assassin also attempted to gun down a female police officer I hired to help uncover the spy. The assassin was shot and killed in a public fiasco reported in the press the other day. Is that the kind of operation you have in mind, Robert?"

"Enough, Philip." Henrí stood up and, uncharacteristically, raised his voice. "It pains me to see such disgraceful conduct coming from someone I have always held in high esteem. You dishonor yourself and our colleagues with your false and scurrilous charges. I can only imagine they are the result of the great strain you have been under lately. Nevertheless, we shall hear no more of it. We are here to see that a problem is corrected, and anyone who threatens to jeopardize our plans must be dealt with in an appropriate manner."

Phil's comments were aimed at getting the delegates to consider the possibility that spies were planted in their institutions. He wanted to drive home the point so that he could catch Henrí in a blatant lie. In what was intended to sound like an reckless charge, he challenged his mentor.

"Do you deny you entered into an affair with my wife and used her to plant bugs in my home in order to destroy me?" It was a grave indictment. Business was never personal, that was an unassailable commandment of the cartel.

Henrí mistakenly assessed his adversary as acting out of desperation, unable to prove such scandalous charges. "Have you no shame left, Philip?" He reached out his hand, as if trying to offer salvation to the younger man. "Of course I deny such nonsense. We are all businessmen here, not some Hollywood actors in a squalid soap opera."

"Then you leave me no choice. I am forced to expose you as a liar, Henrí." Phil's words stunned the group, and created an instant vacuum in the room, as if all the air had suddenly vanished. "Your word can no longer be accepted as the truth." Phil strode back to his chair, reached under the seat, and drew out a large envelope he had planted there before the meeting started.

"Ladies and gentlemen, I am distributing photographs recently taken by the Boston police outside my home one night while I was away. They show Henrí and my wife in a compromising position. I also have a sworn statement from my wife, in which she admits to an affair with Henrí and states he brought Sean Feigen to my home to plant recording devices.

"In addition, I am handing you police reports that verify the fact that recording bugs were found in my home, and that the same types of devices were found in an apartment belonging to Sean Feigen, an internationally-known IRA assassin.

"Mr Feigen, is the person I mentioned who was killed in a recent shoot-out. During that shoot-out he attempted to assassinate a policewoman, Cathy MacKenzie, the daughter of Sterling's Chief of Security.

"Henrí, I sincerely regret having it come down to this, but, as I said, you left me no choice."

Caught red-handed in a false denial, most people will invariably try to offer up some kind of justification as a means of avoiding the consequences. That justification always comes across as a further attempt to manipulate the situation. Henrí fell prey to that irresistible urge.

"I will not allow your cheap theatrics to undermine the work of this cartel. Every one of these delegates knows my only objective is to carry out the will of the cartel, in the best way I can. If I am forced to employ unsavory tactics from time to time it is only because that is what I believe will bring about the best results. My methods and motives have never been questioned before and I can no longer tolerate this insufferable attack on my authority."

"You brought it on yourself, Henrí," Phil interjected. The advantage was his, and he knew how to close out a match. "You never should have allowed things to get to a point where you had to lie. Your mistake came in not giving the delegates a chance to reconsider whether it was wise to go forward with our plans in light of changed circumstances. You assumed it was your decision to make, and once made, the subject was closed."

"How dare you lecture me like some incompetent underling. Your disgraceful conduct will not shield you from the consequences of any further delay in informing this group of the identity of the thief. I demand that you do so, this instant."

The two men stood facing each other with only enough space between them to avoid spontaneous combustion. All eyes were on them as the delegates sat in a state of inanimate shock. The extraordinary emotions displayed during this epic conference were exceeded only by the unexpected revelations being thrown at them, revelations that, at the very least, held dark portent for the future. Even the hint of a scandal could easily sound the death knell of the cartel.

"First, you must admit that it is your intention to have everyone involved in the Sterling thefts, murdered,"

Phil proposed in a strong, steady voice. "Do that and I will name the guilty party."

"Elimination is the only recourse available," Henrí acknowledged. "You admitted that yourself. There is no other way to prevent them from interfering with our plans."

"No, that is not true. In fact I pointed out just the opposite." Phil started to slowly make his way around the table. "At the start of this meeting I asked each of you to keep in mind the fact that $6 million in cash was taken from Sterling. That cash has never come back into the system for one simple reason. The thieves intend to use it to create a black-market. That black-market will, if not cripple, at least hinder any attempt to eliminate the use of cash as a means of commercial exchange.

"The most beguiling advertising campaign will not keep the financial marketeers from hedging their bets once they find out someone is hoarding cash; enough cash to make a difference. It will grow and spread like a cancer, eating away at any confidence you try to build with the public in favor of a cashless economy."

By the time he had come full circle and was again facing his former mentor, the delegates were hanging on his every word.

"No, Henrí, I never said eliminating the thieves was your only recourse. You, in fact, have no recourse. Any action attempted against them will insure the public disclosure of the cartel and all of its activities. Everyone here knows that even the slightest notoriety would destroy the one ingredient that has always made this cartel so successful, anonymity. No outsider has ever known for sure that we even exist.

"That is why I can announce to you and my fellow delegates that I am the thief." He turned and held up his hands to his audience. "That's right, ladies and gentlemen, with the help of some very bright, and very devoted comrades, I planned this entire operation for the sole purpose of bringing a end to the madness of Operation *Sine Dinar*.

Complete silence. Everyone remained still, holding their breath, as if suddenly paralyzed. Their intelligence and experience allowed them to quickly assimilate and analyze the unexpected information Phil has so succinctly laid before them. It added up to a brilliant knockout punch.

A few seconds went by before Henrí recovered enough from the blow to stammer, "I don't believe a word of it."

"Of course you don't, Henrí." Phil smiled at him. "I'm sure there are others here who feel the same way. But I can assure you every bit of it is true. I assumed there would be a certain amount of skepticism over my confession, so I prepared a little demonstration to help gain some credibility in your eyes.

"When you leave here tonight Henrí, I suggest you place a call to your bank. You will find that $2 million worth of francs have been removed from your customers' accounts. As I said at the outset, Sterling was merely a demonstration, an object lesson. I hope that lesson is very clear to all of you."

Henrí fell back into his chair, his mask askew, revealing the gruesome image of ruination. For the first time he appeared to be very old.

Regardless of whether the cartel itself continued to operate, Henrí Bettancourt's fabled mystique, which cloaked him with an almost god-like invincibility for so long, was now completely destroyed. A thorough ablution had taken place, whether for better or worse, only time would tell. All coups are like that. The king is dead; long live the king.

"My friends, there are a few other arrangements you should also be aware of. Outside of the discussions I have had with my fellow conspirators, regarding the objectives of *Sine Dinar*, I have not breached any confidences, nor have I divulged any information about the cartel, its members, or its other activities, to anyone. My actions had one purpose only, which I believe has been achieved.

"However, as you might well imagine, I thought it wise to take some precautions against any reprisals. A complete history and detailed accounting of the cartel's activities has been placed in safe-keeping. It will be released in the unlikely event that I, or any of my friends, or our families, should ever suffer some unexpected accident.

"I realize the revelations I've made today have put a considerable damper on your ability to feel comfortable in my presence and I am, therefore, resigning from the cartel. Notice has been given through the proper channel to the North American Group, and I anticipate my replacement will be appointed in due course."

Mai Wu spoke up. "I have only one question, Philip. Why? You, personally, have so much to lose."

Phil's voice was clear and strong as he responded. "*Sine Dinar* was already being implemented when I came onboard. You may recall that I voiced strong reservations at that time, but it was clear the course had been set. I became convinced it had to be checkmated.

"Robert, I was being completely sincere in my analogy to an invasion. The idea of conquering and dominating people is as old as history, and it's the same no matter what the disguise. *Sine Dinar* should serve as a lesson to all of us that the new opportunities available through technological advances can be every bit as powerful and hard to handle as any weapon of mass destruction. Power is corrupting and until we learn how to prevent that corruption we must avoid placing too much of it in the hands of any one person, or a select group.

"The rest of my plans will be revealed to you in due time. For now, I wish all of you well in your future endeavors. All that I ask is that you give up trying to eliminate cash. For the time being, it serves as a very important safeguard to personal privacy."

Chapter 43

Thursday: July 17th (evening)

Phil slipped quietly out of the room while the others were trying to recover from the shock of their ordeal. He moved quickly down a dimly lit corridor, unlocked a door, and stepped inside a dark room, locking the door behind him. He took out a small flashlight and made his way across the room to a back door that opened onto a staircase.

He hurried down the stairs to a pitch black, empty section of an underground garage. There he used his flashlight to locate a bicycle he'd hidden away earlier in the day. He began to disrobe and beneath his suit he was wearing a cyclist's racing togs. After removing his shoes and socks, he replaced them with special riding shoes that he retrieved from a backpack hanging on the bicycle.

It was his decision to forego using a vehicle for his get-away. He couldn't discount the possibility that Mac and Cathy might figure out where the meeting was being held and arrive before he was out of sight. Paula came up with the idea of pedaling his way to the rendezvous point and Dennis supplied the ridiculous get-up. He felt disrespectful as he rolled up his custom-made suit, shirt, and tie, and stuffed them, along with his bench-made shoes, into the backpack. At least it was dark outside and no one would ever recognize him.

At the exit door Phil carried the bicycle and backpack up an outside stairwell to the dark alley between the two wings of the bank. He glanced around to see if anyone was watching, climbed on the bicycle, and pedaled off down the alley. At the end of the alley he cautiously turned into the flow of evening traffic moving along Atlantic Avenue.

When he reached Congress Street, he turned right and raced for the harbor. Adrenalin was now pumping through his body and it helped him keep up a strong steady pace. There was little traffic on Congress Street, but he kept checking over his shoulder to see if anyone was following him.

Just past the Boston Tea Party Museum he pulled to a stop and looked over the rail down at the wide channel below. He hopped off the bike, carried it down the stairs and over to edge of the wharf. A tall figure standing in the shadows by a launch tied to the dock, waved to him. It was Dennis.

Phil glanced at his watch and noted that he still had five minutes before the launch would have left without him. "I'm not in such bad shape after all," he said to Dennis.

"I won't tell anyone, but you look like you're about to have a heart attack," Dennis laughed, and threw the bike in the launch.

Phil climbed aboard, Dennis started the engine, and the boat moved slowly along the channel. Nine minutes later they came alongside a large luxury yacht, the Flying Carpet, waiting silently near the mouth of the harbor. The small running lights around the deck and a brightly lit wheelhouse were the only indications that anyone was onboard.

The yacht's brow extended down to the waterline and Phil climbed up to the main deck where he was greeted by Paula. "Tres chic, mon amour," she giggled wrapping her arms around his neck.

He hugged her and quickly discovered she wasn't wearing anything beneath the lovely silk shift she had on. As always her abject sexuality added to his excitment. "Is everyone aboard?" he asked, and without waiting for an answer added, "How is Audrey?"

"She's resting comfortably, and the champagne's on ice. We've been waiting for you."

"Then let's get underway, and please help me get out of these ridiculous clothes."

Dennis sent word to the captain to raise the launch and weigh anchor. The deep melodic growl of the huge diesels came alive and the magnificent ship began gliding smoothly through the calm dark waters headed for the open sea.

Phil changed clothes and stepped into the aft saloon to raucous shouts, "Praise be The Lord," as his four comrades raised their glasses and saluted him. He walked over to Audrey lying on a hospital bed and bent down to kiss her on the forehead. "Please forgive me for having underestimated our adversary."

"No big thing," she answered. "I always figured that's why you had Mac watching over me."

Everyone laughed and Sunny gave a toast, "Here's to Mac, the cowardly lion who found his courage in the nick of time." Then she asked, "How did things go with number one?"

"Just like you predicted. When I left him, he was going through a total meltdown. Dennis, I think the withdrawing of money from Henri's bank was a stroke of genius. You all performed brilliantly."

* * *

Cathy and I spent all afternoon and the early part of the evening trying to locate the hotel where Bettancourt was staying. Immigration confirmed he arrived that morning, but when we started checking hotels, we couldn't find any reservation, even under the name of Henry Gabriel. He was obviously using another alias.

We then checked every major hotel for a man fitting his description who might have checked in that day and taken an expensive suite. Finally, late in the day, we were able to pin him down. Several people fitting his general profile were reported, and we went to each hotel and showed his picture before assuring ourselves that we had the right guy. By the time that task was completed we were too late. He'd already gone out for the evening.

That meant we had to check all the cabbies on duty, and by the time we located the right one it was after 8:30 p.m. The cabby told us he dropped a fare off at the Federal Reserve Bank Building on Atlantic Ave., and the guy told him to come back at 9:00 p.m. sharp.

On our way to the Federal building, I had Cathy call Les and tell him something big was going down and to get the whole team over to the Federal Reserve Bank, on the double. I knew that old building well, and showed Cathy where to turn in for the underground parking garage with its special subterranean entrance. I figured the attendees would be using that entrance to avoid being seen in public.

"Now what?" Cathy asked, as we sat in the darkened garage, across from the electronically controlled entrance.

"I'm not sure. I don't have a program."

"It's almost 9:00 and that's when Bettancourt said he wanted to be picked up."

"I know that, but if we move in too soon we could blow everything for Phil."

Les's unmarked sedan, followed by two more cars, drove silently into the garage with their lights off. He contacted me on the radio and said, "I already regret being here, Mac?"

"In case you haven't noticed we're playing in the dark, Buddy," I answered him. "Whatever we do right now could be wrong, and if we don't do anything it could be worse. Makes me think of that time we raided the Gay Palace and caught that scumbag councilman just as he was about to get fucked by a guy with AIDS."

"Yah, I remember that. We couldn't decide whether it was better to be too soon or too late. Well, you got me down here, so we gonna dance or what?"

The darkness settled over us and Cathy took the opportunity to find out what was rattling around in my head. "Don't you think it's time to let your partner in on what's going on here?"

I looked at her and smiled. "You know, that sounds pretty good. Like I said to you in the hospital, I can get used to it if you can?

"As far as what's going on, I'm not sure. When everyone started disappearing today I figured Sunny, Dennis, Paula and Audrey had to be in this together.

" Paula probably found out about this secret operation that Phil was involved in, and ran it by Sunny. Sunny, pissed at the way Phil was treating her, talked Dennis into building one of his gismos so she could get inside the bank's computer system where she knows all the secret codes. They set up a little heist so Phil has to call in Sunny to protect the system from an attack. The crooks get hired to catch themselves, how's that? It was a sure-fire deal, and all they needed to make it work was some character who could pull the fire alarm and still be above suspicion."

"Audrey," Cathy answered.

"You got it, partner. Turns out she has a thing for Sunny and probably didn't want anyone damaging the property. I don't think any of them figured on this

Bettancourt guy going off the deep end and sending a hit man after her."

"What part did you play in all of this?"

"Me, hell, I was the man in motion," I chuckled. "The sap who sends everyone off on a wild goose chase.

"Sunny told me how the money they stole was actually being held for some kind of backward ransom. This crackpot operation of theirs was meant to eliminate cash but it won't work if someone keeps enough dough in his pocket to set up a black market for the stuff. The whole idea is to get everyone on the planet to use plastic for everything so the suits can keep tabs on what's going on. Pretty soon they're telling us what to buy and when, and how much it costs. Big Brother takes over, and all the presidents and kings on the planet can't put humpty-dumpty back together again. Hell, maybe it's like that already.

Phil knew what the cartel was after but is stuck in the middle. He doesn't want Paula and the rest of them to get hurt, so he ends up taking on Bettancourt. Now he's trying to get the cartel to back off and that's where we are right now."

"But Sunny and those guys have skipped town," Cathy argued. "Doesn't that take the pressure off Phil?"

"That's what I'm really worried about. The way I see it, they would only pack up when they were ready to play their hole cards. One last all-or-nothing move, and I think Phil is walking into the direct line of fire."

Headlights lit up the darkness, and a cab pulled into the garage and came to a stop in front of the entrance. Within minutes several more were lined up waiting for their fares to come out.

The lobby lights came on. "The door's opening, let's move," I shouted into the radio.

I jumped out of the car and hustled between two cabs. When I spotted Bettancourt coming through the doorway, along with several other guys, I moved in. "Don't let that door close," I shouted to Cathy and ran up and grabbed Bettancourt with my one good hand.

Les and his guys quickly got all the suits rounded up and told them to stay put and remain calm. The surprise of being rushed by cops put these jokers in a panic mode. I guess they weren't used to being pushed around. They huddled together like frightened sheep, each one trying to nudge their way into the center of the pile, thinking it would give them some kind of added protection against ending up on the front page of a tabloid.

"What is the meaning of this outrage?" Bettancourt complained to me. I know he recognized me, and knew exactly what I was doing there.

"I'm asking the questions, shithead, and you better have some great answers," I growled, pulling him up close. "Let's start with where's Phil Lord?"

"I'm sure I don't have the slightest idea," he answered, sensing the anger in my voice. "He left the room a few moments ahead of the rest of us. For all I know, he is still in the building somewhere."

"What about the others?

"What others?" He gestured toward the people gathered together, and said, "If you will stop these gestapo tactics for a moment you will find that each one of us is covered by diplomatic immunity, and you have no right to be here, or to bother us. We attended a financial conference and no one other than the invitees were present."

"Are you saying no unexpected guests showed up to nail your sorry ass?" I really wanted an opportunity to get back at this pompous jackass for all the destruction and pain he'd been causing lately.

"I can't say, as you so crudely put it, that I was not "nailed," but that was Philip's doing, not some outsider."

"So what did you do to him?"

"It would be more appropriate to inquire what he did to us." Again he gestured toward his flock, milling about, looking dazed and bewildered.

I pulled Les over and asked him to call the "meat-wagon," and haul this crew over to the Dump for questioning. "I'm not sure who they are yet, but I know something major went down here tonight, and it has to do with the stolen money.

"Keep this asshole separated from the rest," I added shoving Bettancourt at him. "Phil was supposed to come up with some evidence connecting this turd to that Irish shooter. All I have to do now is find Phil."

I grabbed a flashlight from Cathy and jogged off into the damp-smelling darkness of the parking garage. I was looking for a specific door that I knew opened onto an alley between the two wings of the building. That alley was used to load and unload trucks transporting the cash that got doled out to and collected from, all the banks in town.

If Phil stuck it to this group of bozos like Bettancourt said, it meant my hunch about who was doing what to whom was still screwed up. The sudden disappearance of Sunny, Dennis, Paula and Audrey must have been part of Phil's plan, but I still couldn't decide if Phil was a victim or the mastermind behind everything. Maybe this whole thing was about taking down Bettancourt and his cronies. If that was so, the why of it all still wasn't real clear to me.

From the looks on the faces of the suits, it figures Phil must have shown his hand and come up with all aces. If so, he and his little troupe of actors couldn't stick around for a victory party because they had to beat it out of town before being busted by the cops. Phil's bunch, like the $6 million they stole, had to be long gone before anyone even thought about looking for them. That meant Phil had a get-a-way car stashed in the alley so he could sneak off while everyone else was getting nabbed at the front door.

I found the exit, got outside, and ran up the stairwell. An empty alley surrounded me, so I ran to the corner and looked up and down Atlantic Ave. I was hoping to spot Phil's limousine, or even his prized Jaguar-XKE, speeding away from the scene. The only thing I saw was a steady stream of cars and trucks belonging to all the ordinary people going about their business, and the back of a lone cyclist pedaling along with the traffic. I stood there for a moment and watched the cyclist turn right on Congress Street, before walking back inside the garage, feeling stupid and disappointed. Phil had used me one more time, and left me hanging on a limb that was ready to break off. There had to be some way of catching that son of a bitch and his little band of smart-asses, before they beat it out of town. I started to scratch my head.

When I got back to Cathy and Les they were packing the suits off to the Dump. I tried to imagine where I would go if I were Phil, and the only thing that came to mind was the possibility that he was still hiding somewhere in the building, waiting for everyone to leave. That wouldn't be a very smart move, so I didn't bother.

"Are you sure things got buttoned up?" I asked Les.

"Look," Les answered, "I've told you, planes, trains, buses, everything's covered. I've had roadblocks set up on a five-mile radius since 8:00 p.m. Unless the guy wants to row himself out of town, he ain't going anywhere without us knowing."

"Shit, that's it," I yelled. "Cathy, dig out your phone and get me the number for the harbor master in Manchester. I don't care if you have to wake him up, but get him to go check and see if the *Lordship* is still at its mooring. He'll know which one it is."

Cathy did as I ordered and had to use all her charm to get the guy to drive down to the tiny harbor in that seaside village, and check for any signs of life aboard Phil's yacht.

The guy called back 20 minutes later with the news the *Lordship* was moored right where it ought to be, and made it clear how much he appreciated this little inconvenience. In the meantime, Les' people finished a thorough sweep of the building just to make sure, and we were finally ready to leave.

"Come on, Daddy, I'll take you home," Cathy said, aware of how dejected I was over the fact that Phil had outsmarted me again. "Those big-shots we hauled off aren't going to talk, and they'll be lawyered-up before we even get back to the Dump. We might as well call it a night."

We drove out of the garage and when Cathy turned onto Atlantic, I suddenly remembered something—the message left behind at Sunny's apartment. "Let's stop for a drink, Honey. Drive me over to Jake's." I wasn't sure what I'd find, but I had a hunch Sunny wanted me to stop there for a reason.

Dugie Russell was behind the bar and as soon as he spotted me, he shouted, "It's about time you showed up."

"What made you think I would?"

"That centerfold you had in here a few weeks back came by earlier and said you'd be stopping in for a drink. She left something for you. I told her if she left me her phone number, I'd call her and let her know when you picked it up."

He opened the cash register, pulled out a slip of paper and handed it to me. It was an I-owe-you, made out to me, for $6 million. "I told her I didn't know you was up to making loans like that, and she said, `He'll hang this on his wall.'"

I looked at it and couldn't help laughing. I finally got the punch-line. "Sonovabitch! The whole goddamn bunch of them were in on it together, right from the start."

"Hey, that ain't all," Dugie added. "There's a package here, too."   He reached down and slid a large envelope across the bar.   It looked a lot like the one that got dumped on my desk when this whole thing began, only smaller.

Cathy followed me to a booth and Dugie brought over some drinks. I sat down and tore open the envelope. The last time I did this, it changed my life. What's up this time?

There were two sealed envelopes and some papers stuffed inside. Each envelope had a name printed on the front. One was addressed to Cathy and I handed it to her.

She opened it and found a short letter from Phil, along with $5,000 in $100 bills. The letter read:

Dear Cathy:

Your employment on behalf of Sterling Bank & Trust to uncover the leaks of valuable bank information has been successfully concluded. The ingenuity and dedication you exhibited were everything I hoped for, and more.   My hope is we can always be friends and that I can call upon you again, in the future, as the need arises.

My fondest regards,
Philip Cabot Lord III

Dumbfounded, she handed it to me to read. I smiled at her. "You earned it, Honey, fair and square."

"It sounds like he's planning on coming back. Wouldn't that be a really dumb move? Even if the cops aren't after him, the insurance company's investigators will never stop trying to find that money. I mean he did steal $6 million, right?"

"I haven't called a single shot right in this whole mess, so all I'm going to say is, he probably has that covered too."

I opened the envelope with my name on it and found another letter from Phil. "It's from Phil. He probably wants to thank me for being such a big, dumb, schmuck."

Dear Mac:

Congratulations! My faith in you and Cathy was well placed, and I couldn't be more pleased with the results. The menace has passed and all is back to normal. Except for one thing: I have no way of getting Sid Moore's offshore funds released. You can assure him I do not hold a grudge, and his job at Sterling is still secure.

As you know, things are over between Charlotte and me. As a sort of settlement between us, you will find enclosed an affidavit from her that should help you connect Henri Bettancourt to that Irish killer. Henri remains a force to be reckoned with, but I think you will find he no longer has the same invulnerability he once enjoyed.

I decided to take some time off and you have deduced by now that Paula agreed to join me, along with Sunny, Dennis, and Audrey. I once told you I know everything about the people I rely on.

You can rest assured Audrey is receiving the best of care and recovering nicely. Everyone sends their regards and wishes you would consider joining us. You will find a ticket in the envelope that will carry you around the world. I'm certain our paths will cross somewhere along the way.

In spite of what you may be thinking, you were never mistreated by any of us. Everyone has a role to play in life and sometimes those roles are not easy to discern. The events that transpired over the past several months, like most events of great import, are often difficult to grasp when you are standing on the playing field. I believe Sunny pointed out to you that the search for truth is not always a worthwhile endeavor, and even less so when the stakes are high.

Timing is always a key to success and your timing in this matter was impeccable. The fact that you are reading this letter assures me that you deciphered the various messages left for you, and by using your detective skills, were able to put those clues to good use. We all counted on you, and you didn't let us down.

Unfortunately, the more far-reaching and important the results, the less opportunity there is to give individual recognition. By the time you read this, the entire episode will have vanished like a bad dream. You will recall, right from the start, I made a concerted effort to keep everything quiet. I never even notified internal audit. No one outside of our little group ever knew, first hand, that anything took place.

Theft was never the issue, at least not directly. Sunny made that clear to you. What was at issue was the ability to demonstrate a technological capability. In case you are concerned about the consequences of the missing money, please rest easy. Anything done electronically can be undone in the same manner. As of right now, no Sterling customer is out any funds and no evidence exists that any crime ever took place. According to the bank's records everything is as it should be.

The FBI was never brought in and the local police have no official report of a crime having been committed. Even the killing of that Irish thug, with the help of your former captain, was listed as an unrelated attempted robbery. No one has any reason, or basis, to even entertain an investigation because no claim has been filed against Sterling's insurance underwriters, and no official loss was ever reported.

Sunny assures me, given sufficient time, even the few outsiders who were drawn in, will lose interest and any memory of the events will fade into the past. And, as you know, Sunny is never wrong when it comes to people's reactions.

Wealth has always been at the heart of any war. Those without it, want it, and those with it always want more. In the past, the path to acquiring great wealth meant conquering lands and subjugating people through bloodshed and violence. Now, all of that has changed.

Modern technology, especially computers, represents a whole new form of warfare. Battles can be fought without the general public even knowing anything is taking place. You are a wounded veteran of one such techno-battle, as are Sid and Cathy.

When you throw your cash down on the bar at Jake's tonight no one will recognize you as a true hero, but you are. They will never know of the battle you just fought for those bills. Oh, well, maybe next time. Justice is a very rare commodity.

Please do consider joining us, you've earned a chance to make your dreams come true.

My fondest regards,
Philip Cabot Lord III

I looked at Cathy and grinned. "See, I was wrong again."

"What does he say?"

"Nothing incriminating, if that's what you're hoping for. But now I understand how it all went down, and I guess the good guys won." I handed her the letter.

"I'm glad you're satisfied, because it sounds like a bunch of rationalization to me. What is he getting at?"

"It's about telling the truth, honey. When you're trying to solve a crime and the perp claims he's telling the truth, if you decide he's lying you're never going to come up with the right answer.

They were all telling the truth all along, just not the whole truth. They set everything up so they could all tell the truth, even Audrey, while I was operating on the basis that they were all lying. I never saw the forest for the trees. Phil was the commander-in-chief and I was his unwitting lieutenant. I was out there trying to fight a battle, while he was winning the damn war.

"Everything they fed me was intended to keep me chasing after the shadows, so the bad guys would think at any moment I was going to uncover the perps for them. It wasn't until Sunny told me to stop trying to figure out who was telling the truth and pay attention to what people were doing, that I began to get the picture. Even then, in my wildest imagination, I never had it figured for some kind of world domination thing. We didn't handle many of those at Special Ops.

"Even that business about Sunny and Phil having a beef when she set up the computer system, was probably a set-up so they could tell the truth and at the same time make it look like they weren't. Dennis told me it was all about assumptions, and he was right. I was just too thick-skulled to get the message." I paused, downed my drink, and ordered another.

"I have no trouble seeing Sunny and Dennis being a part of this, and even Audrey makes some kind of weird sense, but what about Paula?" Cathy asked. "Where did she fit in?"

"Lady Paula was your ever-so-sexy, double agent. Phil, like the rest of us, knew Bettancourt would assume she was trying to sleep her way to fame and fortune. So when Bettancourt came calling on her, she readily accepted his offer to be a mole at Sterling. Phil knew Bettancourt would try to plant more than one person at the bank, and told me the guy never liked to have all his eggs in one basket. By allowing Paula to be one of the moles, Phil figured he could control at least some of the info that was going back and forth. I guess that's why they pay guys like him the big bucks. He didn't miss a trick."

"Well, what are you going to do about this offer? Are you going to ride off into the sunset with the rest of them?

I looked at her beautiful face, a face that I'd only just begun to enjoy again. "Honey, when I was Colin's age I remember telling your great, grandfather, Dougal, that I was going to go to Scotland someday to see where he was born. He gave me a scowl and said, `Na then, laddie, ye wouldna find anything there ye couldna find here.' It took me awhile, but eventually I figured out what he meant."

I reached across the table and took hold of my daughter's hand. "So, how does the name, "MacKenzie and MacKenzie, Private Investigators," grab you? There's a senator I know who might be interested in doing a little digging into an unusual banking issue I ran across recently."

Epilogue

Washington, D.C., October 1998

A select Senate subcommittee hearing is underway and two FBI agents seated at the witness table are looking at each other in shocked disbelief. The Chairman just let loose a bombshell. An empty silence follows, creating a sense that something provocative is afoot, but the sparse audience in the large chamber wasn't been paying close enough attention to be sure of just what it was the Chairman had asked. The longer the FBI guys hesitated, the more the question hung in the air like a ticking bomb, drawing everyone's attention.

Subcommittee hearings rarely draw anyone's attention. Hearings conducted by the Select Committee On Banking Reform are usually nothing more than a photo "op," as each senator, one after the other, grabs their microphone and tries to make the most of their allotted time in front of the C-SPAN cameras. The Chairman's provocative question caught everyone off-guard, and his soft, pliable face offered nothing beyond a lop-sided smile, as an indicator of what he was after.

Elliot Johnson, the senior FBI agent, looked especially distraught. In contrast to the Chairman's doughy features, Elliot's sharply chiseled jaw protruded like Dick Tracy's and the tightness around his mouth made the jaw line even more pronounced. He whispered angrily to his associate. "How in the hell did he find that out?" All he received in response was an exaggerated shrug.

Elliot faced the Chairman and tried to deliver a quickly constructed evasion. His voice cracked, momentarily, from the dryness in his throat. "Mr. Chairman, uhm, I am afraid I'm not able to discuss that subject in this open forum. In fact, I respectfully request that your question be deleted from the public record."

The Chairman, Senator Warren Mills of Massachusetts, didn't hesitate. Ignoring any personal disgruntlement he might have felt over Elliot's obvious rudeness, he delivered another salvo right on that chiseled chin:

"You'll have to do a lot better than that, Special Agent Johnson. You two gentlemen were called here to testify before this committee. What makes you think you can come in here and tell us what can and can't be made public?"

The agents again covered their microphones and whispered anxiously back and forth for several minutes. This time, when Johnson turned toward the row of senators, he proffered his best smile. "Mr. Chairman, I can only reiterate my previous statement and respectfully suggest that you might consider conferring privately with the Director before proceeding further on that subject. Special Agent Walker and I are happy to answer any other questions you, or the members of your committee might have for us."

Senator Mills smiled, stretched out his arms as if to embrace the committee members seated on either side of him, and said, "Senators, I do believe I'm beginning to smell something here. It reminds me of clam digging as a boy, in my hometown of Beverly. At low tide, which, by the way, is the only time you can dig for those tasty morsels, there is a rather unpleasant odor that emanates from the wet sand.

Well, I smell that same odor right now. Our FBI friends here are not talking, and I'm not at all happy about that. I intend to dig up those smelly morsels and get to the bottom of this, one way or another." He winked at two familiar faces in the audience.

THE END
(maybe)

www.ingramcontent.com/pod-product-compliance
Lightning Source LLC
Chambersburg PA
CBHW020336180626
46812CB00001B/235